# Let Them Stare

## ALSO BY JONATHAN VAN NESS

*Over the Top: My Story*
*Love That Story: Observations from a Gorgeously Queer Life*
*Peanut Goes for the Gold*
*Gorgeously Me!*

## ALSO BY JULIE MURPHY

*Side Effects May Vary*
*Dumplin'*
*Ramona Blue*
*Puddin'*
*Pumpkin*
*Faith: Taking Flight*
*Faith: Greater Heights*
*Camp Sylvania*
*Camp Sylvania: Moon Madness*
*Chubby Bunny*

# Let Them Stare

*a novel*

## JONATHAN VAN NESS & JULIE MURPHY

STORYTIDE
*An Imprint of HarperCollinsPublishers*

Storytide is an imprint of HarperCollins Publishers.

Let Them Stare: A Novel
Copyright © 2025 by Jonathan Van Ness
All rights reserved. Manufactured in Harrisonburg, VA, United States of America.
No part of this book may be used or reproduced in any manner whatsoever
without written permission except in the case of brief quotations
embodied in critical articles and reviews. For information, address
HarperCollins Children's Books, a division of HarperCollins Publishers,
195 Broadway, New York, NY 10007.
www.epicreads.com

ISBN 978-0-06-334624-6 — ISBN 978-0-06-345708-9 (special edition)

Typography by Jenna Stempel-Lobell
25 26 27 28 29  LBC  5 4 3 2 1
First Edition

To our younger selves and to all the small-town queers. Wherever you go, wherever you stay, you are loved.

—JM & JVN

# 1

"Are you leaving soon?" I asked. "I really don't want to brave this party without you."

Emma groaned through the phone speaker. We were on FaceTime, both of our cameras face up at our respective ceilings while our hands were busy getting ready. I could see her ceiling fan spinning. "I promise I'm leaving in like two seconds. I just—I swear to god, this second cat eye is going to be the death of me."

"Eyeliner is like brows," I reminded her. "Sisters. Not twins."

"Okay, okay, I'm adding a face gem to one side so the asymmetrical look gives intention, and then I'm there. Love you. Mean it. It'll be okay."

The call ended, and I shook out my hands, trying to flutter away the nerves. This time tomorrow, I'd be out of Hearst. It was a day I'd thought would never come, even if I'd dreamed about it for years. I had made it through every miserable year of middle school and high school. Now I just had to make it through this party, and then I'd be off to my new, non-fat-phobic—*Devil Wears Prada* life as @Lyndzi's go-getter intern in the Big Apple. Rocking this perfect pout, fierce platform heels, and enjoying the glam big-city life I was born for. Like a fucking *Sex in the City* dream come true.

At least that was the plan. I'd talked such a big game for the last few years that I had barely stopped to let myself wonder what it might mean to fail, or to arrive in New York City and hate it. To go all the way there only to have to come back to Hearst because I just couldn't hack it anywhere else. That was the stuff of my nightmares.

I adjusted my makeshift vanity made of two IKEA nightstands and a polished piece of wood from one of Dad's job sites. The summer before tenth grade, Mom had temporarily turned my bedroom into her campaign office, and I'd taken over the basement. It was cooler than the rest of the house, and it was spacious and private. There wasn't much natural light, but I liked to think of it as my recharge den from the hostile rays of the summer sun. And from the hostile denizens of Hearst. Like Ursula's underwater lair—but with less seaweed and more lava lamps and unusual knickknacks from Yesterday's Today, the greatest thrift store in a hundred-mile radius and my former place of employment as of—*dramatically checks watch*—a few hours ago.

Up until, well, today, my makeup collection had been mostly showcased in glimpses. In the basement, I could do whatever I wanted. Overnight hangs with my besties Emma and Guy were safe. So were weekends in Pittsburgh to scope out pop-up vintage shops for work and skim off the major finds for my own online resale side hustle. Even though I had safe spaces, makeup was not for school. And *definitely* not for family gatherings. But today, and every day after, all that was going to change.

I trailed my fingers over the lipsticks in my makeup drawer, selecting Ruby Woo. If I had to grimace through ham-and-egg-salad sliders with my extended family, then it would be wearing my favorite lipstick, please and thank you.

I was leaving tomorrow, and I wanted everyone to remember these perfect red lips kissing them goodbye.

As I finished up my makeup, Mom's kitten heels clacked against the linoleum kitchen floor above me, the sound growing louder and more insistent with each pass. That whole quote about Ginger Rogers doing everything backward and in heels? That was Eleanor. My mom wore power suits to host noontime barbecues when she wasn't running for city council. No really. One time, Uncle Chuck told her that if she was so appalled by bathroom debates and book-banning attempts, then maybe she should just run for local office. So she did. And won. In high heels and a killer blazer.

I guess you could say that I get both my tenacity and my impeccable fashion sense from her. But now it was time for Mama's little bird to spread their wings, and the countdown to freedom was ticking.

"Suuuuuuuully!" she called down the stairs. "Get upstairs and greet the people who are here for *your* party! Your subjects await!"

"Eleanor!" I yelled back. I always used her first name, like we were just a couple of gal pals. "You know art takes time!"

"That's Mom to you, babe! And don't talk to me about *time*. I was in labor with you for thirty-six hours!"

"Then you know I like to make an entrance!"

Even through the floorboards, I could hear her chuckling. Okay, so I would miss this a little bit. But crying would ruin my eyeliner, so there would be none of that.

She opened the basement door then, her voice dropping an

octave. "Get your cute tush up here, please. I may have raised you to be fashionable, but being fashionably late to your own party is *not* the vibe."

I snorted. *The vibe.* Oh, bless.

I straightened my vintage chartreuse chiffon jumpsuit and pouted at my reflection. It was gorgeous. It was elegant. It was . . . too much. Imagining presenting my full Sully Self to the relatives upstairs, I felt something hot rush up my neck that absolutely couldn't be shame. But sometimes it was just easier to pull back so nobody could accuse me of being over-the-top. Maybe the lipstick needed to go. Maybe I should leave Hearst with a whisper instead of a bang. But had I really come this far only to diminish myself yet again?

*Buck the hell up*, I told myself. This time next week, my entire life would be different. I could take solace in that. But for now, I took a makeup wipe to my lips and decided to play it safe. Well, as safe as platforms and a jumpsuit could possibly be. So long, Ruby Woo. Oh well.

"Sully! Now!" Eleanor bellowed.

"I've been summoned!" I yelled back as I ran up the stairs to meet my fate.

# 2

I heard Uncle Chuck before I saw him. His gut-busting laugh echoed from the kitchen, following some joke about the size of Mom's chili bar (which could, honestly, feed half of Hearst).

"I have arrived," I announced, spreading my arms wide and curtsying. Occasions like this, I really wished I'd brought capes back. Was it just me, or were they due to have a moment? Mom twirled around, showing off the sequined rainbow dress she bought last year from Target for Pittsburgh Pride.

I brought my fingers to my lips, giving her a little chef's kiss of approval. "One hundred percent that bitch."

Uncle Chuck sputtered. "Did you just call your mother a—"

Mom slapped his shoulder with a pot holder. "It's a compliment, you old turd."

My cousin Guy saved the day by bounding through the back door like a damn golden retriever.

"Hey Sull! You look, um . . ."

"I think the word you're searching for is *amazing*," I said, helping him out.

"I was going to say *fabulous*." The word sounded like a foreign language in Guy's mouth, but my best friend and cousin grinned and wrapped me in a back-slapping man-hug. "That works, right? Fabulous?"

"It works," I said, grinning.

"Auntie El," Guy added, "thanks for the spread, but aren't you worried you'll run out?"

*Like father, like son.* At least Guy's version of the humor he'd inherited from his dad was mostly charming. Guy was also a Mom Whisperer. All the moms in town just *oohed* and *aahed* while he flirted and buttered them up like the last biscuit at a bake sale. He was starting to be an Emma Whisperer, too, but I tried not to think too hard about that.

Mom laughed, handing him a stack of gaudy gold-and-black GRADUATE paper plates and napkins. Yikes. They'd been the best option at the dollar store, but I'd graduated high school, not lost my eyesight. "Set these out, please, and get out of my kitchen."

Guy gave an adorable little pout and then set off with the paper goods.

To be entirely clear, when I said Guy was adorable, I meant it in a totally platonic non-incestuous way. He's my cousin, technically, but really, he's also my bestie. Even if he was straight. And liked football and video games and had no tolerance for hot sauce. Did I hold that against him? Not in a literal sense. After all, he always stuck up for me around town, which wasn't easy for either of us. True to his name, he was a guy's guy, but he tried his best to understand what life was like for me as the only gender-nonconforming person in Hearst. His friends didn't get it, but he never tired of making them try. I'd given up on most people truly understanding me a long time ago, but it felt nice to have a few good ones in my corner.

Guy ushered Uncle Chuck toward the living room, their wide linebacker shoulders making the two of them look identical from behind. Sometimes it hurt to see the similarities in them. "Dad," Guy said, "you heard Aunt El. Go find a La-Z-Boy and chill until the food is ready." He shot me a wink over his shoulder like *I'll babysit this lug.*

Over the last few months, I'd started to wonder what Guy might become without me here. If the next time I came home—*if* I came home—he'd ask me down to the tailgate for beers and brats with the bros because he'd only have his meathead friend, Ron, and Uncle Chuck for company. Guy's future plans were a rotating door of possibilities. Last I checked he was interested in professional bowling, but just a few months ago it was the navy (admittedly the uniforms were sexy) and then before that it was professional surfing. Emma quickly burst that bubble when she reminded him we were totally landlocked and he couldn't even keep his balance that one time we all attempted standing paddleboards when I was feeling especially committed to a Girl Scout–chic-inspired look I was wearing.

"I'm good for more than just napping and jokes," Uncle Chuck grumbled as he shuffled toward the hypnotic glow of some sporting event on TV.

Soon, having dumped off the paper plates and his dad, Guy was back. He pulled up to my side, whispering, "Hey, so, uh, is Emma here yet? I kind of—"

"Say my name two more times and I'll appear in your bathroom mirror," Emma intoned as she sidled up to my other side. "Like Bloody Mary, but with less conviction."

"Gasp!" I said in mock surprise, pulling my other bestie into a side hug.

Guy's milk-white cheeks turned the color of my favorite blush. Emma had that effect. She looked like a young Stevie Nicks, except with extra curves, bold red hair (straight out of the box), and an upbeat aura that was very Aries with a rising Pisces moon. Her older sister Angelika was my former babysitter and current absolute idol, besides Eleanor, of course. She was now a major department store buyer in Beijing, and the snippets of her big-girl life that I got on FaceTime looked straight out of *Emily in Paris*, *Crazy Rich Asians* edition—and showed me a blueprint for getting out of Hearst. They were two different flavors of awesome.

Emma wrapped her arms around my waist. "Is it too late to beg you to take me with you?"

Guy cleared his throat into his fist. "Hey, Emma."

I looked from him down to Emma and then back to him again. "So are y'all on again or off again this week?"

"No," Emma said, just as Guy said, "Yes."

"That wasn't a yes-or-no question." I rolled my eyes. "Whatever. Just save the drama for after I've boarded my flight."

"Sull," Emma said, her brow furrowing. "What happened to your lipstick? You look like you did your lips then made out with a plate of nachos."

*Damn.* Here she was with the hard-hitting questions before I could even give her our customary we-are-hot-so-shut-up-and-leave-us-alone double kiss on the cheeks.

"Uh, I just didn't want the bold red to clash with my romper, lady!" I said sheepishly, hoping she'd drop it. I wasn't feeling like going into the PhD-level-gender-studies intricacies of why I'd opted out of my red lip at the last second. I was allowed to change my mind, even if I didn't really want to.

Mom peered over her shoulder, probably thinking she was so stealthy, but her telltale gaze landed on my makeup, too. It was lipstick, people! My family claimed to try their best. Even though I used they/them pronouns and had explained all things gender nonconformity to everyone many times, Emma and my mom were the only two who really seemed to get it, and thank god they did. I never would've gotten this far without them. But it was all about to matter a lot less when I boarded that plane tomorrow.

Before Mom could nose in for another "vibe check," the three of us made bowls of chili—decked out with cheese, sour cream, and crispy fried onions, of course—and gathered on the deck. A late spring chill hung in the air despite summer officially starting in a matter of days. Tiki torches lit the backyard while the TV inside the house threw blue flickers against the wall. The bugs hadn't yet awakened to start their droning, so it was almost peaceful. I had to admit that there was something charmingly nostalgic about this moment, though it hadn't even passed me by yet. But it felt like a "before" on the cusp of an "after." The next time I stood on this patio, I'd have experienced the chance to live my own life. Would I be the same person? Whoever they were, I looked forward to getting to know them and seeing them in the mirror. Maybe after some space and distance, I'd find that there were actually things about Hearst I'd miss. Maybe.

"What's your first assignment with this hashtag-Lyndzi chick?" Guy asked earnestly, raking his curls off his forehead.

Emma and I looked at one another and burst out laughing.

"You know it's an at symbol, Guy. Hashtags are completely different. Don't play dumb. Not a cute look," Emma said.

"So you're saying there's a chance of cute?" Guy said with a smirk.

Emma shook her head, but I caught the smile curling on her lips despite her best attempts to hide it. Those two were a mess of feelings.

"Well, first thing once I step off the plane and am whisked away in a town car, I'm sure, is a meeting with the whole team. She has filming and editing people, but I'll need to be on hand for, like, quick little TikToks and Reels and social-media-manager stuff. I think I might even get to help pack her bags for Paris Fashion Week this fall. Where I'll probably see Angelika."

"And Fashion Week is like the . . . NFL Combine?" Guy asked. "Or is it the Draft?"

"The what? Isn't a combine some kind of big farm machine?" I asked. Football terms were even worse than celebrity wellness brand names—complete nonsense.

Emma laughed. "Either. Both. It's like the biggest event of the year outside of the Met Gala."

"The Super Bowl," I leaned in to clarify with a stage whisper. At least I could speak Guy's language sometimes.

Mom left a cluster of my second cousins to wave at me. She was certainly buzzing around tonight. "Sully, when you're done eating, I need you out and about making the rounds. And make sure you say hi to your aunt Maggie. You know she hates driving in the dark, and she's already making noises about going home."

"You're, like, a bride," Emma said to me, then spun to my mom. "And we are totally their maids of honor, Miss Eleanor. Don't you worry, we'll keep them on task with the receiving line. First up, Aunt Maggie."

There were things I *would* miss about Hearst. And Emma was right up there at the top of the list. Aunt Maggie, maybe not so much.

Mom gave us a quick wink before turning on a heel and heading back inside to assemble the dessert buffet and the many "salads" she'd made, which were definitely not salads and mostly consisted of either mayonnaise, for the savory, or marshmallows, for the sweet.

After polishing off the rest of my chili, I drew in a deep breath to steel myself. Time to mingle. This was the part I'd dreaded all day. Extended family functions were always packed with distant relatives who could barely remember how old I was, and all the cousins were defined by whatever sport or hobby they had tripped into at the age of five. I'd learned the difference between biological and found family the hard way a long time ago. Outside of Eleanor, I preferred the latter.

With Emma and Guy following me, I started the greetings with Aunt Maggie, of course, who was sitting inside by the door, wringing her hands and peering suspiciously past the blinds at the gathering dark like it was coming for her.

Guy and Emma flanked me like bodyguards as I made the rounds, and everyone was civil for once. To my relief, there were no veiled insults or "woke" jabs. Maybe Eleanor had read them the riot act on the adult group chat.

As my great-uncle Tim got busy telling us about the fishing trip he'd just returned from, there was a tentative knock at the door, and Emma broke away to answer it. Not a single person coming to this party—at least not this early—would ever *knock* at my parents' house. Then a six-foot-something tall drink of water ducked through the doorframe. Ugh, he wasn't supposed to be here until later.

Guy clapped his hands over his mouth. "What's up, *Bread*?"

I nudged him in the ribs, my eyes wide.

"I mean, *Brad*."

Brad Thompson smirked and nodded to me before beelining for the kitchen to present my mom with a foil-wrapped plate of watermelon, feta, and basil skewers. Most of my family would be horrified at the thought of their watermelon getting cozy with a dairy product, though somehow mayonnaise was okay. Also, basil? Too spicy, too green. But Bread's family was . . . cultured. Like, if Hearst had a country club, they'd be members. His khakis pretty much screamed that he knew his way around a boat. They weren't rich, really, but his parents had lived outside of Pennsylvania at some point—California, maybe? Hence the skewers. Then they apparently chose Hearst when they decided to raise a family, taking a page out of Eleanor's playbook.

"What's the teacher's pet doing here?" Emma whispered as she rejoined us.

"Don't remind me." I'd been trying not to think about Bread interning at Eleanor's freaking city council office for the summer, before he headed to Penn State to wear khakis and study prelaw. I couldn't help feeling that she was replacing me with him, because I'd had the audacity to leave.

Being the only two gay kids in a small town was confusing

enough without Mom swapping one of us out for the other.

"He's buying my car, so at least he has a reason to be here" for this one. But he wasn't supposed to show up until *later*," I said to Guy, pointedly.

This had to be Eleanor's fault. Mom had been not-so-gently attempting to matchmake the two of us since the ninth-grade homecoming dance. She seemed to believe he was my type.

To be clear, I wasn't entirely sure what my type was, but I knew Bread wasn't it. Bread had been my archnemesis for all of high school. He played soccer. He was president of the student council because he wanted to go into transportation and infrastructure after college. Like, what? Bread had also never had a pimple—and I checked. *Every. Single. Day.*

That's probably why Eleanor thought I had a crush on him, but I was only looking for a sign that he wasn't some kind of humanoid robot. Bread had clearly never dealt with an awkward day in his life. Sometimes I envied him, sure, because he seemed okay with playing to fit in. But I also felt sorry for him because he was *Bread*. Boring sliced bread. Though he happened to be the only other person in Hearst who was my age and out of the closet, we had about as much in common as two total strangers who happened to walk into a restaurant and order the same dish.

So what if he was gorgeous? Like a *High School Musical*–era Zac Efron but taller, with a sharp jaw, soft green eyes, and the kind of hair that needed to be trimmed every two weeks by a straight barber named Jim, who also happened to see Guy and Uncle Chuck and pretty much every other dude in town. Bread was the exact "right" kind of gay. The kind of gay that a town like Hearst could stomach.

Unlike, well, me.

He always said he wanted to work toward meaningful change right here at home, but I'm not sure I believed him. What kind of turmoil did Bread know? People liked him, and haters generally left him alone. I knew pain and trauma weren't a competition and everyone's experience was valid . . . but I couldn't help being jealous of how easy he had it.

Brad returned from the kitchen with a plateful of food, courtesy of Eleanor. He even had a few of Aunt Maggie's ham-and-egg-salad sliders, which no one else dared touch due to their grayish hue.

"So nice of you to come tonight, Brad," I said, so cracker-dry that you could've served me with Brie. He didn't seem to catch my edge, though.

He shrugged. "Eleanor said I should come by early for your party."

"Gotta impress your new boss, right?" I smiled, but it felt more like a grimace. That might've come out saltier than I'd meant it to. "I thought we were just going to do our business deal. Leave the money on the dresser and all that."

Bread's mouth quirked just a little at the joke. "I can't believe you're getting out of here."

"I can!"

Before Bread could answer, we were distracted by some movement on the other end of the room. Eleanor stepped out in front of the fireplace. This was a clear sign, in my family, that something important was about to happen. Dad sat at attention in his recliner. He gave her an exaggerated grin and thumbs-up before doing the same to me until I waved back and shook my head at him to stop.

How he, a longtime Hearstian and salt-of-the-earth contractor, ever got involved with someone like Eleanor was a mystery. But he was more than happy to give her the podium whenever she wanted it, which I could respect. He'd probably even build one for her.

She could've gone anywhere, done anything. But she loved this place, its history, her memories. She and Dad met here, and that was enough. I tried hard not to judge her for it, but I didn't get it. I couldn't have this be *it* for me.

Ironically, my delulu great-grandma Josephine's cross-stitch hung on the wall behind Eleanor. Josie's maiden name was Bloom, so she'd stitched the phrase *Bloom Where You're Planted* and surrounded it with flowers. Growing up seeing that silly slogan every day only hardened my resolve to leave, to go bloom elsewhere. And tomorrow, that was exactly what I'd do.

Unfortunately, I had a sinking feeling about why Eleanor was at the podium now. I hoped it wasn't a—

"Speech, speech, speech!" Guy chanted, and Uncle Chuck joined in. Even Bread gave me a smile so wholesome and encouraging it made my cheeks hot.

Fantastic.

# 3

All two dozen or so friends and family turned toward us as my mom smiled, clearly relishing the attention. She reminded me of those teachers who never needed to yell to calm a classroom, one of the qualities that made Eleanor the perfect addition to the city council. I wanted this talent for myself—to command respect naturally, instead of having to ask for it. Or, in some cases, beg.

I noticed that the silence was dragging on a bit too long. And nobody was looking at Eleanor anymore. They were looking at *me*.

"My child. My swan," Eleanor was saying. "My darling little human being, how did eighteen years zoom by so fast? Some people sit around waiting for their dreams to come true, but Sully, my love, you already seem to know what most never manage to learn in a lifetime: the only way things happen is to *make* them happen. You're getting out there, baby, and you're doing it up big."

Dad let out a whistle. "That's my kiddo!"

A man of few words, that one, but that couldn't stop me from smiling at him. For the most part, he didn't know what to make of me, but he was always along for the ride, the steady foundation upon which Eleanor and I built our dreams.

Mom's eyes glistened. "Could you come up and say a little something-something and thank everyone for coming tonight, hun?"

Her watery gaze shifted—almost imperceptibly—into a fierce get-your-ass-up-here-right-now smile. The kind she used on Beauregard Hearst, Eleanor's city council nemesis and descendant of the Hearst brothers (yawn, no relation to the infamous Patty), who were responsible for settling this dump in the first place. She'd miraculously dethroned him when I was a freshman in high school. Mom edged out Beau's platform, which involved reestablishing traditional values to attract families that were just starting out with massive redevelopment plans for housing and schools to turn Hearst into another bland suburb, whereas Eleanor focused on celebrating and preserving Hearst's history. Beau had been angling for that seat back ever since.

I reluctantly left Guy and Emma and stood front and center beside Mom. As I looked at all these people I'd known my whole life, I wanted to feel thankful for them. I did. But right there alongside the good memories were all the times they had been careless and hurtful. They might not have been intentionally cruel, but they hadn't been intentionally kind, either. Memories of their slights, big and small, over the years, drifted over their heads like dust mites.

Like when they'd misgendered me at my sixteenth birthday party.

Called me the F-word at the family reunion.

Refused to invite me to their sleepover birthday parties because they didn't think it was appropriate. That *I* was appropriate.

Laughed at me when I went to the Steelers game for "male bonding" and wore a barrette in my hair. At least I color coordinated it black and gold, but that somehow only made it worse.

And then there was Bread, who'd finally abandoned his ham-and-egg-salad slider and was watching me with curiosity. He could've been a true friend, a confidant. But he'd chosen the status quo, which was a betrayal in and of itself.

This was it. This was my moment to give the speech of a lifetime. The kind of speech that would make everyone see exactly who they'd missed out on. Who they'd never get back.

I cleared my throat and did my best to ignore the nerves fluttering in my stomach. Or maybe that was the chili.

"Thanks so much for coming over tonight, everyone. This means so much to my mom . . . and me," I struggled to add, and was rewarded with a nod from Eleanor. Looking out at the crowd, I spotted Guy and Emma near the back, giving me goofy thumbs-ups, and suddenly I couldn't do it. I couldn't be a smartass, not now. For them, and for Eleanor, I'd play nice. "Sometimes it feels like my life here was like the introduction on a makeover show, you know, before the big reveal, and I'll always remember you all . . . fondly."

I looked over at Mom, not sure whether this was the tone she was hoping for. She pursed her lips into an appreciative, if thin, smile.

Uncle Chuck came up beside me and clapped a broad, beefy palm against my back. This was fine, until I noticed that he was dragging an old department-store bag, which he must've been hiding in the trunk of his sheriff's-deputy cruiser. "Well said, Sully. It's no secret that a little ol' place like Hearst hasn't always been the easiest for a fella like you."

*Fella?* My fists clenched at my sides. Strike number one. Okay, that hurt, but I could be the bigger person here. This was nothing new, after all.

"I decided we couldn't send you off on your new big-city life without a big-city wardrobe."

Someone chuckled from the kitchen. Was I being ambushed?

Before I could say anything, Chuck shook out the bag and dumped its contents all over the floor. I was left staring down at a pile of dusty old prom dresses and nightgowns.

"Picked up some duds at Yesterday's Today!" Chuck said, before doubling over to laugh so hard he wheezed.

So this was me, according to him. Old '80s prom gowns. Drop waists, puff sleeves, and tulle. Satin and lace. Worse, he'd gone to the clearance rack of discards at Yesterday's Today, tainting one of the only places in Hearst where I felt welcome.

Message received, loud and clear. Like those hideous rags, I was unwanted, according to him. My own uncle.

He wasn't the only one laughing.

"You'll finally get to wear all these crazy getups and really be yourself. All these people staring at you around town these last few years"—he didn't seem to notice or care that I didn't appreciate his "joke"—"At least in New York, they don't stare at the oddballs. They're everywhere! You'll fit right in, man."

I felt the color draining from my cheeks as my chest began to burn. I wanted to run out the door. I wanted to vanish from this moment until I was nothing but a puff of molecules and glitter. Because molecules didn't have to be perceived or acknowledged or live through horrifying moments like this. Molecules didn't care about labels; they simply existed.

This, this right here. *This* was why I was leaving. So I could simply exist. Was that too much to ask?

In Hearst I was always the butt of the joke. The little family defect who everyone tolerated, but not really. Their true feelings came out when given the smallest chance.

Just when I thought it couldn't get any worse, Chuck picked up the most offensive dress of the bunch and held it out in front of me, the sequins winking in the last rays of the sunset. "Oh, I think he likes it!"

A heavy, thick silence settled across the living room. Even Aunt Maggie seemed to realize something was wrong. She looked at me, aghast, her spectacles sliding down her nose. I swore my heart was beating in slow motion, either a bass line or a funeral dirge.

And, bitch, I was about to drop the mic.

The rage of a hundred comment sections pulsed up my platform-clad feet, crawling slowly past the belted waist of my chartreuse jumpsuit and into my lungs. *Don't make a scene. Not tonight. Let Mom have this one perfect memory of her homespun goodbye party.*

But it was too late. If I tolerated this, I'd be letting myself down, and her, too. She hadn't raised me to sit down and shut up. The anger quickly turned to pain, and a bit of shame that I had let Uncle Chuck and this . . . this *place*—full of these *people*—have so much power over me.

"*Man?*" I asked through gritted teeth. "A *fella* like me? *He* likes it? No matter how many times I've told you my pronouns, you just don't seem to care or listen! This isn't some slip of the tongue, Uncle Chuck. It's like you're *trying* to hurt my feelings. To embarrass the shit out of me. But guess what? I *can't* be embarrassed if I don't give a flying shit about you or what you think."

I looked around, wondering if anyone would assist. But even Emma seemed suddenly very interested in her red Solo cup, and Mom was frozen in pure shock.

"I'm already getting out of here. Don't pretend you're not happy about it. You won't have to worry about me or my clothes or makeup anymore. So get your last look at the freak show. Right? Is that more like it?"

Nobody was smiling anymore. I couldn't tell if they thought I was deranged, or if I'd gotten through to anyone. I didn't care anymore. Really.

"If people want to stare? Let. Them. Stare."

I felt a hand on my shoulder and whooshed back into my body from the fugue state I'd been in. It was Guy, looking like he was approaching a wounded animal. "Come on, Sully. Let's chill for a bit. He was just trying to be funny."

"Thanks for clarifying, Guy. But there's nothing funny about your own family embarrassing and misgendering you. Family is supposed to be safe. They're not supposed to pick on people and make them the butt of the joke."

The second cousins whispered to one another, their eyes trained on me.

"I'm standing right here," I reminded them.

Guy shook his head, clearly flustered and frustrated. "You know what I meant to say." Mom stepped in then to try to take the attention off me. In a calm, even voice, she said, "Chuck? Guy? I think it's time you headed home."

Uncle Chuck looked at her, confused and hurt, as if he was

trying to piece together what had just happened. I couldn't imagine how he could be so entirely unaware, but I was done giving him the benefit of the doubt and excusing his behavior. He had to run an errand to get those clothes. He'd *planned* this.

A few relatives began to shuffle around, probably eager to escape the awkwardness. Aunt Maggie, bless her, finally leaked out the front door and made a beeline for her car.

"Hey, we don't have to make this a big deal right now. Let's just get out of here. Me, you, and Emma," Guy said, reaching for my shoulder again, but I shrugged him off.

They all just wanted this moment to pass. To pretend like it never happened.

Then the dam of emotions broke loose, and my eyes began to water. "No big deal, Guy? This is a *huge* deal to me. That should be reason enough for it to matter to you."

"It does, Sully. Of course, it does, but—"

"That's exactly it. Everyone accepts me *but*. Everyone loves me *but*. But what? But you wish I could be *normal*?"

"Sully," Emma said softly. "Let's go out to the deck. Come on. You need to cool off."

I turned to her, practically snarling. Not Emma, too. "You know what? This place is a meaningless blip in the universe. And what do you think that makes all of you? Everyone who's too scared to get out of here and discover that the world is bigger than your tiny little boring bubble?"

Mom stood behind Emma, her lip trembling just a bit. And Emma . . . she was wounded. Like the time she realized all the girls in our fourth-grade class had been invited to a slumber party but her.

"I need some air. And *space*." I looked past Emma and Guy. "Sorry, Mom. I love you, but your older brother is a dick."

Uncle Chuck stood there in a puddle of magenta polyester chiffon, looking about as confused as he had the time he'd accidentally tried vegan bacon.

The guests went fully silent, mouths agape. I wanted to relish in the drama, maybe flip a table for effect, send that egg salad soaring, but nothing felt good about the pit forming in my stomach.

Mom's whole face looked like she might crumple into tears at any moment.

"I'm sorry," I whispered to her as I pushed past Uncle Chuck, grabbed my keys off the hook, and slammed the front door behind me.

I sat in the driver's seat of Olivia Newton-John, my green 2012 RAV4, with the key in the ignition and my head thrown back against the headrest, catching my breath. If I just kept my eyes closed, tears couldn't actually escape, though they were threatening. Badly. If no tears were shed, then Uncle Chuck would never have the honor of making me cry.

Mom had asked me to park a few houses down so the relatives could use the driveway and get VIP street access—especially Aunt Maggie. My window was cracked just enough that I could still hear the party going on. Without me. After my outburst there'd been apocalyptic silence, but now the Pirates game was back on, and people were milling around and chatting. Probably about me.

This sucked. This evening was supposed to be like that fantasy of getting to go to my own funeral, where everyone was devastated and only had nice things to say. Instead, here I was almost—but not *technically*—crying in my car down the street from my house.

Just as I was tempted to slide the car into reverse, someone rapped at the window.

"JESUS MARY AND JOSEPH, BREAD!" I shrieked.

Bread smirked, his hands bunched in his pockets. "Hey, Sully, I didn't mean to startle you. Going somewhere? In my car?"

"Yes. No. I mean, she's not actually yours. Yet." I glanced around, my eye catching on the smiley-face sticker Guy had stuck to the volume button once upon a time. I'd tried peeling it off when I cleaned out the car, but that only made it worse, so I guessed Bread would have custody of Mr. Smiley now, too.

"I'm sorry about the blowout back there," he said, seemingly oblivious to the fact that I didn't want to talk about it. To the point where I'd literally left the premises. "It's not a family gathering without a fight, right? I mean, of course, at my house it's mostly my mom saying passive-aggressive things to my dad, them going over his head, and then her getting aggressive-aggressive that he can't read between the lines."

"That sounds . . . exhausting." My knuckles ached as I gripped the steering wheel. "You shouldn't have come, especially just to please my mom."

"Sully." His voice dropped, like we were so familiar that he'd said my name thousands of times. "No one makes me go anywhere."

I tilted my head to the side, giving him a suspicious look. Here was Bread, choosing to come to my party. Being empathetic and kind when even my two besties couldn't quite get there. What was happening?

"Okay, well, sometimes *my* mom makes me go places," he admitted, "but this was not one of those times. Anyway, it's no big deal. Families are complicated. If it wasn't dresses, it'd be something else. I'm glad I was there. I should have said something, though."

My cheeks warmed. That was, like, randomly sweet of Bread. I also kind of liked the button-up-shirt-and-khaki combo he was giving. Thank goodness the pants were flat-front, though. I couldn't bear the thought of unironic pleats, especially in this moment of post-traumatic stress.

"You wanna give me the grand tour?" he asked.

"You were just in my house, though."

Bread laughed. "Of the car."

"Oh! Right! Um, hop in," I said, suddenly aware of how dark it was in the space between streetlights where I'd parked.

Bread jogged around the front of the car, looking like he was in a deodorant commercial, and got in on the passenger side, free and easy, like this was just another evening in Hearst.

"Welcome to Olivia Newton-John," I said.

"Olivia Newton-John?" he asked with a laugh.

"I swear to god, Bread, if you change her name, I will find you, and I will kill you *Grand Theft Auto*-style. Like—"

The corners of his eyes crinkled. "Did you just call me *Bread*?"

Why wasn't he taking this more seriously? "Stop making this about yourself. I need you to understand that you are contractually obligated not to change Olivia Newton-John's name."

"Well, considering I had no plans to name the car in the first place, I guess that's fine. Though I don't see a contract anywhere."

"It's a metaphorical contract." I leaned my head against the headrest once more. "I'm so sorry, ONJ. But it's the best I can give you. You've seen Hearst. Limited options, I'm afraid."

"I'm glad you think so highly of me." Bread smiled again.

"At least I know *you* won't scrape off the progress pride flag bumper sticker."

"I'll keep that one. The 'Save a horse, ride a cowboy' sticker has to go, though. It's going to attract the wrong kind of attention."

I swatted his arm playfully. "Breaaaaaad, you bore. Emma got me that when she visited her dad in Texas."

"I'll take that into consideration, but no promises." His shoulder brushed mine as he rested his arm on the center console. It was obscene how easily he moved through the world. "So, what else do I need to know?"

"Well, the heat always takes the whole drive to school to kick on, so you might want to think carefully about your outerwear budget. The steering wheel alone will freeze your hands off, but who doesn't love a vintage-driving-glove moment, amirite?"

Bread shrugged. "Uh, okay."

"And the stain in the back seat was there when I got her." I glanced over my shoulder. "I swear."

He ventured a look, then cut me a side-eye. "Uh-huh."

I huffed, tears pricking at the corners of my eyes again at the mention of the mystery stain. "I'm, like, feeling really sentimental all of a sudden."

Bread shrugged. "It's okay to miss Hearst."

"It's not—" I said automatically, then stopped. Maybe I would miss Hearst, in a Stockholm syndrome kind of way. "I just . . . I've spent a lot of time wishing for this moment, and what if I get there and find out that I'm the exact same person in New York City as I am in Hearst?"

I desperately hoped he would know his cue to jump in and reassure me.

"I don't want to freak you out, Sully, but I'm pretty sure that's exactly what's going to happen."

"Excuse me?" All he'd had to do was tell me I'd be fine. Even if it was a lie. "Bread!"

"That's not a bad thing! Maybe it's true that being *you* will be easier there than it is here. But it doesn't have to be a here/there, either/or type of thing."

When I didn't say anything because I was furiously trying to will myself to disappear, he added, "You know, when I was a kid, I spent a lot of time wishing we hadn't moved here. I thought California was more my style."

"California isn't really known for its flat-front khaki vibes."

Bread smiled again. "Oh, shush. I'm serious. I was so mad at my parents for moving. I had to leave all my friends behind."

I inwardly rolled my eyes. This just proved how little I had in common with Bread, how little he'd gone through. At least he *had* all kinds of friends to leave behind. "Thanks for sharing."

"But any place can become home."

"Yeah, right!" God, he was one sound bite after another. It was slightly cute, but mostly cringe.

"That's why I'm sticking around and working with your mom. Instead of changing your environment, you can *be* the change to your environment."

"Print that on a bumper sticker and slap it on the car," I said, maybe not as nicely as I could've. *"Anyway."* This conversation had been going somewhere until it simply wasn't, so I took the key out of the ignition and handed it to Bread. *Brad.* "Be careful with that. I don't have a spare."

"Thanks for that key piece of information," he said with a chuckle. "Get it? *Key?*"

"Your humor is as corny as your style."

"Hey, now," he said. "Kohl's isn't *that* bad. Besides, my mom always has spare Kohl's Cash. But I promise to take good care of your car, Sully. *Our* car now, I guess."

I gave the steering wheel a hug. "Goodbye, Olivia Newton-John. We had some good times, even though I never got to christen you."

"Christen her?" Brad asked.

Ugh. The silly admission had slipped out, and now with Brad staring back at me, the air in here felt a little thicker. "You know," I said, squirming, "like have a steamy makeout sesh or something."

Brad's face turned serious. "I could help with that," he said quietly.

"Um, I don't take charity," I said, trying to joke the offer away. Things had just gotten super intense, super quickly, and I was glad that he couldn't see the pink on my cheeks—which was not, in fact, purposefully applied blush.

"You can christen the car and so can I. It's a two-for-one special. They have those at Kohl's all the time." He leaned toward me.

"I, um, wouldn't know anything about that," I said, simply to say anything. What in the *Freaky Friday* was happening? I bit down on my lower lip and mumbled, "But, um, I guess you have a point. About the christening. Not the Kohl's."

What was I even thinking? Bread? Really? Of all the people to kiss? For my *first kiss*? Not that anyone would ever need to know this was my debut outing.

There weren't all that many people to kiss in Hearst, and even though Bread's teacher's-pet energy irked me, I'd be lying if I said I hadn't wondered what it might feel like to make out with him, to feel like the only other queer person in town wanted me. There weren't many other eligible persons here to fantasize about. I'd tried thinking about the straight guys at school, trust, but the fact that half of them had thrown a piece of food at me some time in the last twelve years didn't really get me going.

I wanted to go to NYC and experience plenty of firsts, but kissing couldn't be one of them. The big city would eat me alive, so this felt safe and easy—kissing a guy I'd known most of my life, in the safe darkness of my car, on my street. I was fed up with making things easy for everyone else. It was time for me to think about myself. And as a bonus, whoever I did eventually kiss in New York wouldn't have to suffer through my first time figuring out where the hell tongues and hands were supposed to go.

Tilting my head toward Brad, I met him halfway and closed my eyes, like a Disney princess waiting for her prince to do all the work.

Just as I was about to chicken out and pull back, anxious that I'd misread the vibes, Brad's hand slid up my arm and his lips gently grazed mine. Our noses collided head-on, but then he tilted his head so that there was a place for my nose to go. Was kissing always this awkward? Then again, I sort of liked it.

He tasted like the minty ChapStick from the checkout aisle of the grocery store, and I couldn't help but notice that he was definitely wearing some kind of cologne. God, so many boys I'd grown up with just reeked all the time, so the fact that Brad had even considered what he smelled like put him several steps ahead of the rest. See? Cultured. For a brief second, his tongue ran across my bottom lip.

My heart skipped in my chest, and suddenly this chaste little Afterschool-Special kiss didn't feel like enough. Without even thinking about it, I swept my hand up the back of Brad's head and, holy hunny, I loved the feeling of my fingers in his close-cut hair. His nearly invisible stubble rubbed against my face, and we deepened the kiss.

Immediately, my tongue was down Brad's throat, and, oh my God, he was good at kissing. Was I, though? Would there be, like, some kind of grade at the end? He had clearly been practicing, but with who? I didn't think this was his first time, and his work spoke for itself.

Blood rushed in my ears, and my body was starting to feel . . . a certain way, and—

I pulled back suddenly, leaving us both to pant a little.

"Um, wow. Okay, so that was . . . nice. Uh, good job. Buddy." I died inwardly as I gave him two thumbs-ups, like I was leaving a freaking Yelp review. My lips felt a little swollen, and in the back of my mind was the sudden feeling of wishing we'd had the chance to explore this more.

That was . . . unexpected.

Brad just looked at me and said nothing. My humiliation for the night was complete.

"You . . . uh . . . you and Olivia Newton-John have a nice life together." I fumbled for the door handle, finally finding the lock and practically tumbling out into the street.

"I need to pay you," Brad called out the open door.

"Uh, excuse you. I love *Pretty Woman* as much as the next nonbinary cutie, but—"

"For the car," Brad clarified.

"Oh, right! Venmo me! Be good to Olivia Newton-John! Treat her real cute," I said before slamming the door and hauling ass back up the street, this time like *Runaway Bride*, going from one huge mess to another. I had picked a hell of a moment to be all shades of Julia Roberts.

This had to be one of the most dramatic nights in Hearst's queer history. Probably the only one if I was being honest.

I looked back once more to see Brad sliding over the console and into the driver's seat. At least we wouldn't be crossing paths again anytime soon.

He was a good kisser, though. If only I'd figured that out sooner.

# 5

The next morning, I slept through my first two alarms, which meant I didn't have time for my a.m. skin-care routine, or, conveniently, to think about Bread—I mean Brad. Did I have to stop calling him Bread now that we'd kissed?

Before I could even sit up and let my vision come into focus, the plethora of memories from last night came flooding back. I couldn't decide what was more shocking: Uncle Chuck's bullshit heteronormative prank, me actually being surprised by his behavior, Guy siding with him, or my small-town rom-com moment on the eve of my departure.

I hated to leave town with me and Guy in a bad place, but the memory of him telling me to calm down made my stomach turn. That's what people always told me when I was too much, or too me. I was sure we'd figure things out eventually. Maybe by the time I came home for Thanksgiving. But for now, I felt justified in taking a break.

The only thing that really mattered now was that, tonight, I'd be doing my p.m. skin-care routine in my new bedroom in New York City. Well, more like on a couch, which had so graciously been offered to me by Mara, one of Lyndzi's assistants, until I could get my apartment-slash-roommate situation figured out.

How bohemian of me!

And to get me started . . . *Cha-ching!* My phone chimed with an incoming Venmo alert, informing me that Brad had sent my $2,000 for Olivia Newton-John. The attached message had a car emoji and read: thanks for the car . . . and the memories 😊

I smirked as I sprang out of bed, brushed my teeth, and threw the rest of my toiletries in my bag. If I wasn't literally about to leave for the airport, I'd totally regret kissing Brad. Maybe? But it didn't matter now, because he was just a pre–New York fling.

Gasp!

My first official fling. This was truly a milestone moment. I officially had *romantic history*! Entanglement! Baggage! And not just the suitcase kind. Speaking of which—

"Sully!" Mom called down. "We need to get moving."

"Almost ready, Eleanor!" I sang back sweetly.

When I'd returned to the house the night before, I'd snuck into the basement via the kitchen while the rest of the guests lingered and eventually left. I didn't want to see anyone or talk to anyone, and I certainly didn't care to know whether the mess of dresses had been cleaned up before I returned. By the time Mom came down to talk to me, scold me, or worse, tell me how much I had disappointed her, I pretended to be asleep. I was worn out and not feeling brave enough to have whatever discussion was coming.

Odds were that she was on my side, but I couldn't risk another heartbreak.

And now we'd never know, because this morning, there was no time.

As I zipped my carry-on, I dismissed a few text notifications from Emma that I'd read in the car and began scrolling Instagram for the latest updates.

Nothing super major, but—oh hello, alert! Lyndzi just posted!

It was an impeccable shot of Lyndzi in a form-fitting Givenchy bodysuit, baggy sweats slung low on her hips, and a huge floppy hat. She'd finished off the look with a pair of Jackie O–esque sunglasses while strutting across a commercial tarmac from a black SUV to a huge, shiny airplane.

Looked like we were both traveling today! I wondered where she was flying in from.

Then I read the caption:

Off to Tahiti for the summer! Inspiration only comes when we leave everything we know behind and seek nature and oneness to find perspective. Thanks for the ride @kimKair! #ad #sponsored

I froze.

Holy *shit*.

I was going to Tahiti? Oh my god. I had *not* packed with this in mind. Emma was going to be so jealous! I wondered if that meant I'd need to go to Lyndzi's apartment first, just to chat with the team, or whether we'd meet up on a layover.

My phone chimed again, this time with an email from Gennie, Lyndzi's head of operations. Okay, travel-agent girlie. Had she changed my flight already? Could you fly direct from Pittsburgh to Tahiti? They were so on top of things over there. I began to read:

Dear Sully,

We regret to inform you that due to unforeseen circumstances, your services as a junior assistant at Style by Lyndzi are no longer required. We apologize for the inconvenience. Lyndzi sends her best.

Ciao,
Gennie

P.S. We will not be revisiting this decision until next year when we take applications for junior assistants again.

I read it. Then read it again.
No.
*No.*
I slid down to the floor next to my suitcase, feeling like my whole body had liquefied into a puddle.

Blinking my eyes into focus, I traced the words on my phone screen as if they were an indecipherable message from an alternate doomed timeline.

*regret to inform*
*unforeseen circumstances*
*no longer required*
*not be revisiting this decision*

But the more I blinked, the more real and solid the email became. And the more outrageous! This couldn't be possible. Were Lyndzi and the rest of her team really taking off to Tahiti for the summer *without me*?

My heart began to race, the adrenaline I'd woken up with quickly turning to sick, gut-churning anxiety. Words I thought I'd left behind—like *SAT* and *back-up plan*—rang in my ears. But I didn't have a plan B. I didn't have a college wait-list spot or another job offer. I hadn't even applied to community college as a fallback.

*This* had been the plan. I was going to do the one-year junior-assistant program, and then that would lead to a full-time job or even something with a brand I totally would have made a connection with. So many former junior assistants had gone on to become influencers themselves or to get jobs with a brand. This was my future. My great escape. And now it was as irrelevant as a lightning-charger iPhone.

How could I have been so careless? I had put my future into the hands of someone I'd never even met. A one-name celebrity who wasn't even Oprah or Cher. Or Beyoncé. She spelled her name with a Z, for fuck's sake! And that wasn't even her legal spelling. Lyndzi was really Lindsey, as her old backstabbing high school friends had told TMZ. I should have known she was a fraud!

Anxiety turned to horror. *No, no, no.* The inside of my mouth tasted fuzzy.

Okay. Deep breaths. I needed to think.

Maybe I could get my job back at the thrift store. I could return Bread's Venmo and at least have Olivia Newton-John to my name again. Oh no—Bread! He was in my mouth last night!

That would be so freaking awkward, but I needed transportation. Forward momentum required transportation.

I gave myself ten minutes. Ten minutes to curl into the fetal position and sob. Not that I had a plane to catch anymore, apparently. I briefly wondered if I could get a cash refund on my ticket, for emotional damages, even though Team Lyndzi had paid for it.

"Sully!" Mom called again, cutting my pity party from ten minutes to a solid six.

I had to somehow tell Eleanor that the whole rest-of-my-life plan was off. But speaking the news aloud would make it real. I abandoned my airport 'fit for one of my mom's off-the-shoulder '80s sweatshirt dresses and some biker shorts to give my strongest Princess Diana–post-divorce look. Thankfully, Eleanor had bestowed a wealth of strong fashion references from decades past to uphold me in these troubling times.

The moment I creaked open the door from the basement, Uncle Chuck's voice smacked me in the face, and my resolve crumpled. How *dare* he return to the scene of the crime so soon?

But of course he was here. Uncle Chuck stopped by every morning for a coffee and an egg sandwich on his way to the station, as though Mom's kitchen was his own personal Dunkin'. And by the sound of his chattering, he didn't even seem to remember what had happened the night before. To Uncle Chuck, one of the lowest moments of my life had been just another day in Hearst.

I hovered in the hallway, shamelessly eavesdropping.

"I wonder if Sully will wind up taking any of those gowns with him," Uncle Chuck said with a laugh.

"It's *them*, Chuck. Jesus. Please, let's help Sully leave on a good note," Mom chided. "What the hell were you thinking?"

I'd flipped that party on its head last night, but at least Mom was still in my corner. I wished I'd talked to her instead of hiding in my blanket cave. But now I'd have a lot more opportunities. "Ellie, are you sure you're okay taking Sully to the airport by yourself?" Dad asked over the ice machine, probably Eleanor filling her to-go mug for iced coffee.

"Yes," Mom said patiently. "You know those curbside drop-offs are chaos. Best you all do your goodbyes here without a line of cars honking while you blubber all over our child."

"Nothing wrong with leaking a few."

"It's healthy, even," I said as I stepped into the kitchen, pretending that I didn't mind all eyes on me. I was used to it, but this felt different.

"Morning, kiddo," Dad said just as Mom stepped back from the coffeepot and gave me a kiss on the cheek.

"Where are your suitcases?" she asked as she put the lid on her travel coffee mug. "I packed you a bag of snacks for the ride to the airport, including one of those probiotic sodas you like."

Dread crawled up my spine. I had to break the news to my parents. Unless I wanted to live at the airport after she dropped me off. I just wished Uncle Chuck wasn't there to watch.

"Mom. Dad." My gaze halted on my uncle for a moment. "Chuck." I cleared my throat before continuing. "I have an announcement." I focused on the Garfield mug on the drying rack next to the sink. It was easier than making eye contact and plunging even deeper into the shame. Was I not good enough for Lyndzi? Or had Tahiti really surprised everyone out of nowhere? Maybe if I'd just stood out more, Lyndzi's team would have brought me with them. But I'd spent my entire life trying *not* to stand out, because people like Chuck made it seem wrong. No matter how I sliced it in my head, I couldn't help but feel like this was somehow my fault.

"I will not be heading to New York City today after all. I got fired. Well, not technically *fired* because I hadn't even started working yet. But, basically, Lyndzi and her whole staff took off to Tahiti for the summer, and they no longer need my services, which, in the words of Julia Roberts, is a big mistake on their part. *Huge.* But I will be fine. Don't you worry." I'd been trying to project quiet strength. If it hadn't been for my voice cracking and my chin starting to quake, I think they would have bought it. "Anyway, that's that."

Dad and Chuck sat there in blank confusion, but Mom stepped forward, pulling me into her arms and going into immediate damage control mode. "Oh, honey, this must be some mistake! They can't just do that, can they?"

It felt good to lean into her hug. "Alas, Mom, it seems they can."

"We'll call someone," Dad said, feeling his pockets for his phone. "Surely these people can listen to reason."

"This isn't the principal's office, Dad." I shuddered, chasing away the mental image of Lyndzi and Gennie listening to a stern voicemail from my father and spitting out their oat-milk matcha lattes. "I need to figure out what to do with this summer and, more importantly, my life."

"Hey, there's plenty of fun trouble for you to get into right here in Hearst," Uncle Chuck said brightly, and I was almost overcome with the urge to shake him by the shoulders and ask whether he remembered his stunt the night before.

"Yeah, Chuck. *Such* fun trouble," I said, with a serious side-eye to my mom, who poured me a cup of coffee with too much soy milk—which was exactly the right amount—and a scoop of sugar.

With the caffeine anchoring me to my new—well, old—reality, I sat down beside Dad and sipped thoughtfully. "First, I need to repossess my car and do some groveling to get my job back. Then I can form a new escape plan."

Dad threw a sturdy arm around my shoulder. "You know they say discomfort helps you grow, so maybe there's something to you staying here a while longer. Selfishly, I'm glad you'll be sticking around."

"Thanks, Dad."

I wish he knew just how uncomfortable this place already was for me. His gender identity matched his assigned gender. That was Cisgender Privilege. He didn't have to struggle or fight public opinion at every turn. Nobody seemed to understand that I'd done all the discomfort already. And I'd already grown—right out of here. Or so I thought. Even when I dressed down or didn't bother correcting someone who'd misgendered me, I still stuck out. Some days, I just wanted to contour the ever-living shit out of my face to my heart's content, to be seen for what I felt like on the inside. But that wasn't going to happen anymore, and now I'd have to lower my bar to running errands without being scared that someone would make a scene, try to hurt me, or worse. There was a reason people tended to leave places like Hearst, and it wasn't just the lack of excellent microblading.

"Thanks for being so understanding, people. I know this wasn't part of the plan for you, either."

Mom set her coffee down and walked over to press a kiss to the top of my head. "Honey, I wanted an empty nest about as bad as I want menopause to last forever. This is your home. *We* are your home. You're always welcome here."

Her words soothed my little gay soul. Why couldn't everyone be like her? Just little Mom clones everywhere. An army of kitten heels! Why hadn't her brother gotten the memo?

"Can I give you a ride somewhere?" she asked as I stood to leave.

*Yeah, anywhere but here*, I wanted to say, but kept my mouth shut.

"That's okay," I said, pointing the toe of my cowboy boot forward. "These boots were made for walking. Until I get my baby, Olivia Newton-John, back."

I was sitting on a couple grand from Bread, and I'd have to find a way to talk him out of the car I'd sold.

As I headed down our steep street on foot, I took out my phone and refunded Bread, hoping he would accept. Then I scrolled Poshmark and The RealReal for finds I could now never afford. I'd had a plan to revitalize my wardrobe once I started making some money, but all that had gone out the window. I pined for the bags and shoes I'd never have.

As I turned the corner, my phone buzzed.

A Venmo *REFUND DECLINED* message, with the note: *Sorry, this was a final sale.* 🤠

Clearly, I wasn't getting a break today. *Fine*. I would talk to Brad face-to-face, no matter how weird it was bound to be—then he'd understand. But that could wait, especially since I wouldn't need a car unless I got my job back. It had felt so amazing to quit everything and sever all ties, and now I had to knit them back together. The idea was nauseating. Next up on Sully's Tour of Shame: employment.

Despite having no audience, I hit my best Naomi strut as I walked beneath the canopy of trees on Sanders Avenue. Not much about Hearst was cute or picturesque, but Sanders Avenue was lined with old-growth flowering dogwoods that bloomed in the spring and turned the perfect fiery shades of red and burgundy in the fall. Before I could drive, walking up and down the sidewalks to work always gave me Hallmark movie–main-character vibes. People romanticize that fairy-tale small-town life, but in those moments, I could almost feel it.

Yesterday's Today had always been this amazing old building that not many people saw because it was "just" a thrift store. That was like saying the *Mona Lisa* was just a portrait, though I was probably biased because so many of my good memories had taken place there.

For starters, the address was 728, one of my lucky numbers (because every nonbinary person with a clue needs more than one). Technically speaking, though, 728 was a number I'd seen around town all my life, stamped on the sides of some of the buildings or even etched into cornerstones. I think it had something to do with the factory that manufactured the bricks that went into some of the town's oldest buildings. But as a kid, it became a little game I'd play with myself. *I spy, with my little queer eye . . . Sully's special number.*

Second, because my favorite people in Hearst worked there, making amazing fashion possible for every li'l weirdo in town. (Okay, mostly me.)

The bell rang overhead as I walked inside the Victorian brick building, the familiar scent of the store wafting over me. It was slightly musty, with a hint of Fabuloso, because our manager, Claire, didn't mess around with running a tight ship. But the less-than-great low note of mothball and stale polyester was to be expected whenever a ton of old clothes collected in one building.

Hearst didn't have much to offer on the fashion front—Brad's staple, Kohl's, aside—but this place had always been my own personal haven, with its odd glimmer of couture and glamour. Not only had I unearthed some of my greatest finds within these hallowed walls, but I'd also become the Sully I was today in the fitting rooms and aisles of this shop.

There was something about thrift stores that let me feel like it was safe to play dress-up and find my own personal style. I first took a job as the fitting-room attendant when I turned fifteen, though I probably racked up more off-the-clock hours here than I did working, just hanging out with Emma and Claire. And even when I wasn't here, they'd always text me when a new donation came in that they thought I'd want first dibs on.

So, yeah, this place was just a dinky little secondhand shop to most, but to me, Yesterday's Today was the first public place where I wore a dress and a full face of makeup without feeling one single iota of shame. At the risk of sounding cheesy, I found myself here. Not to mention last night's amazing chartreuse jumpsuit.

Behind the register loomed Clementine, the store mascot, a toy T. rex in a doll dress and glitter-painted nails. I'd dubbed her our sassy little She-Rex, because, obvi. I always rubbed Clem's head for good luck whenever I walked by. But today there was someone new working the front counter.

"Welcome to Yesterday's Today," said the cheery girl behind the register. I'd never seen her before, but she was way too perky for my liking. This must've been my replacement. "Yellow tags are half off!"

"Um, thanks," I said, not sure if I should mention I'd attached those tags last week.

On autopilot, I headed to the back, where Claire was sipping on a green smoothie as she sifted through a fresh box of donations and listened to, no doubt, the audiobook of a bodice-ripping romance through one earbud. She was in her thirties and wore her wild brown curls swirled into a bun atop her head. I kept begging her to let me make her over, but she seemed to know that, like me, she was an odd fish in a small pond.

"Sully!" she said as she took the earbud out. "What are you doing here? I thought Emma said you were flying out today." She stood with a bounce, and a few donations fell out of her lap. "Did you meet cutie Cammie out front? I've never heard her say more than three words at a time, but you know how I like the wounded ones. I remember when you were a li'l baby sales clerk, and now look at you! All grown up and flying the nest!"

A rock sank through my stomach and into my butt. This was my life for the foreseeable future: delivering my bad news over and over and watching everyone react with pity.

"Such a cutie," I confirmed, my voice going up an octave or two. "Love that you won't be shorthanded!"

"God, me, too. And she can work Saturdays. I don't remember the last time I had a day to myself!"

"Live your weekend dream," I said, too cheerfully. She quirked an eyebrow. I'd laid it on too thick, I knew it.

"Sully? Is there something you're not telling me?"

"Well, actually... Claire, my summer plans suddenly changed, so I'm in Hearst at least through the fall. So..." I let it dangle there for a moment, hoping Claire would swoop in and save me the embarrassment of groveling.

"So?"

"So if you, you know, need help training the newbie or even just someone to fill in..."

"Oh. Sully. Damn. I'm so sorry! Between the new hire, Emma going full-time, and our part-time staff, I don't know how many extra hours I'll have."

Emma was going full-time at Yesterday's Today. Why had I not remembered that? This day just kept getting worse. "Totally fine," I said way too quickly. "Yeah. Totally."

Except it totally was *not* fine! How was I supposed to find another job in Hearst? One where I wasn't forced to work with bigots and people who called it "the TikTok"? Yesterday's Today had at least been my safe space. What was I supposed to do now? Bag groceries? I couldn't possibly wear a uniform.

"Don't sweat it," I told her. "I've got my Poshmark side hustle, so I'll be busy with that anyway. I was just wondering if you needed help."

Truth be told, I'd never really had the luck or organizational skills to make reselling work. The truly big-deal people had thermal printers and boxes of bubble mailers and custom stickers. I was an amateur by comparison, and Claire knew it. At least she did me the favor of smiling as if she believed my bullshit.

"I'll still give you first dibs on new merch," she offered, then tipped her head toward a few pallets. "Those came in from an estate sale just outside town. I've been too swamped to go through them."

It was an olive branch, a consolation prize, but... I'd take it. I loved sorting through incoming donations. You never knew what mysteries awaited. It wouldn't hurt to just *look*.

"You're a gem, Claire, and I'll totally take you up—"

It was like time slowed down as my eyes caught on something poking out of the box that she'd been sorting. Something... leather. And exquisite. The rest of the room seemed to go out of focus as my Sully-sense tingled.

"Where did you say you got this stuff?"

"An estate sale, I think, but some of it could have been dropped off in our overnight bin. Or maybe I got it in that mystery bundle at the flea market..."

I got it. A good treasure hunter never revealed their sources. Claire's thrift sense was legendary, and she often covered her tracks. Though normally I might have pressed her, now I couldn't tear my eyes away from the find.

I moved toward the bin as if hypnotized. The calfskin. The stitching... was it? No. It couldn't be. Nobody in this zip code had ever seen a Birkin, and certainly wouldn't drop one off at the thrift store. Maybe my mind was playing tricks on me, but after my too-brief brush flirting with the world of fashion, I was the closest this town had to an authenticator. "May I?" I asked, though my hand was already on it.

Claire nodded.

I pushed aside an old caftan to fully reveal a glorious chocolaty-brown bag that was practically screaming my name.

My heart skipped a few beats the moment I ran my fingertip over the orange stitching. "Oh my god," I gasped as I flipped the bag over.

It wasn't a Birkin. It was *better*.

A Butler.

A motherfucking Butler. One of the rarest vintage handbag finds of all time.

Was Claire too burned-out to see what she had here? Or did she not know? Not everyone had studied the history of fashion with an assist from the internet—and Angelika, of course.

The Butler was as good as an urban legend among fashion and vintage aficionados online. I only knew about it because I perused the subreddits where people drooled about their wish lists. If I found an item on there, I could connect with a collector and make some money. But I'd never come across anything anybody wanted that badly. Until, maybe, now.

Butler Fine Leather had been one of the first luxury bag-makers in the United States, and its brief existence made it all the more fascinating. I'd watched a two-hour deep dive from FashionHerstory on YouTube. Not to mention the ensuing rabbit hole about leathersmithing that I was sucked into so deep, I almost didn't graduate high school.

If this beautiful object before me really was an authentic Butler bag, it could be worth enough to get me out of Hearst and to kick-start my dream life. It was better than crashing-on-Mara's-couch money. It'd be New York City–*without-a-roommate* money. (At least for a few months . . .)

But what was a Butler doing in Hearst, Pennsylvania, of all places? This wasn't *Antiques Roadshow* or Sotheby's.

Even more importantly, how could I make it mine without shortchanging Claire? If she knew what she had, she'd never let me take it. I had to play it cool, though this was literally one of the most amazing things that had ever, potentially, happened to me.

*February 7, 1954*

*My Darling Swan,*

*I thought I'd given up on love, especially after all the disappointments I've been through. But after last night, something seems different between us. Even when we were ankle biters who stayed out too late and ran home barely in time for supper, I think a part of me always knew. It has always been you. It was you then. It is you now. This is the biggest risk I've ever taken, an honest-to-goodness moon shot. If I'm wrong, I lose you and I lose my lifelong friend, my confidant, my protector, my partner in crime, and, I fear, my heart. Please tell me you feel the same.*

*Yours, if you'll have me.*

# 6

"So, um, all this is up for grabs?" I asked, fingering the caftan as if it'd caught my attention.

"Huh?" Claire was back to her audiobook, clearly half listening.

"This stuff." I gestured, faux-dismissively. "I can take whatever?"

"Yeah. Sure." Claire bobbed her head, her messy bun waving. "Oh my god, the other day we got in this anatomically correct . . ."

But I wasn't listening anymore as I dug the bag out of the bin. Claire finished talking, and I quickly checked out with the chirpy new cashier before anyone could ask any questions. Clementine stared down on the entire transaction with what I felt was unnecessary judgment considering her glitter polish needed a fresh coat. The price tag hurt—seventy-five dollars I didn't have, especially since I'd failed to get my job back and I couldn't spend the two thousand dollars I needed to convince Bread to return Olivia Newton-John to her rightful owner—but if this was an actual Butler, nothing else would matter. My problems would be over. I could double what Bread paid for ONJ easy. I'd probably even give Claire a cut of the sale. So lay off the hairy eyeball, Clementine.

Hands shaking just a little bit, I settled into the beanbag lounger in my room and took my first real, good look at her. Mom was still at the office before her usual visit home for lunch, and Dad was down at the workshop, so now it was time to figure out whether I'd truly hit the lottery.

The purse had a kind of medicine bag–shaped body, slightly wider than it was tall, with two very large handles. When I set it on the ground, it came halfway up my calves. A true scene-stealing masterpiece.

I sank back into my chair, studying my treasure carefully. She was gorgeous, and I hadn't even looked inside. What if it was full of diamonds? Okay, okay, I wasn't trying to get greedy. I gently opened the bag, and my fingers ran over a rough edge. Using the light of my cell phone, I peered inside to find a chunky, slightly rusted zipper with a small three-combo lock attached to the end. Um, *excuse me*? A locked bag?

That was just my luck. Who impulse-bought a bag without looking inside first?

It's me. Hi. I'm the problem. It's me. An awkward vision flashed through my mind of me marching back into Yesterday's Today to try and return it to my replacement. Clementine would be so smug.

I lay back on my bed and put the bag beside me, so that I was face-to-face with my new personal nemesis, this rusty-ass lock. How good was this as a security measure, really? Though if it was a Butler, it'd have all the latest and greatest hardware. What if I couldn't crack it?

With a huff, I started trying obvious combinations of numbers I could think of.

Two, two, two.

One, two, three.

Hmm, maybe it was more occult vibes, which would be spicy.

Six, six, six.

No . . . keep going.

Three, two, one.

Nine, one, one. Was there even 911 back then?

Six, seven, eight.

If this bag were an iPhone, it would've locked my ass out seventeen tries ago. I'd never get this hunk of leather open.

Maybe this was destined to be a waste of my last seventy-five bucks. There was no assistant gig waiting for me. No job at Yesterday's Today. I tried not to panic and focused on the combination instead.

*At least the bag is cute*, I tried to tell myself. Except nobody here in Hearst would appreciate it. I'd already seen what looking cute in Hearst had gotten me—a bag of old prom dresses and an afternoon spent in Mom's basement. What was the point of serving up straight looks if I was the tree in the forest falling with nobody to see it?

I closed my eyes, searching for inspiration, but all I could see was movie-theater nachos and a Diet Coke. My stomach growled. *No, Sully*. All this talk of combos had me dreaming of the number nine at Starlight Cinema.

I closed my eyes and tried again. If this was my bag, what numbers would I use?

Seven.

Two.

Eight.

I entered the three digits, my magic number.

*Click.*

The lock popped open.

*No way* that just worked.

I reached into the pocket, and the fabric felt unusually cold . . . and damp. Oh my god, if this bag had water damage, I would actually die.

I removed my hand to check but nothing was wet. I must have imagined it. With a sigh, I went to properly assess the bag's condition. But I couldn't shake the weird feeling.

And then the chill coalesced into a plume of fog, rising from the purse.

"What the hell?" I muttered.

There was a gasp. And it wasn't mine.

I scrambled back across my bed as fog poured from my Butler like dry ice at a rock concert. It pooled on my carpet, getting denser and taller like a column of silvery vapor. As I watched slack-jawed, it slowly solidified into the silhouette of a human.

Whenever I watched a horror movie, I couldn't help but imagine what I would do if some freaky paranormal thing came for me. Freezing in place had never been on my list of possible reactions. That's what got people slashed or possessed. But here I was, completely locked up.

The misty figure—whatever it was—shimmered once and solidified.

It was a . . . ghost? My jaw fell open and I tried to force words out, but all that came out was unintelligible blabber. Fear and something like awe zinged through my bones. "What—who—huh?"

It was a man, although I felt conflicted making any assumptions. The figure stretched and took a deep breath, if ghosts can even breathe, causing the silk, floral robe he wore to slide off one shoulder. The pattern and the way it tied at his waist showed off the curves of his chest, belly, and thighs in a way that reminded me of J-Lo in that break-the-internet Versace jungle dress. A pair of bedroom heels adorned his feet, tufts of marabou above each toe weightlessly floating in the ether. A lock of blond hair swept across his forehead from under a tangerine-colored, bandanna-tied headscarf, and a single dimple studded his cheek, which, like the rest of him, was ever-so-slightly translucent, giving me a view of my desk and the far wall behind him. Unaware of my presence, with one hand he held a tin of soap and with the other a shaving brush, which he swirled along his jawline, then down his neck to his chest leaving a thick, creamy lather behind.

And though this was the least of my problems at the moment, I couldn't help but notice he was *cuh-yuuuute*. There was probably something wrong with me that I was finding an apparition shmexy, but like my suitcase for New York, I'd have to unpack that mess later.

Ghost hottie seemed to realize where he was as he took in my bedroom, gaze tracing my posters and bookshelves before landing on me. His fine eyebrows shot up, then he broke into a grin, eyes gleaming. "What the hell, indeed. Who are you?"

Although I am loath to admit it, I screamed in response. Sure, it was a short scream and I cut it off quickly, but it surprised us both. This was not real. I was clearly having a psychotic break due to massive personal disappointment. Adrenaline coursed through my veins as the nonsense sounds coming out of my mouth began to form words. "Who am *I*? Who are *you*? *What* are you? And not to sound materialistic or anything, but why are you in my possibly priceless bag?"

The telltale clacking of heels echoed above. "Honey, are you okay?" Eleanor cooed. She must have come home early for lunch.

"Mom!" I choked on a gasp as I scrambled to my feet.

"Is someone down there with you?"

Was someone with me? Or was I hallucinating? I had no idea how to answer this basic question. But I didn't have to, because Mom did that thing that moms sometimes do, knocking as she swung the door open, and striding right on down those basement stairs like she owned them.

Okay, well, technically she did.

I spun around on my heels to my new ghostly friend . . . but he was gone.

"Is someone down here with you?" Eleanor repeated as she turned the corner down the steps.

I shook my head frantically. "Nope. Not a soul." Or maybe it *was* a soul, actually. "Not a living soul," I clarified. Ugh, semantics.

The corner of her lip lifted slightly, and she nodded. "Please get through that mountain of clothes piling up, would you?" Then she peered past me, and the smile dropped from her face. "Is that another new bag?"

"Oh." I cleared my throat. "I found it at work . . . after Claire let me know I couldn't have my job back. So not work, exactly. I guess it's like a consolation prize." I gave Eleanor my most mournful puppy eyes. "You know, for my life falling apart and all."

Her furrowed brow softened. "I'm sure you'll figure something else out."

"Thanks, Mom," I said as I made a big show of gathering up a pile of clothes from the floor.

She turned to walk back upstairs, then looked back over her shoulder for a moment. "And Sully, not to kick you while you're down, love, but how much did that bag cost? I just think until we have a plan for the future you might want to be careful with—"

"Oh, this dusty old thing?" I said, whispering *I'm sorry* to it out of the corner of my mouth just in case it—or its weird ghost occupant—could hear me. "Claire felt so bad about the job that she just *gave* it to me."

"Well, that was kind of her." Something seemed to cross her mind. "Why don't I take you out for a mother-kiddo dinner later? Café Al Dente has half-off apps until seven. We can brainstorm what you want to make of your summer. Does that sound good?" Mom bit down on her lip, and I could see her fighting the urge to pry deeper into the state of my room . . . and me in general. Which, I had to admit, wasn't too great at the moment.

I furiously nodded, hoping she'd take the hint. "It's a date. I'll come by your office at five thirty?"

*After having to walk there*, I thought, but didn't add.

"I love how you never get sick of hanging out with your mama. Getting a few extra months here isn't all bad, right? I gotta head back to City Hall, but I'll see you later." Mom marched back up the stairs and the door clicked shut.

The moment she was gone, I threw the bundle of clothes right back down on the floor and plopped onto my beanbag directly in front of the potential Butler.

"Okay, then, um, Mr. Bag Man," I whispered. "Show your face."

The bag sat perfectly still. Not even a wisp of fog.

"I know your ghostly ass is in there," I hissed.

Nothing.

"Fine," I said as I stood up and paced around it like an interrogator. "I guess we'll do this the hard way." I had no idea what I meant by that, but it sounded just the right amount of threatening.

Cautiously, I approached the bag and zipped it back up, reattaching the lock and clicking it shut. Maybe unlocking it had summoned whatever or whoever that had been. I spun the numbers once more, landing on seven, two, eight, and braced myself for . . . something. Chaos? Demonic possession?

The lock clicked open—

But not a damn thing happened. The moment was as anticlimactic as the time Emma and I took so long getting ready for a Halloween party (we were the angel and devil on Guy's shoulders) that by the time we showed up, looks ready to slay, everyone was already passed out, hooking up, or making their drunken exit.

I guessed resummoning the bag ghost—Was I hearing myself? Was this a mental breakdown?—wasn't happening right then. With a groan, I set the bag down and resumed my pacing.

Maybe if I just stared at the bag, smizing my ass off, the ghost would come back out. I steadied myself right in front of the Butler and stared with all my Tyra might. But nothing.

Scooping it back into my arms, I sat on the edge of my bed

and peered inside to see if a mini ghostie might be hiding in there. Maybe he was scared. Eleanor had that effect on most men.

Even if he wasn't, I certainly was. I was scared of this haunted bag, the future, fixing things with Guy, Emma, and (ugh) Chuck, facing Bread . . .

In the last twenty-four hours, my whole life had crashed into a brick wall, and the casualties were piling up. Except now I was either on my literal last sane nerve, or my entire future hinged on evicting a mysterious spectral man from a haunted handbag.

Totally normal summer-after-high-school shit.

# 7

Where in the hell was Angela Lansbury's ghost when you needed her? Eleanor's favorite classic TV show was *Murder, She Wrote*, so naturally I've seen every episode on the Hallmark Channel, twice.

I needed to lure Bag Man out of my Butler again as soon as possible so I could get some answers. I felt like I deserved them, since the rest of my life was maybe hanging in the balance. Getting me out of Hearst was the mission, and no handbag-haunting ghost would stand in my way. Yes, I was hearing myself, and yes, it sounded ridiculous, but this whole day had been a trip. And not the one I'd originally planned.

I turned my phone flashlight on and faced the Butler, preparing myself for the unknown, and jumped about a foot in the air when the phone rang.

FaceTime came up on my screen, but there was literally no one in the universe I wanted to talk to right now. I glanced to check the caller ID and then nearly knocked my lamp over scrambling to grab the phone.

"Angelika!" Okay, maybe there was *one* person I would talk to right now. Actually, the perfect person.

She answered, but the screen was dark, and I could hear muffled talking and laughter in the background. That minx was out and about, living life.

"Sull!" Angelika's dimly lit face filled the screen as she rushed into another room, the background noise dampening. "Oh my god, are you okay? I just saw a text from Eleanor that your thing with Lyndzi fell through. Why didn't you call me?"

Truly, she would have been next to hear me wail about my misfortune. Angelika was more than Emma's older sister and my childhood babysitter. She was the person who had nurtured my early fashion obsession, and not only that, but she got the eff out of this place and did something with her life. She went to Parsons and then became a junior buyer for a huge department store in Beijing. She was quite literally who I wanted to be when I grew up.

No one in Hearst ever knew what to make of Angelika, either. She had shown up to prom in a tuxedo-gown hybrid, even before Christian Siriano made that masterpiece for Billy Porter. The look was still iconic, instant local-legend status for anyone who saw it and got it. (So, just me.) But, seriously, it did spark discussions about a prom dress code, which turned out to be so appalling and depressing that I opted out of my own prom entirely.

Angelika had been so nice and encouraging about my job with Lyndzi, too, even if she did throw a little shade. I distinctly remember her calling influencers flaky, but had I listened? She'd gently encouraged me to apply to a few fashion programs. But that was a no-go, since I'd just spent the last twelve years of my life in a classroom. I was ready for real-world experience.

I really should've listened.

"Uh, yeah," I said, my voice cracking a bit. The concern in her voice made me want to dissolve into my mattress, and I braced for an *I told you so*. "Look, you were right."

Angelika laughed sadly, her blazing red lip peeking through the blue-tinged darkness of what I could only imagine was a bar or club. "I know."

"No need to rub it in."

"You know I'm kidding, Sull. I should have tried harder to warn you, but sometimes you just gotta live something for yourself, ya know? Word in this business travels fast, and let's just say, Lyndzi is on several shit lists. Still, I'm sorry about everything. Hey, are you there?"

My attention and I guess my eyes had wandered back to the Butler. I still wasn't sure if it was going to spew up another ghost. Even though I trusted Angelika with my life, I couldn't tell her I was maybe hallucinating stunningly robed baddies. But if there was one thing Angelika knew, it was accessories.

"I found this bag at Yesterday's Today," I heard myself saying. "Claire took seventy-five bucks for it, which is like all the money I have in the world, hunny, but I'm"—I dropped my voice, even though there was nobody to overhear—"I'm pretty sure it's an authentic Butler."

"Shut the fucking door! No it is *not*. Let me see." She was so close to the screen now that she was basically one big eyeball. This was tipsy Angelika. I obligingly angled the camera.

"I think it might be. But I'm not even sure how I can check to see if it's real."

She bit her lip, accessing her internal fashion encyclopedia.

"Some Butlers were fitted with combination locks, so this tracks. The bag could only be from 1919 to 1929. Despite their popularity the company had to stop producing them due to the Depression. If it's legit an original it's potentially over a hundred years old."

"How do you remember that drunk?"

"I'm not drunk. And I literally took a class in fashion history, hello."

"Okay, queen," I said. Only Angelika could make me smile in the middle of a freak-out.

"Can you look in the interior pocket without tearing the lining? There are rumors about a label hidden there. A lot of designers stuck labels in unorthodox places before serial numbers gained popularity."

"Really?"

I'd learned about Butler bags a few years earlier and was immediately fascinated with their origin story. Despite their hefty price tag and elite status, the Butler had started out as simply a bag for butlers. It was the bag they carried with them during travel, holding all your essentials in one stylish accessory. Like a really nice weekender. Over time, the Butler had become a status symbol, and what had started out as a utilitarian leather bag was now a piece of fashion history owned and treasured by the uppermost of the upper class. And an original? That was the kind of thing people kept under lock and key.

"Different sizes of Butler have different labels," Angelika was saying. She peered at her screen, becoming the eyeball again. "That one seems to be in remarkably good condition and is probably second-generation, but I'd need a closer look."

I brought the camera right up to the bag so she could see better, still not ready to actually touch the Butler in case it tried to eat my soul.

"Do you really think it's real?" I tried to suppress the tremble in my voice.

"If it's real, Sull . . . forget Poshmark and 1stDibs. It's time to get some auction houses on the line. The short life of the company only drove up the value of these bags, essentially making every piece they produced a limited edition. A private collector or museum would pay top dollar for an original Butler in this condition. My friend Paulo is an intern for the historical fashion department at Christie's, but he's in Zurich with some man who is way too old for him, and I don't even know what time zone that is. But, honestly, even a good dupe will net you a few hundred bucks, so you're already cash positive. I'm assuming, given this Lyndzi thing, you'll want to sell it and use the cash as your nest egg to get the hell out of Hearst?"

This was starting to feel too good to be true, which meant it probably was. Because the Lyndzi thing had felt too good to be true, too. But I couldn't contain my excitement for a second longer.

"You are giving me life right now," I told her.

Angelika grinned. "Great. Be gentle with her, and I'll send a voice memo to Paulo." She sighed. "I wish you were here. We're going to get you out of Hearst, Sull. Somehow. To be continued. Ciao, darling!"

"Ciao," I said, but she was already gone, and I was alone again with my possibly priceless, and possibly haunted, handbag.

Emma always said I needed to learn to ask for support more quickly. Sometimes, of course, advocating for myself got exhausting. And other times, it backfired. Like when I was myself around Uncle Chuck—look what happened. I still hadn't been able to shake the ick from his stunt the night before. The near-constant reminder that others saw me as some kind of freak weighed me down sometimes, and it was harder and harder to keep my head up.

But maybe Emma was right, too. I'd long tried to do everything by my damn self, but this was above my pay grade. (Ha, just kidding! *What* pay grade?) If ever there was a reason to ask for help, though, a haunted bag—or my stress-induced break from reality—seemed like a nudge from the universe.

En route to Emma's house, my peasant blouse wafting behind me, I had nothing but time to think. The rhetorical fireworks shot off in my brain, louder than the Founders' Day parade marching band. How would I broach the topic of a ghost in my bag? Emma was cool, but was she I'm-seeing-things cool?

I practiced as I walked over the uneven, cracked sidewalks.

*So I got this great bag. And guess what? Not only are we so not talking about the fight with Guy, but we have a new friend. He's a ghost for a living—or maybe a demon?—and has this amazing bag where he's currently living rent-free. Kinda like me in Eleanor's basement.*

She'd stage an intervention faster than a TikToker could say *follow for part two.*

I tried again.

*So, Emma, darling, last night was a lot to process. Obviously I had to do some comfort shopping at our favorite spot and your current workplace but not mine any longer . . .*

No. It's not like I wanted to guilt her into giving me her job or anything. Did I?

*Anyway, I impulse-purchased this vintage bag that is potentially life-changingly, pricelessly rare, and it just so happens to be haunted by a ghost, or maybe I'm taking a slight break from reality. So how would you feel about a séance?*

Maybe a little too manic. I could also try getting straight to the point:

*Emma, there is a fucking ghost in this purse.*

I shook my head. I'd have to rely on the moment for inspiration because all my efforts were coming out deranged.

After a lovely forty-five-minute high-noon-100-percent-humidity stroll to Emma's house, my hair arrived a whole minute before my body did.

Before I could even knock on Emma's sliding glass door, I was greeted by my bestie, who was somehow waiting to receive me. Maybe she was psychic. This would save me from having to tell her my news.

"Heyyyyyy," I offered, hoping that her anger at my blowout with Guy had been mercifully forgotten.

Emma stood at the threshold, as though she was guarding the house, with her arms crossed and two thick and beautifully tinted strong eyebrows scrunched together (thanks to me and a box of Just for Men on clearance at CVS found on a midnight Sour Patch Kids run two weeks ago).

She was wearing a black linen dress I'd found for her at work while sifting through incoming items. Emma had first dibs on just about anything that came through the store above a size eighteen, because if the general clothing options in Hearst were pitiful, it was even worse for a thick hottie like her. This dress, though, captured her vibe perfectly. It was, like, hot art teacher sundress, but make it goth.

"Sull, what are you doing here? Shouldn't you be fetching Lyndzi soy lavender honey lattes by now?" She was definitely still mad, but I chose to interpret it as curiosity.

"Thank you very much for asking," I started. But I also didn't want to get into the whole Lyndzi thing again. Each time deflated me a bit. This was a harsh reminder that news didn't travel as quickly as I'd hoped. I would now have to explain several things about the last twenty-four hours, and I still hadn't found the right words for any of them. "Unfortch, Lydnzi is having an *Eat, Pray, Love* moment in Tahiti, and my invitation must've gotten lost in the mail. However, I did make a great find at Yesterday's Today that I think you will *love*!"

Emma held a hand up to tap the conversational brakes. "Wait, hang on. What happened with Lyndzi?"

I hated it when she tried to pin me down, because she was so damn good at it. I slipped past her and into the house. "She canceled the internship."

Emma was obviously all kinds of prickly at the moment, but she could never stay mad at me for long, and this admission would at least earn me a few sympathy points. Hate them normally, but today I'd take what I could get. "Sully, I'm so sorry." Her shoulders sank and her nostrils flared with what I hoped was righteous anger on my behalf. But then her face hardened. "That must be really hard. I know how much getting out of here meant to you . . . but—"

I groaned and slumped onto a stool at her mom's breakfast bar. "Why does there have to be a 'but'?"

She shot me a death glare. "But . . . about last night, Sull . . . you owe Guy an apology, not to mention your parents and me."

That was weird. I could have sworn she just told *me* to apologize to Guy. I guess that answered the questions that had been self-consciously looping in my mind. My mom and dad I got, since they'd thrown the party. Even Emma I understood. But Guy? Had Emma and Guy talked about me last night? Sounded like it. Was she on his side or mine? Were there even sides to be taken? I had my answer there, too, but it made no sense, seeing as I hadn't done anything wrong. "So, the bag I got at Yesterday's Today, it is . . . well. You know, this has been really stressful, what with not going to my internship and being stuck in Hearst longer, so I'm not sure if this is a stress-induced hallucination or if it's real but—"

She threw up her arms. "Sully, what the hell are you talking about?" I dug the toe of my espadrille into the linoleum floor and let the words tumble out in one single breath. "This-bag-I-bought-has-a-very-attractive-resident-ghost-man-apparition-living-if-that-is-even-the-term-in-it-and-I-need-help-because-this-is-all-feeling-like-I'm-at-the-tipping-point-of-a-downward-spiral."

"Sully!" Emma gasped, dropping her angry witchy girl mask for a second. "Are you serious right now?"

"What?" Was she surprised about the bag? The ghost? The slightly edgy potential of a nervous breakdown?

Then she rolled her eyes. "Bitch, you will do *anything* to avoid talking about your feelings!"

"Excuse?"

"A haunted handbag? No. This is one hundred percent your inability to talk about what happened with Guy or, heaven forbid, apologize. I'm feeling very caught in the middle with you two. And with you suddenly staying in town after all, I'm going to need you to repair things with him sooner rather than later. We're not all just side characters in the Sully narrative, you know?"

Oof. That hurt. I'd add that to the list of things to unpack later. "But the—"

"The 'bag ghost.'" Emma had the gall to throw up some air quotes. "Right, I heard you. Thing is, last night was awkward for *all* of us, including Guy. I'm not saying you were wrong about how your whole family—except Saint Eleanor, blessed be her name—can be insensitive, but blowing up on Guy after he really does try to understand? Was that necessary?"

Her words knocked me in the chest one after the other. I expected this from literally everyone else. But from Emma? Devastating. "Did you even hear what he said to me?"

Emma softened just a little bit. "I did, and I'm mad at him, too, don't you worry. Is he perfect? No, but you need to talk to him. You can't just ignore it and move on, pretending like nothing happened."

"I'm pretty sure if anyone should be mending this bridge, it's Guy."

"Sully, Guy has the emotional maturity of a baby cow, but in this case you were *both* a little bit wrong. Having some kind of unspoken standoff is just going to make you feel more alienated in a place you already loathe."

Ugh. I was not prepared to hash this out right now. I decided to stick to my script. "Can we please table last night's situation for a sec? This bag is almost literally priceless and could be worth enough to get all three of us out of here! Why aren't we focusing on that? Guy and I will talk it out at some point, but right now we have bigger concerns!" I held the bag up to inspect it as though it might suddenly spit out some kind of operating instructions. "Maybe if I try to rub the bag three times and invoke the power of Simone Biles, the ghost will reveal himself!"

Emma's forehead pinched with concern. "Sully . . ."

"Get on the bag train, Emma. *Choo-choo*, babes!" This was the same girl who had set a fire big enough to shut down the school for two days after she held a sage cleansing ceremony in the drama department costume closet. Uncle Chuck and the Hearst Fire Department didn't seem to appreciate her blessing the space to clear the bad vibes from the previous head costume designer. She wasn't exactly launching into the stratosphere like Angelika had immediately after high school, but there was hope for all of us. Especially if this bag turned out to be the real deal.

So why was she trying to tell me she couldn't buy the story of a haunted handbag? After I had fiercely defended her New-Age, crystal-hoarding, tarot-reading, fire-starting ass?

"*Sully*! You're not hearing me." Emma clapped to punctuate each word. "I know that the internship suddenly falling through is a blow, but we've got to put back the pieces of your life before things are beyond repair. We'll start with Guy, and then maybe we can figure out a job situation. Something to focus on—"

She was right. I *wasn't* hearing her. Or maybe it was more like she wasn't hearing me. Didn't she understand? This bag was about to come alive with the power of one thousand blazing Bianca Del

Rios, and Emma would soon be eating her words off my big gay silver platter.

I rubbed the warm, buttery leather of the Butler, and said, in my biggest and most impressive voice, "By the power of Chappell Roan, I compel you!"

But the bag remained silent and unmoving.

Uh-oh. Desperation began to creep up the length of my body. I'd definitely seen what I'd seen down in that basement.

. . . Right?

Emma crossed her arms, cocked one hip out, and watched me.

If I zoomed outside myself and watched, I could see how this looked. I felt warm all over, and not from the heat. "Okay, okay, let me do a full turn in front of the bag while you go outside, then come back in suddenly. I think the bag ghost needs to be startled to come alive again. But you've gotta make it believable. Okay, GO!"

But she didn't budge. "Sully, this is . . . are you okay?"

She was giving me the same look she'd served after I had petitioned for a recount in the race for seventh-grade treasurer after I wrongly came in second place. I had been *robbed* of the seventh-grade purse strings then, but this was somehow worse. Because this was Emma, my very best friend. And she didn't believe me.

"Maybe he's not coming out because your vibes are sus. Suggesting I apologize for last night? Really?"

"Okay!" She reared on me. Maybe I'd said too much. "So let me get this straight. You yell at my boyfriend—"

"Your what now?"

"Sully!"

"We're going to talk about that—"

But Emma yelled over me. "Then you come here claiming to have found a haunted handbag. And on top of all that, you call my vibes sus?"

"Emma, I know you treasure your vibes, and I was maybe a bit harsh, but I am at the end of my rapidly fraying rope. I am begging you to listen to me."

I waited for her to say something. Anything that would give me just an inch. Fuck. I hadn't even told her about Brad yet. We needed to have, like, seventeen conversations. But the bag! The bag was priority one.

Emma still hadn't budged.

"I guess I'll just take my bag and my cute ass home. I have to freshen up for an early dinner date with someone who loves me." I stormed out the door and wavered for a moment on the porch, wondering whether it was too late to ask her for a ride home. Yes, she was mad, but she knew I couldn't afford a podiatrist, and with these espadrilles . . .

Tears began to swell, and I pulled the stupid Butler up to cover my face without risk of getting any bodily fluids on my priceless bag. Emma had seen me at my worst over the years, but I wasn't about to let anyone know that *this* is what'd sent me over the edge.

"Sully, we *all* love you, and we're all trying to get along. That's the point! Wait . . ."

"No, *you* wait!" I yelled as though that made perfect sense, and stomped off. There were probably better comebacks, but I wasn't feeling inspired. As I marched down the street, the straps of my shoes began to chafe against my ankles, just like Emma had warned me they would when I bought them. (Though I would rather have died than admitted that to her now. What was it with her and Angelika both being right all the time?)

Then, of course, there was the humiliation of being ghosted by the ghost when I needed him the most. Not even the genius rhyme could cheer me up.

The Butler strap tugged on my shoulder, and I began to wonder whether this really had all been a fever dream. Was this bag going to be my salvation, or was it proof that I was having the ultimate not-even-quarter-life crisis?

I hadn't felt this lost since . . . well, ever. And now it looked like I'd have to navigate it alone.

# 8

My heels: blistered.

My spirit: bruised.

My plan: fucked.

My humiliation complete, I sulked home with the Butler to change my shoes. I briefly wondered whether I should stash the bag, but—and this sounded silly, even in my head—it made me feel better to keep it around.

Before long, it was time to head right back outside and hoof it to City Hall, where Mom and I were meeting once she wrapped up her day. If there was one upside, I was absolutely getting my steps in. Not that I had a choice, but whatever.

To add insult to injury, I spotted Bread leaving the employee lot in *my* car. Okay, so technically it was now his car, but the wound was still fresh. It also reminded me of his whole change-the-world pep talk. Here he was, walking the walk and do-gooding. What a nerd.

The Butler swinging from my shoulder, I greeted the security guards flanking the metal detector at the entrance. "Hi, Frank, funny seeing you here," I said breezily to the older guard, who had a mustache that nearly curled over his upper lip.

"Oh, hey there, Sully. Just got wind that you won't be leaving Hearst behind for a while, after all."

A little power suit–wearing birdie must've told them. Word traveled faster than bed bugs around here. "Yeah, but, you know, when one door closes—even if it's on a private jet heading to Tahiti—another opens and all that."

Travis smirked at me, then tapped his baton against the metal detector. "We need to check your, um, purse. It's protocol."

"Huh?" Instinctively, I clutched the Butler tighter to my side. Would they ask to look inside it? Was a ghost about to pop off in the vestibule of City Hall? Would the X-ray hurt the ghost? Had there ever been a more ridiculous thought?

"Ah, we know you. You're good," Frank said. "Oh, and your mom's still at the council meeting, but you can go wait in her office."

After the day I'd had, I couldn't help thinking that my luck was finally turning. Before Frank could change his mind, Phyllis from the records hall approached, holding a stack of papers. "I just got through these overtime logs." She peered at him over her little gold wire-frames. "Were all of these approved, Francis?"

"Okay, byeeeeee!" I cooed as I launched myself past the metal detector, hitting a quick stride, blistered heels still aching.

Soon I reached the brass nameplate that read *Office of Councilwoman Eleanor Hartlow*. I walked inside and sized up the space where so much of my mom's life played out. Anchored by a huge leather desk chair she'd inherited from Beauregard, the previous council member, it was giving boss bitch, but on a city interior design budget.

But she'd also picked up some decent finds from Facebook, like a burnt-orange midcentury-modern sofa and a small bookshelf. She was helping the local economy, hello, even if Marketplace was a cesspool of weirdos and recluses. The walls were lined with framed vintage posters and maps of the town through the decades. I'd insisted on a coat of paint to freshen things up, maybe a nice millennial pink, but apparently painting a city-owned office required more effort than a good tuck.

I set the Butler on the sofa and limped to the desk to perch on the edge as I waited for Eleanor to be done with her meeting. An open file folder caught my eye. I swear, the memo sheet on top of the stack of papers looked old enough to have been written by Phyllis on her Smith Corona. The subject line was low-key juicy:

```
Hearst Redevelopment Plans, CONFIDENTIAL
```

Was this what passed for small-town drama? Clearly, the *Real Housewives* producers weren't going to be scouting here anytime soon.

Unable to help myself—and, really, when had I *ever* exhibited self-control?—I slid the folder closer and flipped through the first few pages. Surely this information was confidential for council people *and* their next of kin. Odds were very low that this was actually important, anyway. Or even interesting. I'd once stumbled upon my mom's journal from college and was extremely disappointed to see it full of recipes and some very tame but adorable thoughts about my dad. (Though some of the recipes did include cannabis. Go, Eleanor!)

Where were all those small-town secrets that they make true-crime podcasts and Netflix miniseries about? A girl could dream.

I began to read.

Upon demolition of the Old Hearst Schoolhouse (est. 1819
and in use until 1947) by landowner Beauregard Hearst,
a cabinet containing historical documents concerning the
provenance of Hearst township lands was recovered. As is
well known, a portion of the Records Hall was flooded in
1968, representing the loss of decades of Hearst history.
This new cache is therefore a significant finding.
Close examination of these documents reveals information
(transcribed and logged by Phyllis Schultz)—

Of course, my girl Phyllis had all the dirt!

—which appears to call into question whether
Beauregard Hearst is the sole heir to the majority of land
in Hearst as established by his patrilineal connection to
the Hearst Brothers, who founded and incorporated the town
and surrounding areas. Though it remains unproven, this
is potentially startling new information, as Beauregard
Hearst's stated intentions for the future of his properties
could be greatly complicated by the revelation of a
new claimant. It is imperative that city representatives
investigate to either corroborate or dispel the existence
of a second property owner.

Sincerely, Mayor Archibald Bevins

I stared at the paper. Um, *holy shit*. That was actually way more interesting than I'd given it credit for. It also made me wish I'd paid more attention when Eleanor talked about work. I vaguely remembered her trying to tell me about this, and in my forget-all-about-Hearst frenzy, I'd blown her off. Turned out Mom's work could be kinda interesting after all! Not full-on interesting, but still.

With a sigh, I closed the folder just as a voice behind me asked, "What's your tale, nightingale?"

I whirled on my heel to find my ghost hottie sitting on my mother's couch below the vintage map of Hearst.

I let out an involuntary shriek.

Ghost Man started and made a show of placing a hand over where his heart used to be, before he readjusted his silk robe to cover more of his chest and crossed his legs, toes pointed. The shaving cream had been replaced by a thick layer of what I assumed was spectral night cream to keep the skin supple and translucent. "Listen, Mary, I'm used to people flipping at the sight of my classy chassis, but screeching every time we meet is getting old."

"I'm sorry, what?" I asked, despite the fact that there were about a million other questions doing laps around my brain. "And . . . and . . . where have you been?"

Ghost Man gestured to the Butler with a shrug.

"I mean," I said, "where did you come from? What are you doing here? Why did you appear again *now*? Where were you at Emma's house? I want answers, Ghost Man!"

"Ghost Man?" He looked offended. "The name is Rufus."

"Okay, wow. *Rufus*. Got it." My heart was hammering, and I felt myself lean back against Mom's desk. "Okay, Rufus. Well, I'm—"

"Sully. Oh, I know your name. And that you've got some *horrendous* manners."

Rufus stood and shook out the lower half of his robe, which seemed to lazily float, along with the marabou on his slippers, on an otherworldly breeze. I could see a wobbly version of the Hearst map through his torso, making me slightly dizzy.

"Excuse you?" Was I really about to have it out with a handbag-haunting ghost? The Butler needed to survive our tussle, but I was getting ready to throw down.

"Oh, I heard the way you spoke to that doll, Emma. Hardly gracious, especially when you were the one asking for a favor. That isn't how you speak to a lady!"

"Emma is *hardly* a lady. And—and you can hear me from inside that thing? Have you never heard of privacy?" Not only did I have my own personal apparition listening to my every word, but now he was giving out etiquette lessons. No way he was about to mansplain gender to me. "We're going to need some ground rules, you purse poltergeist. Listen up—"

Rufus waved a hand at me, pointing a single finger in my direction to cut me off. A red lacquered nail appeared at the end of the flourish and I felt the breeze kick up as it blew papers off my mom's desk all over the floor of the office. Okay, the supernatural insta-mani was sickening especially combined with the drama of controlling the wind like Storm.

"What's with the getup?" he asked.

"I . . . what?"

Rufus gave me a long look, up and down.

Well, this was about all I could handle. My peasant top and I were done explaining ourselves. "You should talk. Flouncing around in a sheer floral dressing gown is certainly a bold choice."

Rufus's nostrils flared, then he grinned and threw his head back and laughed. Red lips that made me long for my Ruby Woo appeared with a cupid's bow that could have been sculpted. "Well, I'll have you know I am nothing if not the epitome of chrome plated. Or I was, at least. Listen, Mary . . . I mean, Sully, I'm not trying to be a wet rag." He crossed to where I was standing by Mom's desk, palms out. "You might get what you want by asking nicely, though. For instance," he pointed a thumb toward the Butler, "I won't be summoned. I'm not your genie. I'm not anyone's anything."

"How am I supposed to know ghost rules? What are you even doing here? I thought ghosts haunted houses, not handbags!"

Rufus frowned and as he did so, the red nail polish and lipstick faded away and the breeze settled. "Now that you mention it, I'm as bewitched, bothered, and bewildered about my current predicament as you are, if you want to know the truth."

Well, this was interesting. But it was frustrating, too. If Rufus couldn't explain what was going on, who could? We stared at one another for a beat.

"My disagreement with Emma is none of your business," I said. Though I did wonder whether I'd have played it differently if I had known someone else was listening.

"Fine. It's just"—he smirked again—"I've always had a deep connection to the ways of the fairer sex, so if you want any advice . . ."

Oh lord. I rolled my eyes. "Rufus, no offense, but things have changed since you were alive—whenever that might have been. I'm not sure if you noticed, but I'm not like the other boys—or girls, for that matter. I'm not even sure how or if you and I are supposed to make a connection, honestly. Except for the fact that you're squatting in my new purse."

Rufus straightened and gave me a long, appraising look. "You think I couldn't possibly understand? I understand all too well."

"How could you *possibly* understand the current set of regrettable circumstances I've found myself in?"

Rufus closed his eyes and took a deep breath. "I understand a lot more than you know, Mary."

"The name is Sully."

"It's an endearment between individuals who share a similarity like we do, *sis*. See, you don't understand everything. And I too have crossed over the line between male and female. Hell, I even danced back and forth across it in heels higher than these." As he spoke, the robe and slippers morphed into a pair of high-waisted trousers and a button-up with loafers, Rufus's hair styling itself into a pompadour like Elvis's. Just as quickly his waist cinched and Rufus looked a lot more like Lucy Ricardo standing in front of me, a voluminous polka-dot skirt blooming over him into a Dior-style dress with white gloves and matching black patent heels and handbag.

My jaw slowly dropped as I stood there completely dumbfounded. I stared at Rufus who appeared as shocked as I was by his sudden transformations.

"Rufus," I began.

Rufus looked down at his skirt but when he looked up, he snapped back into the high-waisted trousers and shirt.

I hesitated before I asked as delicately as I could, "Rufus, did you used to wear men's *and* women's clothing when you were alive?"

Rufus squinted as if concentrating on something in the distance to come into focus. He reached up and patted his perfectly executed pompadour. "I believe I did."

"Same, sis," I mumbled, not sure how I felt about having more in common with a ghost than anyone else in Hearst.

"So, you're dressed like that for a performance?"

"This is just how I dress. I'm nonbinary." My brain was turning over information quickly and I asked, "If you performed in women's clothing, were you a drag queen?"

"I don't understand your meaning," Rufus said, not answering my question as he glanced around Eleanor's office for the first time, as if getting his bearings. As he turned, his eyes caught sight of the map of Hearst and he stopped and reached out a hand and his fingers slipped through the glass.

"Were you born here in Pennsylvania?" I asked. "I was."

"I'm sorry."

"I said I was born here in Pennsylvania."

Rufus shot a coy look over his shoulder, switching back into the polka-dot dress. "Oh, I heard you. I'm just sorry." He looked back to the map. "I beat feet as soon as I could and swore I'd only come back kicking and screaming. Except, here I am. Something brought me back. No, someone—some*one* brought me home. Except this was never my home. He was." His expression fell and he seemed suddenly far away.

My chest tightened at his words. "You had a boyfriend? Here in Hearst? Sometime in the '50s I'd guess from your style of clothing."

"Yes," Rufus exclaimed. "But something doesn't add up." He wrapped his arms across his torso, and his dress faded slowly back into pants. He turned and I could see him concentrating. "We had an argument. Something about another woman. No. That can't be right. That makes no sense. I can't remember. Why can't I remember?"

Without thinking, I reached out to take Rufus's hand in my own, but my fingers slipped through his with no resistance. Despite the clothes and slang and, well, the whole being-a-transparent-apparition thing, sharing some common ground with someone felt good. My experiences weren't just a modern thing. We were from different eras, but we were both queer, we shared history. "Try," I urged. "Anything."

"My memory is so hazy," he said. He looked around the room again then pointed at the Butler, his eyes clearing. "He was the most beautiful boy I'd ever seen. We grew up together. He really thought I was something. He wanted to protect me, to keep me safe."

"From what? Or who? Is that how you died?" I fired off in rapid succession.

"From everything. From everyone." He paused then slowly added, "From myself. And I wouldn't listen. I couldn't. Sully, I can almost see him again. Almost. Except I can't remember how."

My breath caught as he spoke. Here's all we knew: Rufus was a ghost who had potentially performed in women's clothing during the '50s, he had loved another man, and he had died either because of those things or something else entirely. The thought alone was too terrible to contemplate.

He was a ghost in a place where he didn't belong, just looking to figure out what to do next. And maybe, so was I.

*November 30, 1954*

*You know I hate writing letters, but for you I'll make an exception.*

*I've always known who I am, inside and out, because you always saw me as I truly am and stood by me. Supported me. All of me. Even when we were kids, you made me feel seen. Understood. Loved. Like we can achieve anything. Everything. And it doesn't hurt that you're a bit of a dreamboat. But only a bit. Don't let it go to your head.*

*And sometimes I'm so afraid this is a dream because I never want to wake up. I always want to be with you. By each other's sides. At least, as much as we can.*

*I won't sign my name. I know how paranoid you get that McCarthy himself will intercept our transmissions.*

*I will sign instead with all my love.*

# 9

To stop from crying and ruining my eye makeup, I had to remind myself a ghost was now haunting my change-your-life, most-viral-*Antiques-Roadshow*-episode-of-all-time, front-page-of-the-*New-York-Times*-culture-section, new-young-face-of-Sotheby's Butler bag. As if I hadn't been impossibly gorgeous and complicated enough before, we now had more layers going on here than the shag haircut Emma experimented with in tenth grade.

I stood in Eleanor's office, staring at Rufus, papers strewn all over the place. Footsteps echoed down the hallway. The shuffling walk was much too slow to be Eleanor. Frank, the security guard? Phyllis?

Not knowing who to expect, I gathered the papers that Rufus had blown all over, did my best to replace the confidential file where I'd found it, threw the pillows on the couch back to their original positions, and steadied my gorge Butler bag on the desk.

"Rufus," I hissed. "Get. In. The. Bag."

"Beg pardon? Didn't we just discuss asking politely—"

"Someone's coming!"

"Shit!"

Rufus vaporized quicker than toxic masculinity at a Harry Styles concert. And not a moment too soon, because when I swiveled around in a total one-eighty, Mom's door was already swinging open.

"Guy?" Whew. Thank god it wasn't one of Mom's colleagues. Except my relief was short-lived as I remembered I was still pissed at Guy and the rage of the night before hit me all over again.

"Sully, I'm sorry," he blurted. "For what I said. And what I didn't say, most importantly. I don't want to fight with you."

At this, Rufus wafted out of the bag and appeared looking like a fuller-figured happy-birthday-Mr.-President Marilyn directly behind Guy. My butt cheeks clenched. What kind of game was he playing? And was Guy about to be the third person today to say *I told you so*? Emma had obviously sent him, because nobody else knew my plans for the evening. I wondered if she had told him about my little ghost story, too.

I tried to discreetly wave my hand, but Guy continued as if nothing was wrong.

"I know my dad can be . . . a lot," Guy said.

"Uh-huh."

"Sully, don't rush me through this," he said, looking stung.

"Oh, no. That wasn't a brush-off." I stopped gesturing and tried to order Rufus *Monroe* back into the Butler with my eyes instead. "I'm sorry, go on."

"This is hard for me. But I know it's also hard for you."

I nodded, relieved he was empathizing, but I couldn't exactly concentrate. Rufus drifted closer to Guy, examining him curiously. And Guy *was* curious . . . in his denim cutoff shorts, sleeveless blood-drive T-shirt, and the mullet he'd cut ironically over spring break and maintained unironically since.

Sweat prickled at the back of my neck as Rufus hovered over Guy's shoulder while he stared right at me. "I just wish I would have said something in the moment, and . . ."

Rufus reached a hand forward, and I almost leaped out of my skin. Then he put his hand . . . through Guy's head? It took everything in my power not to scream. A third time!

I tried my best to concentrate on Guy and match his intense puppy-dog eyes while also shooting Rufus don't-make-a-damn-scene glances every few seconds. I'd already lost my internship, summer plans, and most likely my entire future. I didn't need any more trouble.

Rufus smiled a cute, crooked grin, as if examining Guy, then made pouty, kissy lips at him. Great, not only did I have a bag ghost, but a cheeky bag ghost full of shenanigans.

"Do you know what I mean?" Guy asked, looking at me expectantly as I refocused on him.

*Shit*. Straddling two realities was tough. Who would've thought?

"I, um, so, interesting perspective. Say more about that," I stalled. "Please."

He pushed a hand through his hair, and I could see him getting a little antsy, like he just wanted to be on the other side of this already. "Look, I can see you're really upset, Sull. I heard about New York, and I feel terrible. Emma let slip where you were, and I was up all night thinking about how difficult it must've been for you growing up in Hearst. I thought I knew what it was like, because all the guys on the football team make fun of me since I love *Mario Kart* and they all play *Grand Theft Auto*."

I nodded as though I knew exactly what the eff he was talking about. Props for coming to apologize, but . . . football? Video games? Like, I was with him . . . until I wasn't.

Guy raised his head tall and puffed out his broad, all-American chest. "Just because I like to play as Yoshi doesn't mean I'm not a fighter. It doesn't mean I'm not strong. It just unlocks a core memory for me."

"Right? Yeah, I can see that. Me too," I said quickly, trying to give him the benefit of the doubt here. But even Rufus arched a gorgeously drawn-on eyebrow at this, possibly the clumsiest apology of all time.

"And then I got to thinking that, like, your core memories are all probably of you getting made fun of and not getting to do anything you actually like because people can be mean."

"Yes, they can," I said.

Rufus drifted around the room in a sultry, slinky way, weaving behind Guy and nodding as if he understood something. That made one of us.

"So I can see how Dad giving you dresses last night was crossing a line," Guy admitted, then shuddered. "Is there a draft in here?"

He spun toward Rufus, who had already *whooshed* back into the bag.

"Sorry." Guy blinked a few times. "Where are your shoes?"

"Oh!" I looked down at my feet, my toes curled in from the stress of it all. "Long story. Emma can explain espadrilles to you."

"Oh. Anyway," Guy said, straightening up to his full height

once more, "I want to say that I support you. You're a Yoshi, and you *should* be a Yoshi."

"Guy, that might be the sweetest thing you've ever said, even if I don't fully grasp the meaning."

"Cuz, we really gotta get you to clock some *Mario Kart* time this summer. Now that you're staying. Seriously, I'm glad. You're one of my best friends, and even though I don't always understand, I do love you and always want to protect you. Not that you *need* protecting, but I bet it's nice when someone has your back. That's where I failed last night."

There was a distinct prickle at the corners of my eyes, and it risked spreading to my sinuses. This was all I'd ever wanted. Expecting true understanding from someone else was difficult and, at times, impossible. After all, I didn't always fully understand myself. I didn't need Guy to always get it, because that would be unreasonable, but I would always need his respect. He clearly understood more than I'd given him credit for.

"That means a lot," I told him. "I get so angry sometimes, you know? For the most part, people are trying, but it's awful to feel like I'm constantly explaining myself over and over, especially when it's to the same people. It's exhausting."

"Oh, man, Sully, I mean . . . um . . . oh, *person*, Sully," Guy said very slowly. I could almost feel his brain heating up from the friction of thinking so hard. "I can totally see how that would be annoying. It's almost like when you're fourth down and only half a yard away from a first down, but Coach makes you punt the ball, even though we all know we could totally get that half yard. It's like we're so close but so far all at once."

Jesus, Mary, and Joseph, I needed to get Guy a chiropractor or a massage chair or both. The weight of all this emotional labor was *this close* to throwing his back out.

Distinct Mom-like footsteps sounded on the marble floor in the hallway, bringing me back to focus.

Rufus peeked out of a corner of the bag, his eyes and mass of curly, bleach-blond hair just visible over the bag's lip in a way that was both cute and also a bit unnerving. When Guy closed his eyes to wipe away a single tear, I gestured for Rufus to hide again. While I wanted Emma to see him, Eleanor would flip, and I wasn't ready for that, especially after this heart-to-heart. I needed to get Guy—and my resident handbag ghost—under control so dinner could be somewhat normal. I was starving, and this day had been bizarre, to say the least. Sully deserved a treat.

"Guy, that is almost *exactly* what it's like. Thank you so much, and everything with us is hunky-dory. I love you to the moon and back, cuz!"

Frantically, I moved to shoo Guy toward the door. I glanced over my shoulder to find the purse one hundred percent Rufus-free. Maybe this ghost with more outfits than Paris Hilton's closet and I could work together after all.

"Wow, really? What a relief! So we're good?" Guy asked.

"So, so good!" I said, lying just a teensy bit because never in my life had I let go of a grudge in less than forty-eight hours.

As soon as Guy left the room, I fell into the chair behind Mom's desk, pretending to be idly waiting. But the sounds of clicking heels passed. All that hustle for nothing? I didn't know how much more I could take feeling so on edge. I peered into the Butler, which sat there like a very ordinary handbag. Then—*whoosh!*

A very moony-eyed Rufus appeared, hands clasped under his chin like a Disney princess. "That was positively ginchy!"

I could have squeezed the life out of him if he'd had any. "What were you doing? You almost blew your, well, my—*our* cover! Guy almost saw you!"

"He sounds like he really cares about you, Mary."

"My name is Sully."

"Truth be told, sis, I only understood half of what he said—"

"Well, yeah, same here actually," I admitted.

"But I know how hard it is to forgive, especially when family is involved." Something dark seemed to pass through Rufus's thoughts, though it was hard to tell with his slightly see-through features. "It sounds to me like you've got some true friends."

"I do!" I said, not sure why I sounded so surprised. "But listen, you've only got half the story. Last night, my uncle gave me some dresses as a joke, but it was mortifying."

"I thought you like dresses," Rufus said simply, gesturing at my Free People skirt. "I love them. And gowns. Oh, and hats. Millinery is a true art form."

I did my best Pez dispenser impression, mouth popping open. "I know, but . . . but . . . he did it to embarrass me. Not to be nice."

Rufus raised an elegant eyebrow. "In my time, a man wearing a dress could be arrested. Being laughed at would be the least of my worries."

As invalidating as his words were, I didn't have a snappy response. We surveyed one another, and I felt the fight draining from me. "I don't get why you're even haunting me. Is this, like, some kind of Ghost of Christmas Past situation where you're supposed to get me to learn from my mistakes?"

"Ha!" Rufus clapped. "Well, I certainly never mind giving advice but I don't think so. What would I get from the gig?"

"Well, I've never been haunted before," I told him.

He shrugged. "And I've never haunted. I didn't even believe spirits were real until I suddenly became one."

Rufus drifted over to the window and looked out over the town square, then after a moment he turned back to me. "It's baffling to think someone like you can exist in a place like this. That wasn't possible when I was your age."

I hadn't fully thought about what it must've been like for Rufus, especially in a very different time. Yeah, I didn't have many people I could relate to here in Hearst, but I had Instagram. I had TikTok. I could see trans and nonbinary and all other kinds of people, living their best lives, even if it felt like I wasn't yet living mine. Rufus must've felt completely alone, because he had no way to find his people. And it seemed as though he'd died young, too young by his lack of crow's-feet and smile lines, without getting a chance to live a full life. The very prospect was gutting. I could relate, having just been shut out of my own bright and shiny future.

"What's funny is that this place feels familiar to me. This square"—he gestured to the fountain in front of the biggest intersection in town—"Seems like I should recall something happening there. But as I said, my memory is spottier than soiled panties."

I wrinkled my nose. "Gross. You really don't remember how you died?"

He smiled sadly and shook his head. There was something in

his eyes like maybe he was worried what I would say next. I realized suddenly that Rufus had nobody—nobody but me anyway. What was he going to do? What was *I* going to do?

Maybe I was disassociating from the absurdity of what was happening, but a part of me liked the thought of solving the Problem of Rufus. Figuring out where he came from. Discovering where he was meant to go next. How he loved. How he died. Mainly because it took some of the heat off trying to piece my own future back together. And if I could figure him out, maybe I'd have better luck with myself. Every question I asked him meant one less question I had to pose into the mirror.

"What if I can help you remember?" I asked.

Rufus's expression brightened. "You'd do that for me?"

"No offense, but I don't really have anything else going on at the moment."

Rufus grinned. "Then let's make a deal. From what I overheard you tell Emma, you're broke."

"That's an understatement, but yeah."

"And you seem to think that this old bag might be just the ticket." Rufus gestured to the Butler.

"That's a resounding yes."

"If you help me figure out what happened to me, and the guy I was going with," he said brightly, before pausing as though he was considering something nostalgic and almost painful. His face turned animated again, the moment passing. "And how I might have met what I can only imagine was a very unfortunate and tragic ending . . ."

"Go on."

"And if you still want to leave Hearst after all that—"

"Which I most definitely will," I said confidently.

"Then I will vacate your bag so you can burn rubber right out of here and never look back, just like I did . . . at least I think I did."

We would get to the fuzzy memories later, but right now I had another concern. "You can do that? You can, like, exorcize yourself from my handbag? How?"

"How do you breathe? How do you bat those big pretty lashes of yours, my darling? You do it because you know how, even if you don't know how you know. So believe me when I say I'm tethered to that bag until I choose to let go. I can feel it in my . . ." He patted his chest. "Well, not in my bones, obviously. But I know. Trust me?"

Maybe it was because of how well I knew the power of those internal certainties that I did believe him. I considered the bargain at hand. Apparently, it came with strings attached, like any good bargain with the beyond. I had no idea how I'd find out about Rufus, let alone *another* person from his time period, but I wasn't about to let that stop me. These were all problems for Future Sully, that poor fool.

"Done. Let's shake on it." I grabbed Rufus's outstretched hand, but mine shot right through it. He looked embarrassed by this as well. We fumbled for a moment longer before I lost patience and finally said, "Metaphorically. A metaphorical handshake."

Rufus grinned. "You have yourself a deal. A lot like I did when I found that old thing at the consignment store."

"Do you mean the Butler?"

Rufus nodded, his Marilyn curls bobbing. "I needed a bag to stash my outfits in whether I was a guy or gal on the go and it was the least expensive one I could find."

And I'd uncovered it in a secondhand store too. I didn't believe in the whole fate thing, but up until today I hadn't believed in ghosts either. Then it hit me. "Rufus, you remembered that! This deal might be easier to settle up than I thought."

"Don't get cocky. My memory is full of more holes than . . ."

"Don't finish that," I said as Rufus made a show of wiggling his hips down into the Butler.

I sank back in my mom's office chair, all her town maps peering down at me like only decades of disappointment could. As much as Rufus's returning memory was a good omen, digging into his past would mean getting better acquainted with our least favorite place on earth: Hearst.

# 10

An hour later, I sat across from Eleanor at Café All Day, which was what everyone in Hearst called Café Al Dente, one of the only "fine dining" establishments in town. And it was exactly that. It was *fine*.

We'd chosen a table on the back patio, between a pond and a parking lot, and were picking over the last of our caprese appetizer while flicking away the occasional mosquito. The Butler was perched at my feet, a napkin protecting its underside from the sticky flagstones. On the drive over, I'd been half-terrified Rufus would show himself in a brand-new getup and make Eleanor swerve off a bridge. But since we'd struck our deal, he'd been remarkably quiet.

"So if Claire's got nothing for you, what now?" Eleanor asked. Coming from any other mother, it would have been a loaded question. *Why aren't you hitting the bricks, kid?* But not Eleanor, or not entirely. She had mentioned me evacuating the basement at some point, but I could only assume that was the stress of that city council or life talking. I knew she trusted me to solve my own problems.

If only I had that same confidence.

I sighed dramatically at the hunk of mozzarella on my fork. "Let's be real: I'm unemployable in this town. A pariah."

Eleanor pursed her lips in something between a smirk and a scowl. "I'm not saying try Dick's Sporting Goods, but are you going to send around résumés for the summer or just sulk in the basement?"

"Um, ouch?"

"Honey, I love you."

"Don't say it."

"But."

"I said don't say it!"

"You do sulk."

"No I don't!" I said automatically, before breaking out laughing. She didn't need to remind me of my childhood nickname, Sulky Sully. At least it was one of the nicer ones. "Okay, I sulk. But don't I have cause?"

How to explain to my mother that I did have a plan for my financial future; it was just under the table and occupied by an adorable ghost? Eleanor, awesome as she was, didn't have Emma's openness to the weird and occult, and I didn't want her thinking I'd finally snapped and started talking to inanimate objects like dear old Great-Grandma Josephine.

"Anyway," I said, forcing a grin, "tell me what's going on at work. What's with all the land development? I was so interested when you told me."

For the past few weeks Eleanor had been buzzing about some major land deals and Beauregard, which I assumed had to do with the confidential document I totally hadn't read in her office that afternoon. Thankfully I could play dumb, like any good snoop.

Eleanor looked confused. A fly tried to investigate our

remaining tomato slice, and she waved it away. "You mean the parking permits?"

"What? No. I thought there was something *juicier* going on," I pressed. "I thought you'd mentioned something about the old schoolhouse demolition? And finding some, uh . . . some documents . . . ?" I trailed off innocently, waiting for her to take the baton.

But Eleanor's expression pivoted from confusion to suspicion to fury. "Sully!"

"What?"

Eleanor glanced at our neighboring diners, a few of whom had turned their heads at her outburst. She continued in a harsh whisper, "Did you read something on my desk that you shouldn't have?"

"I don't know what you're talking about. I was reclining beautifully, exactly where you found me, doing *nothing*," I said, innocently surveying the patio. "Did that waiter forget our drinks?"

"I swear, child, I cannot leave you alone," Eleanor said with a sigh. Then added, "Well, it actually *is* pretty juicy."

I smiled. Eleanor could never stay mad at me. Besides, gossip trumped parental outrage any day. "Okay, so spill."

Our waiter, a girl a year behind me at school, whose name I couldn't remember, chose this moment to appear with our entrées.

"Lemon pesto chicken for Mrs. Hartlow," she said, "and flounder for Sully."

I suppose some might have found it weird that a random waitress would know both our names, but Eleanor was always in the local news for one thing or another, and me, well, let's say you couldn't miss me. I decided to own the irony of ordering flounder, since that's what I was up to this summer.

When the server left, Eleanor made sure no one was eavesdropping before leaning across the table. "Well. The documents recovered seem to suggest there is someone besides Beauregard who has a right to the land. We're thinking there could be a distant relative, or maybe"—Mom raised her eyebrows for dramatic effect—"A secret love child. Because whoever this person is, he doesn't have the family last name."

"Gasp!" I said. But was this really news? "How would that change things for Hearst *today*?"

"Well, it could mean a number of land titles held by the Hearst family might belong to someone else, or their descendants, anyway. I'm sure they'll be glad to have what's rightfully theirs."

"And that warrants an investigation on the part of the city?"

Eleanor repositioned her napkin on her lap. "Normally, no. It's not only that Beau may owe someone else money if he sells property or turns it into condos or a strip mall or whatever. Even with Beau having lost the city council seat"—Eleanor gave a small, smug smile—"he owns such a large amount of land. That gives him a certain power around here. If he decided to level a building, there are only so many grounds we can oppose him on, for example. Another stakeholder may own enough percentage of the property to throw a wrench into Beauregard's plans for Hearst, assuming they don't share the same vision. It's about the future of Hearst and how drastically that direction can be affected. You probably saw this on the memo"—Eleanor rolled her eyes—"But we lost a lot of the original records in a flood. The truth is, we know a lot less than we should about the town's history. What we *do* know is there's no one currently living here named Cobpen."

*"Gesundheit."*

"No, that's the guy's name. The one who might have a claim to the land. Cygnus Cobpen."

"Now that's a mouthful!" I waggled my eyebrows.

"Sully, behave. We were actually getting to a civics lesson."

"How could I forget?"

Mom's shoulders sagged. "You know, that's exactly the problem. Most people in Hearst today wouldn't notice or care. But our history is important. It's our context. It's what we grow out of."

If that was true, Hearst's growth spurt was a long time coming. I leaned back in my padded chair and admired my passionate, dedicated mother. I wished again that we could pack the Butler and run off into the wide world together. Sure, bloom where you're planted but dandelions spread their seeds far and wide, so let's go far and wide. But Eleanor didn't seem to see things my way.

"I bet you told *Bread* all about it—" *The perfect gay son she never had*, I thought.

"Don't call him that." Eleanor shook her head, then smiled. "He's great. He reminds me of, well, a young me!"

"Because he's your new pet. And I bet he lapped it right up."

Eleanor gave me a look. "Sully, are you *jealous*?"

"Of course not!" I was about to say something about Bread's eager do-gooder golden retriever personality, but realized I'd be insulting Eleanor, too. Maybe there had been a time when I was jealous of Brad, but maybe now the whole *Bread* thing had more to do with some unresolved post-lip-lock tension.

"Well, I haven't told him about any of this yet. You feel special again?"

"Of course. This even makes me marginally interested in Hearst and its lack of interesting history." Which certainly had nothing whatsoever to do with the inconvenient truth that I did, in fact, want Brad to kiss me again.

Eleanor frowned, cutting into her chicken. "Look, I'm not blind. I understand why you want to leave. It's natural. But when I look around this place, I see everything I know and love. Did you know your father and I had our first date here?"

"No." I was surprised this little family detail had never come up, since I'd heard the story of how they met (rainstorm, gazebo) too many times to count.

"Before it was Café All Day, it was the worst Japanese restaurant you've ever been to. The owner's last name was Macdonald, okay? They made these cheeseburger spring rolls. I am not kidding."

"Good lord. But Pennsylvania *is* credited with inventing the Philadelphia roll, so . . ."

"They were so gross, your dad and I couldn't stop laughing." Eleanor smiled at the memory. "Some people want the world, and that's great. But my world is here. Especially now that you're staying for a bit longer."

One entrée and a few mother-approved sips from Eleanor's Chablis later, I excused myself to the restroom, trying to picture Eleanor when she was my age. I wondered if there had ever been a moment she'd considered leaving. Part of me wished I had some of her pride in this place. Who wouldn't want to feel that? But I also couldn't fake it. Because at the end of the long hallway decorated with black-and-white photos of Hearst, I was confronted with something my parents never had to think about—choosing a fucking bathroom.

No, this place wasn't for me. It hadn't ever been and that wouldn't change.

Coming back to the table, I felt weirdly energized. I gave the Butler a reassuring pat, hoping Rufus had been listening. Because our talk had given me an idea.

"I want to help out with researching the heir," I said.

Eleanor nearly spit out her sparkling water. "You do?"

"You're right, I shouldn't be sulking. And I need a project. Something to keep my mind active." I put up a hand before she could cut in. "*In addition* to looking for a job."

Eleanor was almost beaming, and my heart broke a bit.

"Well, that's very civic-minded of you," she said. "Right now we've got about five years of microfiche from the *Hearst Bugle* to get us started on uncovering who this Cygnus Cobpen is and where he is now. The city's going through the issues and putting them online, but it's slow going. If you're really serious, I'll show you how to access the digital archives. Just don't tell Phyllis. She's territorial."

"Ah, the inner digital sanctum," I said, steepling my fingers.

"That's just the tip of the iceberg. You think anything in the records hall is digitized? You won't find anything before the 1970s online."

"Oh. *Great*."

"And I doubt you'll find much, but it makes me happy to see you getting involved in something."

We clinked our glasses, and I tried not to feel like the worst child in the world. I wasn't being completely dishonest. I *did* want to dig through Hearst's past, but not in search of some love-child, secret land claimant Magnus Corncob, or whatever. If I was going to hold up my end of the bargain with Rufus, I'd need all the help I could get, including access to the town's records, on the off chance he really did have a connection here.

"I have to say, I'm not mad about having you around," said my mother, putting down her wine.

I took another sip, feeling the Butler against my leg, and smiled.

"Well, don't get used to it."

As soon as I cracked this case and sold the bag, I'd be out.

# 11

Hearst obviously had its fair share of shortcomings, but at least we had some very adorbs coffee shops and robust broadband 5G coverage, so one could get their best Nancy-Drew-paranormal-investigative-journalism on in public. As I settled down with an iced chai and a scone, the only thing I didn't appreciate was the café's name: Mom and Pop's.

As a nonbinary person in the midst of a massive life change, could I just say how tired the term *Mom and Pop* was? What about all my *Mom and Mom* shops? Where were all my *Two People Who Love One Another* shops at? Maybe brainstorming a better and more queer-inclusive title for cutesy family-owned stores would be next on my gay agenda after I figured out what the hell happened to Rufus.

The only problem? I had no idea where to start, and I kept getting distracted.

Tragic name aside, Mom and Pop's had strong internet and even stronger coffee. I settled into the corner booth, where I could watch people coming and going, and typed away at my screen like Bella googling *vampires*, searching for even a whiff of Rufus's past in Hearst. It probably would've been easier if Rufus hadn't been so intent on playing an endless round of twenty questions about all modern things from inside the Butler.

It was probably very disorienting to have switched decades, but if he wanted my help, he wasn't doing himself any favors by whispering up at me constantly. Most annoying question so far today had to be: *Since everyone seems to have a jalopy nowadays, where's your ride?*

Talk about a long story, and we did not have time to cover Olivia Newton-John's star turn in *Grease*, or my recent romantic entanglement (which I'm almost certain Rufus would have had a lot to say about). Speaking of entanglements, I had to call Bread sooner or later to get my car back. But this research errand was the perfect excuse to put it off.

Eleanor had shown me how to access the town's newspaper archives, but so far they hadn't yielded much. I'd tried wading into the larger world wide web, but googling *Rufus Hearst PA* only turned up a website for Rufus Hearst, Public Accountant, in Orange, New Jersey. I needed to up my game. My social media stalking skills were so good I could be an FBI recruit . . . as long as the FBI was interested in whether Corey and Gretchen, the longest-running couple in my class, had secretly broken up before graduation. (Spoiler: They did. He cheated. A lot.)

I combed my brain and every interaction with Rufus thus far for words or phrases I could possibly use that might bring up a result specific to his identity. But this was all so obviously useless. What did I expect? To come here and magically unlock this mystery with a single keyword? Google had ruined me for analogue research.

"What is that newfangled device making those fancy, foamed

coffee concoctions?" Rufus asked. I couldn't see what he was wearing but he told me his hairdo was known as the jelly roll and had been very in. I'd propped the Butler on the seat beside me where it was mostly hidden from view. Rufus was peeking out of the bag like a pet Pomeranian as he nodded to the espresso machine. "That certainly isn't drip or Nescafé."

"It makes coffee much more delicious and cuter," I answered absently as I typed.

"Cuter?"

I shot him a look, not really wanting to get into the intricacies of latte art at the moment.

He squinted at the chalkboard bakery menu. "What's a *cronut*?"

"It's fucking delicious," I muttered out of the corner of my mouth, suddenly aware that, to anyone else in the room, I looked like I was talking to myself. Whatever. The people of Hearst would probably find that to be the least shocking thing about me. They expected some kind of freak show, so why not lean in?

I popped in my AirPods in the hopes that I might fool everyone into thinking I was on the phone as I continued answering Rufus's questions and went back to snooping around. No matter how I sliced my search terms, nothing was coming up. Not even in the Hearst archives, which were located on a website from before I was born that still had a visitor counter and guest book. They were definitely a vibe, but one that made my head hurt and my browser slow to a crawl.

*Beauregard Hearst Elected to City Council*, read the headline from the time capsule. And there he'd stayed until Eleanor's shocking election. He represented the establishment in more ways than one, so his loss had rocked the town to its core. Even his black-and-white portrait made me shudder.

I glanced at the Butler. I needed more than Rufus's first name, but we'd established pretty quickly that his surname was one of the many things he couldn't recall.

"Not even a first letter?" I asked. Then, remembering yesterday's dinner conversation with Eleanor, "Does the name Cygnus Cobpen mean anything to you?"

"Is that a new model car or coffee maker?"

"No he's a person—"

"I was joking," Rufus said. "I may be dead, but I'm not humorless. And no, I've never heard of him."

Then Rufus's eyes snapped to the photo on my phone screen. "But who is *that square*?" Rufus practically recoiled.

"Beauregard Hearst."

"Like the name of this city?" Rufus mused out loud. "Lord Square of Squaresville."

"*Exactly* like that."

"Oh! Oh!" Rufus shouted, and I lunged to close the bag before we got kicked out of the coffee shop.

"What?" I hissed out of the corner of my mouth. "You have to be quiet."

"I remembered something. *That* name is familiar."

"Don't tell me you're Beauregard's relative. I'm not sure we could be friends." The very idea gave me the ick.

"No, I'm not thinking of a person."

"Phew!"

"But is there a train station here?"

"Maybe once upon a time. Why?"

"Beauregard. *Beau. Gare.*"

I stared down at him blankly.

"Those words are familiar. I think they mean 'beautiful station' in French. They were laying tracks near my home as I was growing up. Everyone was worked up over it."

"Railroad tracks?"

"What other kind would they be?"

Well, this was new information. Maybe I'd been *getting* nothing because I'd been *giving* nothing. While we didn't have a railroad in town anymore—because why would anyone want to visit Hearst?—that hadn't always been the case.

I went back to Google, feeling energized, and typed in: *Beau Gare train station Hearst*

This landed me back on the geriatric city archives page, with an article about the demolition of our sad one-room train station sometime in the late '90s.

Ugh. Well, what had I been expecting? A picture of Rufus atop an engine as the first search result? I took a nervous sip of my coffee. "Is that all you remember from your, um, story?"

Rufus reared back as if affronted. "That's what *you're* trying to figure out."

"No, I mean—ugh." There'd be nothing more embarrassing than saying the wrong thing here. But I also realized part of my own discomfort was that I didn't know much queer history. Not really. Rufus's knowledge of the past may be hazy, but I was coming to understand how holey and superficial mine was. And clearly there was a lot to learn. Was Rufus gay? Queer? Something else entirely?

Based on his reaction earlier, the term *drag queen* didn't even seem to apply to him when he was alive. And yet . . .

"What did you say people called you, you know, back in your time?"

"Ru-fus," he said, very slowly. I could practically see his faith in me dying before my eyes.

"How did people *identify* you, I mean? You said you were a performer?"

"Oh!" Rufus laughed and his jelly roll split in two and separated into two victory rolls, large eaves flowing from them and pouring down over his shoulders. In a blink, he was painted for the back row in a dimly lit club. "I was. A starlet, really, with my youth and beauty."

"But definitely not a drag queen?"

Rufus wrinkled his nose. "Most definitely not."

"So you performed as a man?"

Rufus winked dramatically. "And how. If birds did it, bees did it, and even educated fleas did it. I was determined to do it too."

It was my turn to wrinkle my nose. "Rufus! I wasn't asking *that*."

When Rufus was done laughing, he said, "I suppose if you loosely consider walking around daily in male attire as an unremarkable, functioning person who was afraid Eisenhower would pass another law against you for being too sensational, then yes, I performed as a man."

"Fair," I mumbled sheepishly, seeing how my question wasn't phrased in the most enlightened way. I took a moment to reword what I was trying to ask. "Did you get on stage or put on a show for an audience in your slacks and button-down or other male clothing?"

"Absolutely not. I had beautiful garments with petticoats and beading. No matter how beautifully tailored my suits were, they were nothing compared to my costumes."

"Right, right, right," I said, not convinced about Rufus not being a drag queen, and went back to the search bar.

*Hearst drag queen*

No results. I got asked if I meant *Hearst drag racing* instead.

"Siri," I said to my phone, "how far back do public records go for the town of Hearst, Pennsylvania?"

Rufus's eyes widened. "Who are you talking to? Who or what is a Siri?"

I was about to explain when Siri disappointed me with her answer: The Hearst Records Hall had digitized everything back to 1968, then the basement flooded. But for all the earlier stuff, I'd have to go through old newspapers and microfiche in person to see what remained, which was exactly what Eleanor had said. I gritted my teeth, because this all seemed like a real crapshoot. There was no telling which documents survived the flood.

"Sis, I promise to explain the intricacies of the modern age to you, like, ASAP, but what we need to do right now is figure out how we're getting across town to the records hall without a jalopy."

"It's called a car, *Mary*," Rufus fired back.

"Touché."

"What about that Brad your mother goes gaga for? The one you call Bread? Maybe *he* has a ride?"

I had to admit, Rufus was surprisingly quick on the uptake. I don't even remember mentioning Bread. In fact, I'd done my best not to even *think* about him, so it was rude of Rufus to bring it up. Clearly, resisting this topic wasn't working. "Okay, so that's a loaded question. Bread-Brad is not a friend, even though he does have a car. But it is *my* car, and he won't let me buy it back, and it's just complicated, you know? I sold him Olivia Newton-John, and we kissed . . ."

"You sold and kissed Olivia Newton-John?"

"No. Rest her soul, she's a triple threat from down under."

"I met one of those once. He had a reputation for being a great time."

"That's . . . something," I say. "But it's the name I gave the car I sold to Bread after kissing him in it."

"*Bread* meaning *Brad*?"

"Yes."

"Did playing back-seat bingo with Bread in Olivia Newton-John up her sticker price?"

"No! There was no game played anywhere in the vehicle, most certainly not in the back seat."

"Why not? Are you not a good kisser?"

"How very dare!" I exclaimed, at the same time wondering if I was a good kisser or not. "Focus, Rufus. I tried to return the car and sent a Venmo request, which Bread rejected, and now it's awkward."

"What's a Venmo—"

"It's not anything involved with making out, before you go there. It's like virtual banking meets Facebook. It's actually kind of cringey."

"What's a meats face—?"

"Rufus! The questions!" I yelled. "We need to focus or I'm never going to figure out how you died!"

At that exact moment, the music stopped mid–Selena Gomez track.

The barista with the very cute septum piercing gave me the stink eye.

"Sorry, I'm writing a murder mystery," I yelled, putting on a big show of typing into my Notes app.

"At least you get to kiss people out in the open," Rufus pouted.

"Well, this was more in the dark spot between two streetlights, but, yes, point taken. Queer people can kiss one another now for the most part. But it's still fairly dangerous depending on where and who you are."

Rufus looked at me with a piercing kind of longing and I checked myself. Yes, shit wasn't easy right now, especially for trans people, but how amazing it must be to consider that queer people can be out in public. Sure, that wouldn't be the case if certain legislators had their way, but there had been so much progress made compared to Rufus's time. I guess the pendulum was constantly swinging. Sometimes it felt like five steps forward and ten steps back, but I had to remember that we gained a little ground every single time.

"What was it like back in your day?"

"I don't remember much, though I can tell you that I had to be on guard. I didn't know who to trust." Rufus's makeup and hair retracted into the single jelly roll. "They could fire or even arrest you for loving another man. And want to work for the government, or even be in politics? Well, you can forget that. In some places, they put your name in the paper so everyone would know. Or even threw you in an asylum. Not only were there no laws to protect us, but they designed laws to harm us. They were conspiring against us. To root us out. Anyone could be watching. Anyone could tell on you. There was this feeling of being . . . haunted."

How ironic. This hit me like a jolt. You always heard of ghosts having unfinished business and being stuck in limbo. I never really considered how lonely that would be.

Rufus seemed to shake it off and paint a bittersweet smile back on his face. His victory rolls and paint reappeared but slower than the first time. "Anyhow. Time's a-wasting, and Bread-Brad's dance card is probably filling up. Get on the horn with him and your Olivia Newton-John, too!"

"We don't need any of those people." I had no time to explain. "I can figure out another way to get us there."

"You're blushing," Rufus said simply. "Ask your Siri to send him a letter or telegram."

"It's called a *text* mess—oh, never mind!" Even as I said it, I became even more aware that my cheeks were radiating heat. "I don't like him, anyway."

"I see through you, Sully," Rufus said. "Even though it seems *I'm* the ghost."

Burning with embarrassment and most definitely *not* swooning, I sprang up and grabbed the Butler. Even if I had to walk the whole way there, I'd march into the records hall and get this infuriating relic into the afterlife, or wherever the hell he wanted to go, as long as it wasn't here in my bag.

My phone buzzed with a text from Emma as I fumbled with the Butler while bussing my plate:

I heard you made nice with Guy really appreciate it...

When the store closes tonight we're having a little summer kickoff shindig come by after 8 and say hi

I didn't necessarily want to go back to my former place of employment that no longer cared to employ me, but a thought struck me. If I could figure out who'd dropped off my presh Butler, or ask Claire when she was in a better mood, I could get some more information on it. This was a risk, of course. I didn't want the original owner asking for the bag back—or realizing that they'd donated it by mistake. But I was desperate for any leads on Rufus.

I texted Emma back:

See u there

"Stop staring at that glowing rectangle and get to the party," Rufus grumbled.

"You sound like my dad," I told him. "And it's not for a few hours."

With no ride, I probably couldn't get us to the records hall, home to change, then to Yesterday's Today in time. I made the executive decision to look cute first and research later. It was time to kick off the summer that was never supposed to happen.

# 12

I walked to Yesterday's Today, my feet *still* punishing me for those espadrilles the day before. My fabulous floaty, folksy chiffon dress rippled in the stiflingly warm breeze, and I did my best to ignore the sweat dripping down my back. I'd planned on debuting this look in NYC, but if I couldn't bring this iconic fashion to the Big Apple, far be it from me to deny Hearst.

I'd paired the dress with a cute platform Converse high-top to keep it edgy (and cover up my blister Band-Aids), grabbed the Butler, and made my way to the party. As the sun dipped below a cluster of clouds, the summer breeze ruffled the skirt against my legs and, for a moment, things felt sort of right. The sunset painted the front of the old brick building a dazzling orange.

Judging by the number of cars in the parking lot as I rocked up to Yesterday's Today, this party was giving. But it also reminded me that I no longer belonged there. Not officially, anyway. I could always visit, but it didn't feel the same.

If not for the sound of laughter emanating from downstairs, I might have just scooted back home. But the bag under my arm reminded me that I had a purpose, as did the 728 above the door.

The world worked hard to make me an outcast, but I didn't have to do it to myself. Not here, where I could easily slip around the corner to the employees-only entrance at the back of the building. This wasn't exactly the velvet rope VIP experience I had planned for this summer, but at least I could guarantee I'd be the best dressed.

When I ducked into the basement, the familiar scent of mothballs and musty sweaters greeted me. But I didn't have time to start feeling sorry for myself, because Emma caught my eye immediately and waved me over. Based on her rosy cheeks and glossy gaze, she was a few drinks deep.

The rest of the basement was stuffed with people, including every freshly graduated theater kid who was—surprise, surprise—still hanging around. Basically everyone from high school who hadn't made athletics their whole identity tended to band together.

Claire had shoved aside the break-room tables and stacked stock boxes against the far wall to clear some space. That's where she sat now, perched on some crates while half a dozen teenagers listened, a captive audience to whatever wild story of her youth she was reliving. Eleanor was an amazing mom, but we misfits had also been lucky to have Claire as a matriarch. I'd take as much support and solidarity as I could get.

Emma made her way over to me before my Chucks even hit the basement floor, brandishing a dark cherry seltzer. "Sully! Look who's here and thriving!"

"Thanks for dragging me out of my cave. This is nice."

She kissed me on the cheek. "Guy is here somewhere. And

so is Breeeead," she sang. "Who was asking about you. Hmm. I wonder *why*."

"Uh-huh. Great." Settling in with my boozy seltzer and my Butler, I did my best to give cool, unaffected, unbothered, undercover-celeb vibes. Barely even a few swigs in, and I was already feeling a little more at ease. I bopped along to an Olivia Rodrigo classic from 2021, while Emma scampered off to find Guy.

"Is this what music sounds like now? I love it! Who *is* this songstress?" Rufus echoed from somewhere under my armpit. "How are you barely moving your shoulders? This beat was meant for a gallop. Let's rattle!"

I whispered, "Rufus, we are *not* doing a dance number at this party! My social capital is at stake here. These are basically the only people in Hearst who tolerate—"

Before I could finish my thought, Guy and Ron, the class clown and Guy's best friend from football, made their way over to clap me on the shoulders. Thank goodness they didn't try to lean in for a stiff-armed, awkward man-hug. It was clear Guy had volunteered to babysit Ron, who'd had a few seltzers too many already. I tolerated it because Ron was pretty cool . . . for a bro.

"What a staple accessory you have there, Sull!" Guy said, smiling wide. "Is she new?"

"OMG, Guy! I love that you just said 'staple' and 'accessory,' and used both correctly in the same sentence!" I didn't say it, but he also got major points for saying this in front of Ron. "And while I can't be sure, I do think the new bag identifies as she."

"Only when I shake, rattle, and roll!" a small voice shouted from beneath my arm.

I cupped my hand around my mouth so it looked like I was covering a sneeze, then looked around. It didn't seem like anyone could hear Rufus, but we had to be careful. I was nowhere near ready to explain the rules of my ghost companion when I hardly knew them myself. "We're not having a *Ghostbusters* moment at this party, king! I said *the bag* was a she. You think I'd misgender someone? Pipe down!"

"Pipe down?" Guy looked confused. "I thought I was doing good with the lingo. Really speaking your language."

"No, no, you're wonderful, love. Thank you." Then I clocked Claire breezing past us. "But I have to talk to Claire."

Guy scratched behind his ear, his brow furrowing. "Oh, um, okay?"

"Go get her, tiger," Ron bellowed, so wrong for so many reasons.

I made my way through the party like Moses parting the Red Sea, but Claire was hustling and I kept losing sight of her. The basement wasn't *that* big, but she was on a mission. Just as I caught a glimpse of her, Bread stepped directly into my path, looking cute in a white T-shirt that hugged his biceps, and low-slung jeans. He seemed more relaxed than usual. To be honest, I hadn't realized he owned shirts without buttons, or non-khaki pants.

"What a dreamboat. Wait, that's not *Brad*, is it?" Rufus asked from inside the bag, just as Bread said, "Sully! It's good to see you!"

"Shut *up*!" I snapped at Rufus.

"Huh?" Brad said, looking confused.

"Brad, I'm so sorry. That was, like, a *nice* shut up. Like an are-you-serious shut up." I took a nervous gulp of my seltzer, cherry fizzing on my tongue and the buzz going right to my head. We had to stop meeting while I was all flustered.

"Are you okay, Sully? You seem . . . stressed." Bread's eyebrows creased together in concern. Why did he look so adorable when he was worried?

My tongue felt too big for my mouth as something in my stomach fluttered. "Stress? I don't know her. Everything's great."

"You're sure?" Bread asked, leaning in a little closer. "You tried to send back my money for the car, which was . . . weird."

A breath hitched in my throat. He was near enough that I could smell the crisp, clean scent of his detergent. And cut grass maybe? He definitely struck me as the type of son who cut his parents' grass.

Rufus gasped. "The way he's eyeballing you!"

"That is none of your business!" I yelled.

"Oh, I'm sorry," Brad said. "It's just that Emma said you lost your job. The one in New York."

I *had* to stop trying to have two conversations at once. "Well, technically it was a paid internship. But, yeah, it totally sucks," I said with a winning smile. "The whole Venmo thing was because I was hoping to get Olivia Newton-John back. I could really use a car. Now that I'm, you know, stuck here, I don't want to be *stuck* here."

Bread smiled, and for a brief second, I had hope. Then he said flatly, "That's not happening."

"What?" Bread refusing was so not on my bingo card. What was I supposed to do now? "Why?"

"I need a car." He shrugged.

"So do I."

"I'm starting my summer job and I need to drive there."

There was a lot to unpack here, obviously, including the issue of Brad spending all summer with Eleanor. Too bad I couldn't really be mad at him since he was literally devoting his summer to supporting my mother.

"Oh, I know! Maybe you two could ride together!" Rufus offered with all the earnestness in the world.

"You mean he could *give* me a ride, boo." Though the second I said it, I knew it didn't sound any better.

"What?"

"I just said, since I'll be here after all this summer with no car, could you at least give me a few rides for a project I'm working on? I mean, if you're not going to sell Olivia Newton-John back to me, that is."

He squinted. "Did you call me 'boo,' though?"

"I said, 'Ooh.' Like, it's a good idea for us to share a car." I decided to play dumb and laugh it off. "It's loud in here."

He leaned in closer so that each of his words tickled my neck. "Okay, well, yeah, I could give you a ride. But we'll have to work around my internship schedule. And I'll probably be playing a lot of pickleball after. I *really* want to get into pickleball."

"Thank you, Bread," I said, swallowing back the ridiculous giddiness budding in my stomach. "I mean Brad. Bad Brad."

"No more nicknames, please." He shook his head, clearly trying to decipher what exactly was wrong with me. "Are you sure you're okay?"

I desperately wanted to stay, to flirt, to see if we could re-create the good parts of my graduation party . . . wait, what was I saying? I had ulterior motives today and couldn't get distracted. I hoped my scurrying away wouldn't seem like a cold shoulder. "Yes. Um, I have to go."

"Oh-kay, then. I guess I'll see you around."

I darted off, practically stumbling over my own feet, before the conversation ventured even farther into the weeds.

That had been a little hot, though, hadn't it? Or was it the seltzer hitting my brain? Honestly, I was sort of into Brad refusing to sell my car back to me. Like maybe I wanted him to make me beg, but, like, in a charming way? And pickleball? I could be into it.

Fully blushing from head to toe, I finally found Claire and swam toward her like she was a lifeboat. Doing that awkward crowded space dance between couples and trying not to walk through any people's conversations, I finally got within earshot.

"Claire!" I waved. "So nice to be back at my old haunt."

She blinked at me slowly. "Weren't you here just yesterday?"

"But you're missing me already, right?"

Her eyes went wide, and a wave of horror washed over her expression. "Oh, Sully, we really do! The new part-timer tried to relocate Clementine the dino to the back office, and she gags every time she smells pennies. It's a real vibe killer."

I grimaced. "I mean, to be fair, pennies do smell gross. Though she shouldn't turn down that money, hunny. But hey, listen, I'm so obsessed with this new bag."

"I'm so glad!"

"You said something about an estate sale, though? *Super* curious about where you got it."

"Oh, I got my wires crossed. I thought I got it at this old building cleanout on the edge of town, but that was something else. I want to say it came off the donation truck from Philly?"

Bless that woman, but she could be so scatterbrained, from one ADHD warrior to another. What had started out as a promising lead was completely falling apart. "Are you sure? You seemed convinced it was the first place."

"Or you know how the auctions sometimes put together a flat-fee lot?" Claire said, scratching her head as if trying to remember.

"Sure," I said, trying to hurry her along to her point.

"And it's a lot of garbage but any good stuff is finders keepers?"

I had to admit, I liked the sound of that. A hodgepodge of junk, hiding a treasure trove, with no way to trace it back to the owner. Good news for me, but terrible news for Rufus.

"I can check my receipts tomorrow, but it's sort of a mess down here right now." She gestured toward the folded-up tables where her workstation usually lived.

Before I could fully answer or think about what this meant for my investigation, Ron drunkenly climbed onto a rather tall and quite obviously unstable stool. He teetered for a moment before waving his arms over his head. "Hey, everyone! Quiet down. I'd like to make an announcement, I mean toast! Hear ye, hear ye!"

"Hey, Ron, buddy, we hear ya. Get down before you get hurt," Claire urged.

Ron chuckled and in a mock-wise-old-man voice said, "Getting hurt is part of life, Claire. Don't you get it? We're all just beating hearts, you know? If you think about it, we're all walking around, bleeding on the inside—"

The stool wobbled and then tipped, sending Ron backward into a blur of shaggy hair and cargo shorts. But instead of hitting and bouncing off the basement wall, his whole body crashed through the drywall in a plume of dust.

"What the hell?" Claire yelled.

Rufus snickered, muttering, "Looks like he'll be bleeding on the *outside*, too."

Guy staggered away from the seltzer bucket, took one look at the scene, and swore.

Everyone covered their mouths against the swirling particles, which slowly settled to reveal a Ron-shaped hole in the wall.

"I'm okay!" he managed to shout.

"Come on, buddy," Guy said, hauling him to his feet with a look of grim determination.

"What is *that*?" someone asked as cell-phone lights revealed a completely intact old storage room just behind Ron.

Ron glanced over his shoulder at the damage, looking squeamish. "Whoa. I'm, like, so sorry . . ."

I rose to my tiptoes for a better look. "What the—"

Even Rufus seemed stunned into silence.

Shaking her head in disbelief, Claire made the inevitable announcement. "All right, everyone, party's over. Let's wrap it up and go home. I'm going to be in deep shit for this."

Turning to me and nodding to the gaping hole in the wall and the room full to the brim with a lot of dusty, old stuff she said, "*That* is a tomorrow problem."

This was why Claire and I got along, as I blithely ignored Future Sully sagging under all of Today Sully's problems. At least I could rest easy for now, knowing that the Butler likely had no owner wanting her back, at least nobody we could trace. If we couldn't find them, they probably couldn't find us, either. Unfortunately, it also meant I had no trail to discover who had owned the haunted handbag and if they had some sort of connection to Rufus.

"Let me know if you find anything good," I cooed as I made my way up the stairs with the rest of the crowd, petting Clementine as I passed.

"Yeah, yeah." Claire looked around at the mess and drained her can of seltzer, crunching it in her fist automatically, which was one of her quirks. We always knew who'd been drinking all the Diet Coke.

I kept my head on a swivel, looking to see if Bread-Brad had left yet. What was this nervous excitement rippling through my entire stomach right now? Butterflies? Drywall dust going to my head? Would it be a bold move to cash in my first ride request so soon after we'd struck our deal?

"I better not be asked to clean up your mess," Emma was saying as she and Guy helped Ron up the stairs. "You all want to take this party to a park or something?"

Guy looked to Ron. "I think I gotta get this one home."

"Wait a moment," Rufus said. *"Wait."*

When I was out of earshot, I pulled the bag closer to my mouth to explain what a party foul was. "I know you liked the music, but Claire is kicking everyone out. I'll play you some Olivia Rodrigo at home and other hits from the last seventy years."

"But for a moment I felt like I might . . ." He shook his little ghostly head, sounding exasperated. "It's probably nothing." He shrugged.

"I swear we'll come back another day. We'll figure it out. I learned some new stuff," I said, even though I had nothing that would help *him* and didn't know if I should be making promises. "Tomorrow, we'll go to the records hall and get some more information."

I looked around for Brad but didn't see him. He must've left, which made me nervous.

But I had to focus. The Butler wasn't just about me, after all.

# 13

The next morning, I woke up to a 3:00 a.m. text chain from Emma:
 I kissed Guy again or maybe he kissed me I don't know I can't remember
Then, moments later:
We said we were done fooling around but then after we helped ron sneak back into his room we kissed in his backyard but it's a blur and I can't remember who kissed who first
Punctuation? Don't know her. Then:
like how do I even know if I should apologize or be mad at him for breaking our no-makeouts pact
And:
HOW ARE YOU ASLEEP ALREADY

Last year, barely a weekend went by without some new Guy and Emma drama. Now, with my head full of Rufus and the Butler and Brad, watching it play out all over again was almost reassuringly familiar. I smiled to myself as I started to text her back.

"You're smirking at your light-up rectangle again."

I jumped, fumbling my phone onto the floor. Rufus perched on the beanbag, semi-transparent and examining his ghostly nails, which perfectly matched the beaded roses on his dress. A hat that looked like a cake made out of feathers sat atop an updo that formed a mass of lustrous curls. He glanced at me and grinned. "Is it Brad?"

"It's Emma," I said. "She's having a meltdown."

"That sounds serious. Will she be all right? Which part of her is melting?"

"No, she's not literally—ugh. It means she's freaking out about a kiss," I said, retrieving my phone and resuming my text. "I'm being helpful, and a good friend."

"You two seem to have a lot of drama surrounding necking. Wouldn't it be more helpful to actually speak to her?" Rufus waggled a finger at my texting. "Instead of doing whatever this is?"

I sighed, preparing a speech about the wonders of modern life where voice calls could be avoided like scabies, but then realized he had a point. Four texts merited more than a text back. Emma deserved to hear the mellifluous tones of my voice.

"Sully?" Emma's voice was thick.

I pictured her still in bed with her lavender comforter pulled up to her chin, surrounded by her army of monster-size plushies. Then I remembered that she'd been up until some ungodly hour and regretted calling so early due to peer pressure from a stunningly attired ghost. Oh well. She had seemed eager to talk, so I piled on the charm. "Hello, Sully's emergency relationship service. How may I direct your crisis?"

Emma groaned. "I think it was me. I think I screwed up." There were rustling noises, which I guessed were her turning over. "I'm a bad friend."

"I'm pretty sure Guy was very eager to kiss you, too," I said. "He's been giving you the lost-puppy-dog eyes for weeks now."

"This can't keep happening, though," she said. "It can't."

"Why not?"

"What's she saying?" Rufus hissed, hovering over my shoulder. "Is she melting like the Witch of the West or a nuclear reactor?"

I shushed him.

"Is someone there?" Emma asked. "Oh my god, did you bring someone home from the party?"

"Oh my god, Emma, no! TikTok video somehow still playing," I said, turning the phone away from Rufus. Nobody could hear him over the noise at the party, but as much as I needed my "I told you so" moment with Emma about the haunted bag, this was way too much to explain right then. "And this conversation is about *your* love life, not mine," I hedged.

"It can't be my love life, though!" she moaned. "Not unless . . ."

"What, what is it?" I said, pinching the phone between my cheek and shoulder as I tugged on a pair of sweats.

"Forget it."

This stopped me dead. Emma had never not wanted to talk about a hookup before.

"Hey, come on," I said. "What could you possibly not want to tell me? I told you about my bag ghost."

There was a long pause, and then an exasperated sigh that, coming from Emma, was like an eyebrow pencil to my heart. "I love you, Sully, but you wouldn't understand."

"Um, excuse me. You are talking to the relationship whisperer here. I mean, not my own, but other peoples'."

"It's just, I'm not really going anywhere, and Guy's doing community college. At this point, if we get together, we might never . . . get un-together."

"Oh." The full enormity of the problem hit me.

"You're goofing this up," said Rufus, and snapped his fingers. "Let me talk to her."

"Shhh!" I hissed.

"I should really let you get back to your . . . TikTok video," said Emma. "I'm sorry, you're right. It's not a big deal."

"I didn't say that!" I protested, just as my phone buzzed in my hand.

It was a text from Bread, like he was some kind of psychic:
Still need that ride?

"We're not done talking about this, okay?" I said.

"Okay," she moped. "Thanks, Sull."

I hung up and glowered at Rufus, who gave me an innocent look.

"We need to work on your phone manners." When Rufus went back to examining his nails, I decided to fib. "In this day and age, interrupting someone on the phone is considered incredibly rude. In fact, it's punishable by death."

Rufus smirked. "Is it, now? I suppose I should consider myself lucky I'm already dead. Are you still sore that I said you had bad manners yesterday?"

Huh. Check and mate.

I scowled and opened Brad's text to compose a response that was both the perfect level of casual and most certainly avoided opening the door to discussing the potential ramifications of my *own* hookup. I typed:

Yes, your services are still required . . . pick me up in an hour?

Too bratty? But then Bread hearted it.

"You're smiling again," Rufus said.

"Rufus!"

He threw his hands up. "You weren't on a call, were you?"

I couldn't wait to get to the records hall and continue my search, with Bread's help, of course. The Butler was an amazing accessory. The talking ghost watching my every move? Not so much.

Eleanor was already at City Hall for the day, and Dad was at work, which was why I didn't bother asking Rufus to tuck himself away in the Butler. He trailed me around the kitchen while I made myself a cute little morning coffee.

As I pulled the creamer out, there was a knock at the door.

Rufus angled for a look. "Must be the milkman or the postal courier at this time of the morning."

"You shush!" I hissed, because apparently Brad was *very punctual*. An hour, to him, meant an hour, not an hour and a half. But there was his yummy frame, silhouetted against the living room drapes. "Get in that bag right now!"

"Oh, cool your jets!" Rufus said, vaporizing into the Butler, which teetered on the edge of the table with the force of his disappearance.

I hurried to the door to let Brad in, but not before stopping at the mirror to do a quick once-over. An hour had hardly been enough time to get fully ready. What had I been thinking, setting such a rigorous schedule for myself? My floaty floral shirt ever-so-gently skimmed the top of my bike shorts.

Hair? Meh.

Skin? It could always be worse.

"I'll tell you this much," Rufus's voice echoed from the bag, "in my day when you primped like that for a knock at the door, you dug your trick. You seem rather besotted, darling." Of course, Rufus had to say this while looking like a total glamour puss.

"Rufus, get back in that damn bag and shut up!"

I popped the door open with a flourish, trying very hard to remember to use his real name. "Oh, hello, *Brad*. I was just about to put my homemaker hat on and make breakfast. Would you like an omelet before we head over to the records hall?"

Brad looked around, seemingly confused. "Who were you talking to?"

"Oh. Um. Siri. Or Alexa. Or both!"

"Oh, nice. Alexa! Play Mitski!"

The silence in the house was deafening. We didn't have an Alexa.

"Um, she's probably just doing a software update and can't hear you. Anyway, forget breakfast, we can grab something on the road."

Time was ticking, and we needed to get on with our field trip moment. I grabbed the Butler and locked the door behind me before I reunited with my beloved, four-wheeled Olivia Newton-John.

I slid into the passenger seat, immediately noticing the clip-in air fresheners. I leaned forward and took a whiff.

"Fresh pine," Brad said. "I hope you approve."

Truthfully, it smelled wonderful. Fresh and . . . reliable? If something could even smell reliable. Oh, Bread. Okay, *Brad*. Bread didn't exactly feel right anymore. I reminded myself that most dudes our age would've tried to find an Axe body spray scent. "I'll allow it," I said.

The corner of Brad's lip curved as he reversed Olivia Newton-John out into the street. I wasn't about to lie—I liked how he handled her. A pang of longing struck me, but whether it was for the car or the boy, I couldn't quite tell.

"You never told me what's happening over at the records hall," Brad said after a moment. "What are we doing there?"

"Oh, um, my mom needs me to do some research on title deeds. Incredibly boring, obviously," I rushed to add. "I wasn't planning on being here this summer, of course, but here we are."

"But what specifically are you researching?" he asked.

Why couldn't he just buy my flimsy excuse and chauffeur me in style and *silence*? I'd had a lot of time to think of a plausible explanation, but no dice. And I had technically promised Eleanor that I wouldn't talk about the whole potential missing heir mystery. "Sorry, that's on a need-to-know basis."

"Huh."

I angled a look his way to see if he was hurt, but he seemed fine. Good old, dependable Brad. The houses slowly yielded to lush farmland as we drove along the outskirts of town. I managed to expertly navigate Olivia Newton-John's sound system—it still remembered my phone—to turn on some Bad Bunny.

"Have you heard from that Lyndzi chick?" Brad asked. "Any chance you might end up working with her later on?"

It was so cute that he was concerned about me that I instantly forgave him for saying *chick*. I sighed. "No, actually, I haven't. Ew, right?"

My phone buzzed. I glanced down; it was a block of text from Emma. But before I could read it—

"Sully, have you always not liked me?" Brad asked suddenly.

I choked on the pull I'd taken from my refillable water bottle. "I'm sorry? What? I do like you, I mean, as a friend—"

"No," Brad said. "I meant, like, as a *person*. You've always kind of looked at me like I was contagious. But then after the other night . . . I thought if you liked me, I would have known. Yeah, I've had a crush on you—"

"Stop sign!" I screamed.

Brad slammed to stop at a sign he was about to blow through, then took a deep breath as if he was trying to gather his thoughts. If only it was that easy to stop this conversation.

"Sorry about that," Brad said, breathing a little hard.

"No worries."

There were definitely worries. Specifically, that he'd start talking again. I could barely hear anything over the sound of blood rushing in my ears.

"Um, as I was saying," he continued, apparently not one to be deterred by a literal stop sign from the universe, "I like you, but I don't like-like you unless you *want* me to like-like you. But I can't tell, because you're not exactly easy to read."

"Me? Seriously? I'm an open book!" And holy hell, had he just said the words *crush* and *like-like* all at once? To me?

"I spill my guts and that's what you pick up on?" Brad asked. "Typical."

"Typical? What exactly does *that* mean, Bradley? Or should I say Breadley?"

"What is with the Bread thing? And don't tell me it's just a nickname again."

"I thought . . . it sounded . . . cute."

He snorted. "Okay, Sully. Well, for starters, my full name is Bradford. And I'm only saying this because I care, as I just said and you ignored, but you're self-centered, Sully. I get it. It's not easy being you, and you *should* be making yourself the priority in a place like Hearst. It's actually something I love about you, that you're in your own planetary orbit. Your own atmosphere! But do you even notice all the people rotating around you?"

"I notice people," I told him, really, really, really trying not to think about how he said he *loved* something about me. "I notice all kinds of things."

He leaned back into *my* driver's seat. "Fine. Tell me five things you know about me."

I dropped my water bottle into the side of the door and crossed my arms. My pride quickly sank as embarrassment floated to the surface. Was Brad right? "One, you like Kohl's. Two, you bought my car. Three, adults love you. Four, you're gay. And . . . and . . . five, your favorite color is khaki!"

He nodded curtly. "Cool."

"You said five things! That was five things!" I said. Five flimsy, ridiculous things, but that didn't mean I didn't like Brad. Okay, wow. I liked Brad. I shook my head gently.

But what if the way he irritated me had less to do with him being a goody-goody and more to do with me trying to avoid the fact that I really, really wanted to smash our faces together like two Barbie dolls?

He pulled into the parking lot and found a spot on the far end. It was unusually packed. "We're here."

"Oh-kay," I prompted, but Brad sat in the driver's seat, gripping the wheel, his eyes fixed straight ahead of him. "Should we . . . go . . . or . . . ?"

"I know you call me Bread because you think I'm dull and boring."

Well, shit. Okay, so I wasn't always the picture of discretion, but it was a touch mortifying to get called out like this. Who knew butch guys had such soft hearts?

I tried to catch his eye to see whether he was mad or just curious. He didn't look at me. My heartbeat pulsed in my throat. He'd been so honest, and he was right: I hadn't paid him the same respect. I had to say something, and quickly.

"I don't know, *Brad* . . . I guess I've been"—I sighed. Why was this so hard?—"Jealous?" The word felt so revolting coming out of my mouth. I was also trying not to make it about me—ouch, by the way—but it was tough. Because I especially hated the thought of admitting there was someone I'd rather be than myself.

"What?" He turned his whole body to face me. He looked truly stumped. "Why?"

"Shouldn't we be going inside?" I asked.

"I think we have time," he said a little sternly. "How could *you* possibly be jealous of *me*?"

"Because you're masculine and straight-passing. You play soccer and were voted class president by some of the exact same people who tortured me for years. Isn't it obvious? You always had it easier. You wear your khakis and button-down shirt, and people want to eat you up with a spoon. I stick out everywhere I go, and you, you just have . . ."

Ugh. Saying all this made my head and heart hurt. I couldn't tell whether it was the right thing or the wrong thing to think or feel. Speaking it out loud felt like an absolute betrayal. Of both of us, maybe. But what else did I have to lose? *Bradford* wanted me to talk, so here it was. The full, ugly truth. Maybe he'd learn his lesson and wouldn't ask again, because I wasn't just keeping a bag ghost secret. He thought I was myself and out and authentic with everyone? Well, there was a layer beneath how I presented, and here it was.

*May 16, 1955*

*That was close. Too close. We were careless in our happiness. Because of our happiness. Being questioned in the street? It's too much. And yet, we can be, because people like us are always suspect.*

*I'm used to it, mostly—there's no hiding any of my light under a bushel basket. What worries me is you. You're made of a different light. One that brightens my every day but one that doesn't shine too bold, too obviously, too dangerously. You're able to control the burn. And I am a person set ablaze. Especially when I'm near you.*

*You're quick to tell me you're proud of me, you admire me even. Who I am and what I do. You tell me I'm brave and brazen . . . and brash. And you're equally quick to remind me of McCarthy, Eisenhower, and Executive Order 10450, and that we are never truly safe and can't be too reckless.*

*And I worry that this will all be too much for you. That I will be too much for you given your dreams and ambitions to enter politics and affect change. I worry that I'll be left in the dust if you decide my image doesn't align with yours and it's simpler to put pedal to the metal.*

*I may burn this letter before sending it. I'm not sure how you'll receive it. Or if I truly want you to. It is the shadow of my flames, and I can't stand to live only in shadows.*

# 14

The admission that I hadn't planned on making in a million years hung in the air between us. The Butler nudged against my leg, as if Rufus was listening. Great. This was definitely going to be the last ride Brad and I ever took together—innuendo fully intended.

"I like that you stand out, though," he said. "I always have. I like that you know exactly who you want to be. But also, Sully, I like soccer. And the guys are hot. But don't tell them I said that. Most of them had just finally gotten over changing in front of me by the time the season ended."

"They were uncomfortable around you?" This was absolute news to me. But Brad had always had things easy. Hadn't he?

Brad looked at me like I was crazy. "Of course."

"Oh."

"And I want to go into politics. Class president felt like a good place to start. Your mom is a badass, by the way. And khakis make me feel a bit more dressed up, you know? Besides, whether or not I'm likable, cool, masculine, straight-passing, or boring as fuck, that's for other people to decide. I know who I am, and I like him."

Actual tears almost sprang to my eyes. He thought I knew who

I was? *He had* confidence and self-assurance. Maybe I was right to be jealous. Brad somehow just managed to be okay with all parts of himself. I'd thought I'd known who I was, too, but since Uncle Chuck's shitty stunt, Lyndzi's betrayal, and having to stay in Hearst, I was beginning to doubt that more and more.

We stared straight ahead at a field and flat horizon line. Then my Sully Drew senses perked up. Wasn't this where the railroad used to run? I had to remember that detail from Rufus, especially since it was a real memory, and those were so few and far between.

"We should go inside," Brad finally said.

The records hall was normally a pretty sleepy country building on the outskirts of town, but not today. It had classic red bricks and a portico, if watching HGTV had taught me anything about architecture. A few windows had seen better days, and weeds usually choked the parking lot, but for the first time in maybe *ever*, it seemed like a ton of people had gotten interested in Hearst history. The lot was full, and people were gathered outside.

"What's going on here?" I asked as we walked to the entrance.

"I thought you'd know. You're the one who wanted to come here today." Brad stopped and pulled the door open for me like a total gentleman. He squinted at the sun, and it was so cute. My gaze wandered to the vein on his forearm.

Brad was . . . hot.

"Are you going in or . . . ?"

"Oh!" I snapped out of it, hugged the Butler, and skipped inside. Close call, though. Brad was proving irritatingly good at reading me.

But I almost came to a crashing halt in the lobby. Like, the whole town was in here, the line stretching from Phyllis's desk like she was running the TKTS booth in Times Square.

"Okay, Sully," Brad whispered. "I think you need to explain what's happening here and how you knew about it."

Jack Spangle, proprietor of the feed and tack store, who'd never met a pickup-truck gun rack he didn't like, whirled around. "Haven't you heard, young man?" Then he saw me and his eyes narrowed.

"No, um, sir," Brad said, ducking his head.

See? Acceptable gay. The Jack Spangles of the world could immediately identify him as a "man" without getting all confused.

"The *Bugle* did a cover story on it. But your generation doesn't bother with the newspaper, I suppose."

So much for keeping Eleanor's secrets. Apparently, Rufus was the only purse resident left in this town, because the cat was out of the bag.

Brad turned to me with a question in his eyes.

"There's a land ownership fiasco," I whispered. "As much as it pains me to know this much about the inner workings of Hearst, Pennsylvania. But my lovely mother told me—"

Brad pouted a little, looking hurt.

"Just yesterday. You didn't miss anything. I would've shared the gossip with you. Eventually. Your brownie points are safe."

That seemed to cheer him up. "Anyway. Beauregard Hearst the First—which sounds incredibly stupid when you say it aloud—and Harry Hearst are credited with establishing the town. And as we know, because Beauregard Hearst the *Fifth* won't let anyone forget it, he is the sole surviving patrilincal heir to a shit ton of land around these here parts. Or, at least as far as we know, since so many of the original records were lost in that flood. Right?"

"Right." He nodded. That lineage had been drilled into every child in town from a young age.

"Well, what if he wasn't?"

"The heir?"

"The *sole* heir. They found some records in the old schoolhouse that point to the idea of another claimant. So Eleanor—"

"Wait, a different Eleanor?"

"No, of course not. There is no other Eleanor."

"You don't call her Mom?"

"Brad! Focus! I'm pretty sure *Eleanor* wants to potentially track down this other owner and announce the findings at the Founders' Day Festival. Shake things up a little. And put Beau back in his place so he can't decide he'll bulldoze half of Hearst on a whim. But we need to locate these records so she can get them to the historian she's working with."

"It looks like pretty much everyone in town beat us to it."

I rifled through the Butler, wondering if Rufus could feel me grabbing around in there. "Yes, but not everyone has *this*! A records requisition form, signed by a councilwoman."

Brad grinned. "*God*, I love bureaucracy."

I choked back a snarky response because I needed Brad on my side. And also, his enthusiasm was a li'l bit cute.

From the head of the line, Phyllis was getting increasingly agitated, yelling, "As I told you all already, I'm afraid I cannot offer access to the historical records without a requisition form. They are fragile, there has been damage, so you are welcome to what's already digitized, as is every Hearst citizen, but we cannot risk the integrity of the original paperwork."

"Well, look at that. Priority boarding!" I said, grabbing Brad by the elbow and pushing past the assembled crowd. The smell of really old paper—with a slight bass note of water damage—greeted us as we crossed the black-and-white-checkerboard tile floor toward a knot of people grumbling at Phyllis.

The energy in here was as frenetic as I'd ever seen it. Especially once I noticed the contemporary Beauregard—speak of the literal devil—holding court with his supporters and no doubt trying to sow a culture war. It must've burned him up that he couldn't sign a requisition form for any of them. Or himself. Oh, the sweet irony. Good for Phyllis for holding her ground.

"I'm sorry, but this needs a signature from the council," she was saying.

"I was *on* the council."

"But you're not anymore. Everyone in this town has to play by the rules. No special treatment."

"But this is about my land. I have a right—"

"That's to be determined. Isn't it?"

Ooof. That Phyllis was one tough bitch. Iconic. I waltzed over, cutting between her and Beauregard. "Good morning, *Phyllis*, darling. You're looking lovely. I have a *signed* requisition form for you from Councilwoman Eleanor Hartlow." I produced the document with a flourish and could almost hear Beauregard's butthole puckering.

Brad snickered beside me.

"Can we please check into the records room for the 1920s to the 1960s?" I asked.

"Of course you can," she said pleasantly and shot Beauregard a *look*. If I didn't know better, I would say there might've been some fire between them in a previous century.

"Let's have you two sign in here. Now, actually, Sully, those years take up two different rooms. We are currently in the middle of digitizing, so we've separated what we have already scanned from what we were able to salvage after the flood. Down the hall, second door on the left you'll find the 1900s to the 1940s, then the 1950s through the 1990s is the third door on the right."

Based on the side-eye Beauregard gave me and Brad—who was totally innocent here—when Phyllis waved us back, he was clearly up to no good. I couldn't have possibly felt better sashaying down the hall to the exact rooms he was interested in.

"Thanks, Phyllis!" I cooed as we made our way around the corner.

I couldn't believe we'd pulled it off, and right in Beauregard's face. "Brad, how do you feel about dividing and conquering? Would you do the 1900s room, and I'll haul ass to the 1950s? I wish we could zero in on the right time period, but we can get more done that way. Besides, I really need to get these records for Mom's committee. Imagine how much they'd love *you* if they found out you helped."

I was really laying it on thick, but I figured an appeal to Brad's civic duty would seal the deal.

"I do love efficiency." Then he paused. "But you have to tell me *exactly* what we're looking for. You've been sketchy on the details."

"Great question," I said, like I was channeling my inner Eleanor and holding a press conference. "Anything that seems out of the ordinary. You know most of the key players—the people with the statues, the last names on the buildings. Look for anyone who isn't *that* but who had prominent land or business holdings. Someone who could be the long-lost descendant of one of those statues." Then I froze. "Shoot."

"What?"

"Eleanor said an important name. I can't believe I forgot it. It sounds like Walrus Trash Can? That can't be right." I dug out my phone to text her but saw the time. The city council was in session, with a strict no-texting rule because we were apparently in the Stone Age.

"Walrus Trash Can?"

"It's not exactly that, but it sounds similar. Something that would absolutely catch your attention." I smiled widely. "I believe in you."

With those orders, Brad marched off to his room, leaving me, the Butler, and Rufus to get down to business. It could not have worked out any better, because now Brad couldn't see me talking to my purse. I quickly scanned the ceiling to see if I was being surveilled—an instinct left over from my brief flirtation with some light shoplifting at the Aéropostale at Elmwood Mall, long before I both got some fashion sense and understood the plight of the retail worker—then ducked out of the lone camera's sight line. I combed my way between the suffocatingly narrow aisles of tall bookshelves. Obviously, keeping the Butler free of nicks, scratches, and cobwebs was mission-critical, so I tucked her even more securely beneath my arm.

At the end of one row of shelves, I found an out-of-sight clearing big enough to unleash Rufus. I took a step back, marveling at how much my life had changed in the last week. Seeing the Butler in this vintage records hall made me think of all the things she must have witnessed over the last hundred-plus years. The good. The bad.

The fabulous. I wondered again why and when Rufus had moved in. Here, in this place steeped in history, it seemed possible that we might actually figure all that out.

I opened the clasp, and Rufus rushed out to greet me in a very somber and understated gray two-piece suit. "I get why you call him Bread now, since he's the greatest thing since the sliced variety. I think he's smitten with you, yes sirree Bob!"

"Sir? Bob? Rufus, first things first: just say buddy, hunny, babe, or whatever. I'm nonbinary."

"Non-*who*-nary?"

I slowed down, remembering that some things were second nature to me, but totally new to Rufus. We had a whole divide to bridge between his time and experiences and mine. "It means that I don't identify as a man or a woman, I'm somewhere in between. So instead of sir, man, or he/him, I like they/them, person, or words that don't correlate to the idea of gender as a strict binary idea. This is the new lexicon."

"And this is widely accepted now?" he asked skeptically.

I laughed. "I mean, yes, but no. Maybe not in a small town like Hearst. But with our phones—also known as light rectangles—we're all so much more connected. It's easier to accept that there are a lot more ways of being, and to find community, even if only virtually."

Rufus stared back at me with wide eyes, clearly shocked. "A lot of us would use they and them to avoid admitting we were talking about another man. But you're fine when I call you *Mary* or you call me *sis*?"

"I know, it's a lot to take in. And, as you said, those are terms of endearment for people we feel a kinship with. But it means a lot that you thought to check, sis." I proudly claimed they/them. If anything, my pronouns made me feel more myself, not like I was hiding a secret.

Rufus nodded thoughtfully and cast his eyes around the room. "Right, Mary . . . that map on the wall! I recognize that river." He rushed up to it to take a closer look. "And this—"

"Beau Gare," I read, and a lightbulb went off. The train station Rufus had mentioned at the coffee shop. I checked the bottom corner. The map was dated 1954.

"So you lived around here somewhere?"

Rufus studied the map, tracing his semi-translucent fingers across a radius close to the train station. The landmarks and houses were labeled in impossibly small block lettering.

"Do any of these ring a bell?" I started reading off landmarks. "Byron Gates? Galeton Place? Boalsburg Hill?"

Rufus shook his head, looking dejected.

I kept scanning. "Gratton Farms? Um, Chester—"

"Wait! What did you say?"

"Chester?"

"No, before that." Rufus crowded next to me to look at the map.

"Gratton Farms?"

My pulse jumped. Were we on to something?

"That's it! Gratton! That's my last name!"

"Seriously? Well, well, well! Gratton Farms. Maybe there are some records about your family in here somewhere."

Lo and behold, there were. Brad had better watch out, because

I'd spent a lot of time in the library with Eleanor as a kid and could be pretty handy with research. Rufus followed me as I pulled a binder of old records off the shelf.

Rufus and I scurried over to the reading table at the end of the aisle. He couldn't manipulate the pages himself, so I tried to read as much as I could and keep flipping through at the same time. "Tell me if you see something, okay?"

After a few minutes, Rufus looked up at me with what appeared to be pearlescent ghost tears in his eyes. We were in a portion of the book from the 1960s. "Thomas Gratton. That was my father. He owned the farmland, but he wasn't a farmer. He hired people to do that." Rufus pointed to the page. "It even looks like he ran for mayor of Hearst himself! But I see no mention of a son, Rufus, anywhere in here. And I remember now I didn't have any siblings. So as far as history goes, it's as if I never existed . . ." His voice broke on that last syllable.

I knew a thing or two about erasure, and my heart ached for him. "Maybe we should check another binder or decade?" I wanted anything else to be true, but I suspected that we wouldn't find Rufus anywhere. "We'll keep looking. One way or another, we'll get some answers, I swear." I squinted more closely at the page, then traced my finger down a census but didn't find Rufus listed as a resident of Gratton Farms. I went back to the shelves and scanned the spines of the other binders. "Shit! Brad is in the room with the older files. There may be a birth certificate or something but it won't be in here. We'll find it, Rufus. I promise."

He began to pace and his outfit flickered back and forth between the gray-suit and beaded-rose-dress looks. I wondered whether the changes were involuntary or Rufus causing them.

"Why can't I just remember? It seems so cruel, doesn't it? To not know my own memories. My own story. Because obviously no one else was troubled enough to document it."

I began to flip through the book myself, hoping to stumble upon something that would turn this whole thing around. We came to a picture of a house on a significant amount of acreage. "There it is, Gratton Farms."

Rufus gasped. "I was right! Sully, this is the home where I grew up. Look at the address."

"Millroad Lane? Are you *sure* you recognize it?"

"As sure as I'm Tallulah Bouvier Beale!" As Rufus finished saying it, his dress tightened and lengthened into a full-length gown. The beaded roses sparkled and bloomed from out of the fabric of the gown into silk flowers while his hair gained height and his makeup shimmered. He looked down, his mouth dropping open.

"Rufus," I whispered in awe.

He looked at me, bottom lids lined with tears, which he quickly used a fingernail to delicately wipe away. "I remembered. That was my stage name."

"Rufus Gratton and Tallulah Bouvier Beale."

"The one and the same." Rufus, or Tallulah, jutted one hip out as he did a dramatic flourish.

"We've got a lead! Just like Celine, it's all coming back to us now."

Our heads snapped toward the door we had entered through as we both heard hurried footfalls coming in our direction.

I snapped a photo of the sketch of Gratton Farms and returned the binder to its place on the shelf. Then I opened the Maps app on my phone to double-check before saying, "That's just fifteen minutes from here!"

We needed to get to Millroad Lane, and the boots I'd happened to wear today were not made for walking. This research was triggering Rufus's memory, and we had to follow that trail of breadcrumbs in Olivia Newton-John.

Brad burst into the room, zipping down the stacks. He brandished his phone, which glowed with pictures of dusty brown pages. A smile lit his entire face. Rufus whooshed back into the Butler just as Brad turned the corner with big teacher's-pet energy. "Sully! I found this rogue folder with newspaper clippings from one of the Founders' Day celebrations in the '50s. Guess what?"

"What? I hate the suspense!" Besides, I was bursting to tell him my news.

"I found a picture of your grandparents as babies with *their* parents—your great-grandparents, including Josephine—at the parade! How cool is that? Who knew their granddaughter would grow up to be on the city council one day!" He zoomed in on the screen, his phone filling with a grainy image.

I deflated a little. "Wow, that is pretty cool, I guess." I didn't want to sound ungrateful, but my mind was so focused on Rufus's story that I didn't really care much about some picture that was probably also gathering dust somewhere in our attic. "Say," I began as casually as I could. "You didn't happen to see anything like old censuses or birth records or anything like that?"

Brad shook his head. "I'm afraid the flood wiped out more than the city council would like to admit. The council would have to approach other counties or go to state archives to see what we could recover."

"Drat," I muttered, aware it wasn't a word I'd normally use. I guess Rufus was rubbing off on me.

I could practically feel Rufus's sorrow emanating from the Butler. He'd gone from recovering his name only to find out all traces of him had been wiped away, either by a flood or perhaps because his family had preferred it that way. How would I have made it this far if I hadn't had parents like Eleanor and my father?

"Hey, so, this is great," I told Brad, who was still holding out his phone. "But we have to mosey. I'll explain on the way."

And it wasn't a moment too soon, because what sounded like a stampede of men's loafers echoed from the hallway. Beauregard burst into the room, and his team of lackeys scattered out from behind him. He looked me up and down, blocking the doorway for a claustrophobic second before his shoulder purposely bumped into mine. "We'll need you to leave now," he said.

"We were just going, so don't worry, you guys can all hold hands and make out in peace."

Beau sneered as I squeezed the Butler under my arm in what I hoped was a protective and reassuring way. In a surprising plot twist, Brad began to scratch his forehead with his middle finger. Me-ow! Aggressive! I was here for it.

At least that hideous Beauregard was a universal nightmare to everyone, and not just me. I wondered how he'd finally worn Phyllis down.

Making our way back to dear old Olivia Newton-John, I had a new goal in mind. Two, actually. I needed to get to Gratton Farms to try and figure out what had happened to Rufus and whether his family had kept any records of him. Then I'd need to look further into the whole lost-landowner sitch. Something was just not right—Beauregard was clearly on the warpath and likely to pull some kind of stunt, and Eleanor and I couldn't let that stand. Since I was stuck here for the summer, I might as well shake shit up.

As we exited to the parking lot, blinking in the bright sunlight, I thrust my phone into Brad's hand, GPS already locked and loaded.

"What's this?"

"Old Gratton Farms on Millroad Lane."

"Um, okay. But why?"

"For research, obviously."

But Brad seemed to have something on his mind. "Sure, but look, Sully. I'm happy to give you rides whenever you need them, but if you were trying to get rid of me back there because you're talking to someone else, you can just tell me. It won't hurt my feelings. I just don't really want to be driving you to a booty call or whatever."

"Excuse me?" I could not even imagine what Brad was talking about. He'd been my first kiss just a few days ago. Forget a booty call. "Do I look like the type who lets anyone have a go at back-seat bingo with me?" Okay, there was no doubt Rufus was influencing me. "I'd like to think I've shown more discerning taste despite recent lapses in judgment."

Brad did not take my bait. "After we split up, I heard you talking to someone. And I heard you talking to someone at your house, too." He gave me a look. "You don't have an Alexa. I'm not an idiot."

*Think fast, Sully.* "I talk to myself, okay?" Ugh, a mortifying admission, but it was technically the truth. Besides, I'd already poured out more of my soul to him today than I'd ever expected. More often than not, my internal monologues became external.

"Is that the story we're going with?"

Clearly, my excuses weren't working on Brad, who was smarter than he looked. But I couldn't tell him about Rufus. Not yet, and maybe not ever.

*No.* "Absolutely."

Brad frowned but moved toward the car anyway. "Because you can tell me if you have a boyfriend, you know. Or a . . . person-friend. Is that what it would be called?"

"Oh my god! Brad. Stop. I was talking to myself, and maybe you hallucinated the rest. Or you heard Beauregard's henchmen making out in the broom closet? Now, that would be a juicy plot twist."

"Sooo . . . you're not dating anyone else?" Brad seemed to brighten.

"Good lord, Brad. Who would that even be, anyway? Of course I don't have a boyfriend! Hearst is not exactly resplendent with potential suitors for someone of my caliber. If there's only a single option, I'm lucky." I had no idea how to handle this. Brad was asking me if I had a boyfriend. Brad had said *love* to me earlier. I practically floated into the passenger seat. "Some T-Swift for the ride?" I knew she was one of Rufus's newly discovered favorites.

Brad nodded, smiling again.

And so did I. Because it seemed Brad like-liked me. And maybe I like-liked him too.

# 15

"Before we head to Gratton Farms, I have two questions for you, Sully." Brad looked at me across the console. "One, I need coffee—"

"That's not a question."

"You didn't let me finish. Do you want any?"

"I've never turned down an iced chai in my life. Why would I start now?"

Brad flashed a smile. I waited for the second question, but Brad had already pulled into the one and only Starbucks in town, which was a completely separate business venture from Beauregard's development plans for Hearst, but it still might have been a harbinger of them.

"What was your other question?" I asked over the crackling of the drive-through speaker.

"Is this mission still only about your mom's land ownership project? Because you know I'm all over that. I even started digging into that Cygnus Cobpen guy."

"Who?"

Brad rolled his eyes. "You called him Walrus Trash Can. I had his name stuck in my head. It's so unique. So I started poking around."

"Oh. Right." These old-timey names were sending me. "But you got all that from Walrus Trash Can?"

"I may have talked to my boss."

"You mean my Eleanor?"

Brad sat up a little straighter in Olivia Newton-John's luxurious bucket seat. "A perk of the internship. But—"

"But nothing!" Brad with the hard-hitting questions! I almost wished we were back to talking about coffee. He clearly wasn't having any of my half-truths. I chose my words carefully. "Okay, well, it's not *exactly* about that."

Half his mouth dipped into a frown. He'd been asking me directly whether I was lying, and I'd been evasive. Somehow, it made more sense in my head. But Brad was a rule-follower, and I knew I had to rescue this without making him feel bad for already going out on a limb for me.

"Okay, so I was looking for one thing and then I think I might have found another thing, but the first thing is . . . a little hard to explain, so—"

"So it's like when someone posts the vague lyrics to a song and"—he handed his card over to pay for our order, like a true gentleman, before continuing—"It makes perfect sense to them but not to anyone else?"

I thought about that for a moment before nodding. "Yeah, so like, if you can just trust that I know what the lyrics mean, then we're good. But I can't really explain just yet, if you get me?"

Brad collected his iced caramel macchiato and my grande iced chai from the window and shrugged. "Okay."

"What?"

"You got it. I won't press until you're ready. I can tell this is important to you."

"Um, wow. That's, like, really elevated of you." Emma and Guy would always be my ride-or-die duo, but I could never imagine them going along with this without a full-on PowerPoint presentation. Emma, especially. But even beyond my besties, so few people in this town trusted me to know myself. It was refreshing to feel like I was capable of leading the way—even if I so wasn't.

He blushed a little. "I'm just along for the ride."

"Okay," I said.

"Okay." He took a sip of his coffee. "On *one* condi—"

"Nope! You already said okay! No backsies!"

"How old are you?" Brad asked, but before I could get offended, I saw that he was smirking. Pulling out of the drive-through with our treats, we got back on the road toward Gratton Farms, which was on the outer edge of Hearst. Soon, the GPS was leading us down what I was sure was the wrong road, because *road* was almost too luxurious a term for it. At some point, the city must've given up on paving it. Gravel sprayed behind Olivia Newton-John's tires.

One little brain cell wondered if Brad and I were about to become the next victims on some true-crime podcast. What would they call us? Friends, probably. Tragedy upon tragedy.

Another part of me was mystified that there were apparently parts of Hearst I'd never seen before. But Sully and farms didn't go hand in hand.

"That must be it," Brad said as the car rolled to a stop next to a driveway. "And, uh, looks like we're not alone."

I rolled down my window to take in the view. If I wasn't already thinking about how emotional this visit would be for Rufus, I'd think the place was beautiful but not at all a farm. In front of us was a rambling old manor, the kind you see in movies with *Condemned: Do Not Enter* signs out front and witches or whatever lurking inside. There were no barns or fields, but overgrown lawns and gardens.

"But, farms?" I blurted, making no sense.

"This was the estate house," Brad explained, discerning what I was trying to ask without any further clarification from me. "The working farmland used to be behind that line of trees in the distance, out of sight and probably smell of the owners."

But in sight were giant dumpsters and an excavator. Men in work clothes moved in and out of the front door, tossing trash bags into a dumpster parked out front. Even from the car I could hear hammering and what sounded like a power drill whining somewhere inside. Had we arrived literally a day too late, after all these years?

"Is she about to come down?" I gasped.

Inside, something fell with a crash, followed by several workmen shouting.

"Oh no they didn't!" I grabbed the Butler, doing my best to angle it so that Rufus could see the house without revealing himself to Brad. Maybe this was just the groundskeeper's cottage or something, and the *real* Gratton Farms was safe down the road, I tried to convince myself.

A small voice issued from the bag. "Why are they wrecking my house?"

So this *was* the right place. "Take it easy," I mumbled.

"What'd I say?" said Brad, sounding stung.

"Oh, no, nothing," I stammered, catching myself between conversations again. It seemed that Rufus was becoming more able to interface with the world, because Emma had heard him earlier too. But if he made himself known in the car, I had no idea how I'd spin it.

We continued to watch out my window as a man with a beard and a checked flannel shirt appeared on the front porch. He held a cell phone to his ear and looked as though he was in the middle of a heated conversation. As he paced, he seemed to spot Olivia Newton-John parked at the end of the driveway and gave us a look that was two parts inquisitive and three parts *get off my lawn*. He'd fit right in here in Hearst.

"Maybe we should go," I said, catching serious cold feet. What was I supposed to say? *Hey, can we have a look around—my bag ghost maybe used to live here?* I turned to Brad, ready to pull the rip cord. "Did I just hear your stomach growl? Are you hungry? I could eat too—"

Rufus huffed and rattled inside the bag, making his views on the subject crystal clear.

Brad shook his head. "Come on, Sully. We didn't come all the way out here to turn back. I trust that you wouldn't have come if it wasn't important. That guy looks like he's in charge. Let's go talk to him."

I stared at him, mouth open. No way Brad was being more adventurous than me. But he was right. I wanted to help Rufus, and this was where the trail had led us. "Okay, fine."

I grabbed the Butler and reached for the door handle.

Brad glanced at the bag. "Oh, you're . . . gonna bring your antique purse?"

"It's a *vintage bag*, Bradford," I said. "Besides, it might be an intimidation factor. 'Hey, let us look inside your house or I'll shame you with my crushing fashion superiority.'" I didn't add, *And Rufus will haunt your ass for eternity.*

Brad stared for a moment then burst out laughing.

I smiled. I couldn't help it. "Or maybe I'm just a crazy bag lady."

"You're not a lady," he said. "You're a theydy."

My lungs swelled at the recognition, even if it was just in response to a silly joke. I felt my face turning into the personification of a heart eye emoji. "Are you trying to woo me? Because it's working."

He grinned and nodded for me to lead the way.

Whatever resolve I'd had started to evaporate as soon as we walked up the drive to the front porch. Cell Phone Guy hung up his call and stood with his hands on hips, waiting for us to approach him. A total cis-het power move. With his beard and flannel shirt, he reminded me of a lumberjack. Or that guy from the story with the big blue ox. What was his name?

"Can I help you boys?" he asked.

"There's only one boy here, but yes, we hope so," I said. I may not have been great at striking up conversations with obviously straight adult men, but I was way too practiced at being misgendered to let that slide. "This place is beautiful. Did you just buy it? You have great taste."

The flattery seemed to work, as I knew it would. The guy's stance loosened and he glanced over his shoulder at the house. "Yeah, I guess I do. It's a beautiful old Victorian. Shame about it."

"Why a shame?" Brad asked.

"It has to come down," the guy said.

Rufus practically bounced the bag out of my grip. I squeezed the Butler and tried to keep a look of abject horror off my face. "Wait, why would you tear it down?"

"We were hoping to just gut the place, but the foundation's rotted all to hell," the guy said. "Mold, too. I was hoping to restore it, but whoever last owned it let it fall into disrepair. It's a shame they didn't care for the bones of this old place. But the new recreation court we're building will be awesome." He tried a salesman grin on us. "You boys like pickleball?"

"Again, only one boy here," I said, right as Brad said, "An *indoor* pickleball court?"

"Not now, Brad," I hissed, then returned my attention to our new neighborhood pickleball enthusiast. "Would you mind if we took a look around?"

"Yes."

"Oh, great!" I started toward the steps, but Flannel wasn't moving out of the way.

"I mean yes as in I *would* mind. Who are you two? What are you doing here? And I can't let two kids go traipsing through a building being demo'ed. It's a liability issue." He made a shooing motion with his phone hand. "You can't be hanging around here. I've got calls to make, so . . ."

"Their mother is a city councilor!" Brad burst out.

I felt myself die a little inside. Talk about the least intimidating brag ever. I also was a bit better than Beauregard with the name-dropping, so I didn't love seeing Brad sink to this level. I wanted to succeed on my own terms, rather than riding Eleanor's very fashionable coattails.

"Wait, seriously?" Flannel's eyebrows made a slow climb to his hairline. "Is that, like, a mayor?"

"Not really," I said as Brad went, "Pretty much."

The guy looked back and forth between us. "Because someone from Hearst Sanitation or whatever seriously needs to call me." He waggled his phone. "I got a notice saying dumpster pickup is eight hundred dollars. Eight hundred!"

As we'd been talking, construction dudes had been silently moving past us, carrying shapeless hunks of wood and drywall, though I wasn't a contractor or anything. As we spoke, load after load of debris was chucked into the dumpster that took up most of the mansion's front lawn. I glanced inside and saw what looked like a busted grandfather clock, half a chair, and what might well have been a box full of papers. My vintage radar pinged—this seemed promising. Rufus must've felt it, too, because he almost vibrated inside the Butler.

I pulled the bag closer to my side. Seeing all these old, smashed things hurt my heart. It went against my thrifting ethos. True, I'd never thought about all the history in this town that was already gone and forgotten, family treasures loaded into dumpsters because they seemed too dirty or broken to be useful. Flannel guy clearly didn't have any connection to it, but it meant something to someone.

Hold on, was I actually feeling *defensive of Hearst*?

"You're just throwing all this stuff out?" I asked. "I mean, I can call my mom about the trash removal. So I have to, um, know what you're dumping and how much."

"Trying to," the guy said. "But I'm sure as hell not paying eight hundo for dumpster pickup. Some Beau guy told me Hearst was a family-oriented community ready for progress, but all I've experienced so far is red tape and hidden fees."

My neurons started to fire. The part of my brain that was scrambling for a way inside Gratton Farms suddenly pivoted to a whole new angle. "Actually, I know a secondhand shop that would take this stuff off your hands," I said. "For free."

Flannel scowled. "This is trash, kids. Believe me, nothing in there is going to *Antiques Roadshow* or anything. I already checked."

"No, of course not. It's trash, like you said." I resented the implication that we were trying to stiff him out of some antiques, but I had to convince this guy, so I kept smizing. "What do you say, then? Save yourself eight hundred bucks? We also don't have to call in the city. Save your capital for, you know, permits and stuff. With the way this town handles historical buildings that might be up for *landmark status*, you might need all the help you can get." I had no idea what I was talking about, but it seemed to put some serious fear into Hearst's newest homeowner.

He looked at us, the dumpster, then back at us, running a hand over his lumberjack beard and reminding me even more of that dude with the blue ox. Babe? Or was that the ox? He finally stepped off the porch and extended a hand.

"You've got a deal, young . . . person," he said, and we shook.

"Sully," I said. "They/them."

"Saul Bunyan, Bunyan Properties," he said. Then, when I started cracking up, "What's so funny?"

Even Brad shot me a puzzled look.

"Nothing at all. Sorry. You'll see a truck from Yesterday's Today a bit later, okay?"

But Saul was already heading back into Rufus's old home, his phone glued to his ear.

# 16

Forty-five minutes later, Claire and her trusty pickup pulled onto the lawn of Gratton Farms. Brad and I had been hanging out waiting, in case Saul Bunyan changed his mind or did anything with the dumpster haul. Thank goodness Claire had agreed to come by, because the ice had melted out of my chai and I was getting antsy. I hustled over to greet her.

"Still holding on to that bag for dear life, I see," she said as she climbed out of the cab.

I pulled her into a *let's change the subject* hug. "Thank you for doing this."

"A chance to raid the old Gratton place? Please, I've been dying to get my hands on some of that stained glass. They don't get the color variation in the panes like that anymore." She glanced at the dumpster, the workmen, and Saul Bunyan approaching her with a hand already held out for a firm, manly shake.

"Saul Bunyan," Saul said, pumping away.

"You're kidding," said Claire.

"What about?" said Saul, apparently oblivious to his resemblance to the lumberjack. He continued to grip Claire's hand and she didn't seem eager to pull it away.

I waited but when neither moved, I jumped in to explain the situation as best I could, steering Claire toward the dumpster. Saul followed like a baby duck that had imprinted on the first thing it saw as its parent. Claire eyed the mess, looking seriously underwhelmed by our haulage, but that was her default. I never knew if she was tired and grumpy about something specific, or simply tired and grumpy.

"Sully..."

Okay, she was definitely tired and grumpy for a reason, probably because I *might* have referred to it as an "antiques smorgasbord" on the phone, rather than "a dumpster full of mostly trash."

"Why do I get the feeling I've just been bait-and-switched?"

"Don't you worry your beautiful self," I whispered.

Saul cleared his throat. "A good eye might see something with potential. And you've got two. Eyes, that is. Good ones at that."

"Thanks for noticing," said Claire. "You've got two yourself."

Saul and Claire laughed harder than need be. I glanced back and forth between them wondering if these were two oddballs making small talk or the most awkward flirtation I'd ever witnessed.

"May I help you into the dumpster?" Saul asked, offering his hand.

"I'd appreciate that, but I'm still not sold on finding anything promising."

The great thing about Claire was that she complained a lot, but she also didn't let it stop her. The job took all afternoon and several trips to Yesterday's Today. Bunyan thankfully told his crew to help us load up and lingered nearby, lifting garbage for Claire to peer under or steadying her as she climbed over the heaps. But by the time the sun was dipping behind Gratton Farms' gabled roof, I felt like we'd successfully saved everything salvageable from Rufus's family home that wasn't bolted down. And some of the stuff that was, too.

In the end, Claire had even managed to negotiate the front door's stained-glass window panels for herself in a back-and-forth with Saul that felt ripe with sexual tension, so I felt less terrible about roping her in. Actually, it was like I'd done her a favor—or more than one depending on if Claire was picking up what I was on the Saul front, though I didn't want to push my luck by bringing it up.

"A recreation center," Claire said, shaking her head as Brad and one of Bunyan's crew hefted the front door gingerly into the back of the pickup. "So much of this town's history has been lost or buried. But history matters. People need to know where they came from."

"Totally, but hey, you're preserving some of it," I said, trying to sound cheerful.

"If we don't, who will?" Claire said, placing a hand on my shoulder.

"You sound like Eleanor," I quipped. I was *not* preserving Hearst history. No, hunny. I was solving a mystery. And all for a vintage bag I planned on selling for cold hard cash once it was . . . unoccupied. To get as far away from here as quickly as I possibly could.

As Claire got into the driver's seat, Saul came trotting over. He closed her truck's door and leaned on the ledge of the open window. "You're someone with a lot of style. Would you mind coming back here tomorrow? I'd love your opinion on whether any of the old bones of the place could be restored or re-created as part of the new rec center."

I could see in the way Claire held the steering wheel and her jaw, she was about to shoot Saul down.

Before she had a chance, Rufus and I said loudly, "She'd love to."

Saul straightened and patted the truck's window frame. "Tomorrow. I'll see you then. With my eyes. The two I've got."

Claire shot me a very dirty look as she pulled past Brad and me getting into Olivia Newton-John.

Brad smiled. "What was that?"

I shrugged. "It was getting painful for everyone. Mostly me. Someone had to put them out of their misery. And who knows, maybe Claire is Saul's type and maybe part of Gratton Farms gets salvaged or rebuilt or she manages to score some more vintage windows."

"Seems like you care about Hearst."

"I care about Claire," I say with finality.

Back at Yesterday's Today, Claire, Brad, and I turned the basement into a makeshift sorting center. Claire had cleared off several big tables, which Brad and I quickly covered in piles of Gratton Farms' old *stuff*. There were crushed chunks of latticework, shards of painted tile, a soggy footstool, a whole collection of mismatched table and chair legs, and tons of other unrecognizable odds and ends.

"Anything with resale value, I get to keep," Claire said, repeating the agreement we'd reached on the phone. "Except for whatever you need for your little history project or whatever."

"We'll have all this stuff cleared out of here by tomorrow

morning," I promised. "Thank you, Claire, I owe you."

"Just lock up when you're done," she said, tossing me her keys. There was a time when I'd had my own set, but now I was there at Claire's largess. "And try not to burn the place down. We're still dealing with the wall collapse." She nodded over at the drywall with the Ron-shaped hole in it.

"Yeah, good luck with that. Such a bummer," I said.

Claire opened her mouth and, for a second, I was afraid she'd tell us to clean up the entire basement while we were at it, but then she just shook her head and went up the stairs.

"*We'll* have all this stuff cleared out?" Brad asked when we were finally alone again, and I felt a twinge of guilt for monopolizing not only Claire's day, but his, too.

"*I'll* have all this stuff cleared out," I correct. "I don't expect you to pull an all-nighter with me. Unless you want to." That came out slightly spicier than I meant it, but Brad didn't seem to pick up on any innuendo. Thoughts of Brad and me lying side by side in a dark room flooded my head like memories that were just waiting to be made, and I blushed.

He shrugged. "You've got me curious now. I can stick around for a few hours." A sound like a bullfrog croak rumbled from Brad's midsection and he covered his stomach, blushing now too. "But we should probably eat something."

"Pizza?"

"Antonio's?" He raised an eyebrow. Antonio's was our local pizza place, and it was worth the hassle of their cash-only policy.

"They don't deliver," I reminded him.

"I'm not doing Domino's."

I gasped like a southern belle. "My hero."

"You get started down here," he said, his hand briefly running down the length of my arm, like we could just casually touch each other without my head spinning. He rocked back to step away, but then he leaned forward and kissed my cheek, his lips brushing the corner of mine. "I'll go for pizzas."

Um. Did that count as a kiss? Surely it did. My heart stuttered in my chest as he turned to go upstairs and I watched the muscles of his back move as his thighs and, finally, calves disappeared upstairs. Call me old fashioned, but a man going to get me food made me flutter a bit in that *be my caveman* way. Not that Brad was caveman-like, even with that physique.

*Stop it, Sully.*

No sooner did I hear the upstairs door shut with a jangle than Rufus came rocketing out of the Butler like a spirit scorned. He was wearing a flowing black taffeta number that swooped and swooshed as he darted through the air. "Oh, I could have clawed that man's eyes out! The two of them! Mold? Rot? Show me! The staff kept Gratton Farms pristine!"

"Would you keep it down?" I begged as Rufus did his usual manic loops through the air. Brad might have left, but seeing Rufus out of the bag in public—even if we were relatively hidden away in the basement of Yesterday's Today—made me feel panicky. I prided myself on not caring what people thought, most of the time, anyway, but I also knew I didn't want to be caught hanging out with a ghost.

"That was my house!" Rufus moaned. "And they're tearing it down."

"Hey, don't be like that. You only remembered it was your house this morning, anyway," I tried. He shot me a glare, so I switched tack. I couldn't imagine how painful it was for Rufus to start remembering, only to be confronted with his childhood home in ruins. "You know, I'm amazed it was still standing at all. It was in lousy condition, and at least Saul seemed interested in preserving something of it even if only to impress Claire. And look, we might be able to find something in all this. Is there anything you recognize?"

Rufus rolled onto his ghostly stomach and draped himself across the table. "This is all that's left of my life. Three tables of trash in a basement."

He considered the stack of gilded picture frames and one large wooden board that looked as though it used to frame out a small window.

"This was from my bedroom, I think. I'm amazed at how snatches keep coming back to me." He sighed, giving me a pathetic look. "I remember watching the birds through the window this board came from while I sat on my little footstool and sketched costumes into my diary. I wonder if they saved that."

"Bunyan?"

"No, my parents. I wonder if they were sentimental about anything to do with me, or if they jettisoned it all when I split the scene with another guy and two suitcases filled with Tallulah."

"They found out?"

"My father discovered enough to know *enough*. He urged me to make better choices for my life. But I knew who I was. Both sides of me. I'd been performing on weekends, and I was good." Rufus's black dress sparkled as if a spotlight was shining on him. He raised himself into the air and worked his curves in the garment to show off his ample hourglass figure. "Really good. I was becoming a star. And I had a man who loved me. All of me. I was happy. My father could have been happy for me too."

"He kicked you out?"

"I left. I swore I'd have to be dragged back. He told me he wished he never had a son, his was dead. He was never very original. Those are the last words I remember exchanging with him." The color faded from Rufus, and not only from his cheeks and lips but all of him, as if someone was erasing him. He sank lower in the air until he was touching the floor.

I wondered how Rufus had been erased while he was alive and if this was keeping him lingering between worlds. I reminded myself to give Eleanor and my dad a hug the next time I saw them as I began to pick through some of the larger pieces we'd transported.

I kept glancing at my friend, surprising myself at how easily it was to think of him as such. Especially now that we were sifting through his history, side by side. Despite his still dim pigment, he was becoming so much more solid and was having no trouble touching actual physical objects now even if he couldn't fully handle them. I'd point it out, but it didn't really feel like the time. Every so often, Rufus would gasp, but by the time I came over to see what he'd found, the photo album had turned out to be blank, or the folder of possible business documents soaked through, the ink a smeared purple mess. It made sense that the crew had wanted to throw this stuff out. Bunyan didn't have any nostalgia for it, and none of it looked remotely recognizable, let alone valuable. Or resalable. Claire was going to be more disappointed than usual, but I'm not sure that mattered as much.

One of the biggest pieces was an old desk, legless but with the drawers still intact. We'd turned out the drawers when loading the thing into the back of the pickup truck, and they were stacked on top of it now.

"Nothing in Daddy's old drawers?" Rufus asked, adding, "Okay, even *I* know I could have phrased that better."

At least Rufus got double entendres, unlike Brad.

"No, they were empty," I said, picking up one of the wooden drawers. "But, actually, this isn't as deep inside as the others. Weird, it looks exactly the same depth from the outside."

"Oh, that's because there's a trick compartment," Rufus said. "I remember my father kept his Colt in it. There wasn't much to do for entertainment, so of course I snooped."

"It's like you're getting *my* childhood memories, because same," I said, feeling my excitement return. This was maybe the lucky break we needed. I flipped open the drawer and felt inside for a latch. There was definitely *something* there, but I hoped it wasn't like one of those puzzle boxes that were impossible to crack. I also hoped the pistol was long gone, or at least unloaded, because I didn't want to shoot my hand off before Brad could arrive with pizza.

An object shifted around inside. Finally, my nail found a small gap cut into the underside of the drawer. Emma would turn into a Muppet if she knew I was risking my gel. She was always saying, "Nails are jewels, not tools," but this was important. Rufus hovered over my shoulder as the hidden compartment opened with a *click*.

Something large and rectangular thumped onto the floor,

then settled. The Colt was nowhere to be found, thank goodness. "Holy shit," I said, lifting the object up into the light. "You weren't kidding. I can't believe that worked."

I laid the object on the table and unwrapped the thick fabric folded around it to find a frame. I turned it over to reveal a cross-stitched chart and the words *Honor Thy Father & Thy Mother—Exodus 20:12* sewn across the bottom. "Ack! It burns!" I pulled my hand back in mock horror.

"There was mold, rot, *and* a fire?" Rufus asked with obvious concern.

"No, sorry. Commentary about the Christian right."

Rufus quirked an eyebrow.

"Never mind."

We bent over the frame and fabric within, which were actually in great condition. Each stitch was tiny, neat, and precise.

"Our family tree!" Rufus said in a hushed whisper. "My grandmother made this for my mother when she wed." Rufus ran a finger over the stitches, names and dates of births going back into the 1800s. "This is it. Our family. My mother added my name and birth date right there." Rufus pointed.

But no writing was there.

*June 1, 1955*
*My son,*

*I had to ask your schoolmate for your address. Curious that you would still be in contact with him given your lifestyle. Do you have no care about losing your reputation? Your aspirations? Or your eternal soul? Once made public, this is a blight that can never again be hidden. You might as well kiss any hope of a political career goodbye. And if I found out, surely others will.*

*I implore you to return home. Your mother and I will help you right the mess you've put yourself in. You are no longer a child, and it is time to do away with childish fantasies and childhood friends, especially the one who has led you astray with their perversion of feminine wiles. You have your future to consider. We would see you marry an appropriate young woman before you are too far past the age of being a viable provider, husband, and father.*

*No good can come of your current choices. My forgiveness is yours if you choose to receive it. God's forgiveness requires you to turn away from the sin you so eagerly embrace.*

*Father*
*P.S. I haven't told your mother to spare her the disappointment and pain of your disgrace. It would break her heart to know what the child she bore has become.*

# 17

I found the name of Rufus's father, Thomas Gratton, easily. Then, branching below his name, not a thing. Wait, not nothing. The fabric puckered and was frayed if you looked carefully under Thomas and his wife's name. Someone had spent time carefully removing each stitch from that area of the family tree. Such a deletion would have been painstakingly slow and methodical, but more importantly, intentional.

I turned to Rufus, who had gone uncharacteristically quiet. It suddenly seemed too heavy to say anything. Shoulder to shoulder, we stared down. And for the first time, my life didn't feel so impossibly distant from Rufus's.

"I see," Rufus said. I wondered if he was piecing things together as I had, or if he'd unearthed some more memories. Painful ones, which he wasn't ready to share. "Even hidden away where no one would see, he made sure there was no record of me."

"Let's put it away," I said, lifting the frame from the material it had been wrapped in. Before I could flip it over and rewrap it, an old photograph dropped to the floor along with a yellowed, folded piece of paper. "Sorry," I said, swooping down to retrieve the paper and a photo of a beautiful building, rising grandly above a picturesque lake, surrounded by rolling hills. It certainly wasn't Gratton Farms.

The word *Knollwood* was written on the back and the year, *1956*.

The paper was a pamphlet for gay men and written on the front were the words: *If you are arrested . . .*

Have you ever had that moment when you realize that, suddenly, your jaw is clenching, your feet are flexed, and you are gripping something so hard that your knuckles ache? Everything in me tightened as I tried to imagine what this meant.

Rufus was entirely without color, almost like an old black-and-white television broadcast, as he tried to take the pamphlet. "They could round us up and arrest us for nothing. We were seen as criminals. We were targeted. We had to know what to do not *if* it happened, but *when*."

I remembered a book I'd seen in the library's LGBTQ+ collection titled *The Lavender Scare* about laws the American government instituted after World War II making it legal to persecute gay men. I'd put it back because it was so long and looked boring. But now, seeing how thoroughly Rufus had been erased during his lifetime, and after, made me think of all the others like him. It put a lot into perspective. I was suddenly overcome with a sense of gratitude—it obviously wasn't a competition, everyone faced hard things in their own time and space, but I was fortunate even when my existence wasn't perfect, even when it was a pile of cheap prom dresses dumped on the living room floor. There was still a long way to go, but society *had* changed.

I was embarrassed to admit that I didn't know much about these pockets of history, but I could only guess that, for all the problems of our time—including queer, nonbinary, and trans youth being legislated out of existence—it was still much easier in today's America than it was during Rufus's era. I made a vow to ask Rufus to help me close some of those knowledge gaps so I could learn about our shared history. If he wanted to, of course. I wasn't about to demand his emotional labor.

"Rufus," I started, but stopped myself. His gaze slid from the spot on the family tree where his name had once been to the pamphlet and back again. His eyes seemed to be sparkling despite none of his color having returned. For a moment I wondered if this was some kind of new ghost power I didn't know about, and then I realized the sparks were really gleams—ghost tears.

"I, um . . ." he began. "They . . . I . . ." He held one hand to his chest as he swallowed hard and the other one up between us in a stop position.

I nodded, giving Rufus space. I'd never been very good at being quiet, but even I could recognize a moment. I needed to let him share in his own way, in his own time.

"I had to be Tallulah," Rufus finally managed. "I *was*—no, I *am* Tallulah. I couldn't *not* be who I am."

I know he had objected before, but I couldn't let go of the Rufus-drag similarities. "Did you know anyone else . . . like you . . . when you were alive?" I asked, choosing each word carefully and precisely so I didn't ask the wrong thing.

"Of course." Rufus's cheeks gained a hint of color, or maybe I was optimistically imagining it. "But not here in Hearst." Rufus put both hands on his hips and swung them from one side to the other before saying in a Mae West–sounding voice, "And when the men couldn't come to the mountain, this mountain shook it on over to the men."

I didn't want to ask again, but something kept niggling at the back of my mind. I decided to take a different approach and pulled out my phone, bringing up a compilation video of drag performers. "Rufus, I want you to watch this on my phone—"

"That's still not a phone as I know it."

"Fine. Light rectangle. Whatever. Watch it anyway."

Rufus came closer to me and his shoulder went through mine. As we watched, Rufus's eyes gleamed with the joy only a well-executed death drop can bring. The color pooled back into him as he flickered in and out of looks that resembled the kings and queens we watched.

"Were you one of these types of performers?" I asked when the video ended.

"Yes. No. Similar but not, obviously. They're from your time."

I kept following my hunch and searched the internet for *1950s drag queens* and was validated when I managed to pull up a copy of a book written in 1954 called *Femme Mimics*. There were photos and the names of men who were brave enough to perform in drag during Rufus's day. I held my phone up for him and slowly scrolled so he could see the images of the book's pages.

"Una! She showed me how to properly glue down a paste-on, and how to fix my paint so I didn't look like I slapped a brick."

"Rufus! You actually knew them? You were one of these performers?"

"That's what I've been trying to tell you this entire time," Rufus said, his appearance settling into a bright yellow dress with draping around the neckline that revealed a hint of shoulder. A wide-brimmed hat appeared, cocked jauntily to one side.

"That's what I've been asking this entire time. Rufus, you were a drag queen."

"Tallulah was nothing of the sort. I was a rising star. I was an impersonator."

I threw my hands up in the air. "Impersonator. Mimic. Drag queen. Same difference!"

"Hardly. I never had to work the night as a drag queen. I had one trick, and we were steady. We even moved to the big city together." Apparently, we were unlocking some memories that he hadn't had until this moment.

"Work the night?" I asked. "What do you think I mean when I say drag queen?"

"A man who dresses as a man by day and then as a woman by night, pursuing the oldest profession, of course."

Ah, so he meant sex workers who cross-dressed, but weren't trans? There was so much that could be lost in translation just because of our massive generational divide. We were getting off track, though. "Do you remember which big city? New York? Boston?"

"Pittsburgh!"

This was actually a beautiful moment, so I had to hold back a laugh. I fixed my face. Pittsburgh? The big city? Another reminder that things had been very different when Rufus was alive. He hadn't had easy access to New York City, and certainly wasn't taking a private jet to Tahiti. His world had been much smaller back then, and so were his options.

"Your trick—you mean your boyfriend, right? He went with you?"

Rufus closed his eyes and shook his head, as if hearing invisible music. "He was my best friend, my heart, who I had known since childhood. He came with me. Somebody who loved me, even when my family couldn't, wouldn't, and didn't."

"And he knew about you performing as a woman?" I asked for confirmation.

"He was the one who first dared me to try it out when I complained that all of the impersonators were more waifish than *robust*." Rufus sensuously slid his hands down his sides. "I loved the attention. I always stood out, but it finally felt like it was for the right reasons, at least in that circle. People appreciated how different I was. I could be brazen and irreverent. So when the weekend rolled in, I put the *big* in *big city*. He was always so proud to show me off as we walked into the clubs with me on his arm, even though I towered above him."

"He sounds like a really decent guy," I said, my mind going to my own decent guy.

"Better than that. He was the best."

"Can you recall his name?" I prompted gently, hoping a little nudge would lead to another breakthrough.

Rufus shook his head, looking pained.

"What can you remember about him?"

"We moved to the city. And it was expensive. Even when I scored a gig performing, it was tight. I learned to sew my own costumes, not being an off-the-rack body, and managed to get some work making outfits for other performers, which helped. We had to rent a larger apartment with two rooms. We couldn't live together without raising suspicion. Then we had a big fight. I think it started over him worrying about money . . . no, about us being discovered and some letter his father had sent warning him about losing career opportunities. He thought someone would report us—but that's where my memory goes completely blank. I don't understand what happened."

Rufus tucked a lock of hair behind his ear, looking deep in thought.

"What is it?" I asked.

"I'm thinking of our fight, the aftermath, getting dolled up and going to dance and drown my sorrows but . . . that's all I've got. Even those details are choppy." He hung his head.

"Until the click of the lock and the bright light, and you exploding out of the Butler in my basement?"

Rufus nodded.

He looked so dejected, I searched for something to say to rally him. "Well, that's why we're doing all this, right?"

Rufus smiled, though it didn't quite reach his eyes but at least his color remained. "This photo is something else, though. The year is troubling. My memories get worse the closer to the end of the decade I get."

"This is so much to take in at once. Do you think this Knollwood place is somehow related to what happened?"

"You saw the date. It says 1956. My memory doesn't go that far, but I'd bet my best pumps that Knollwood is somehow connected. I'm afraid I have a bad feeling about it."

I hadn't known Rufus long, sure, but it hurt to see him so

forlorn. That word didn't come to me easily, but it was true. It made me so sad that his own family had never appreciated him for his true self. And even though he'd found a guy and seemed to think fondly of him, there might've been trouble there, too.

Rufus gave himself a shake, or maybe it was a shimmy since it was a touch glamorous. "All right, you're using the mystery that is moi as an avoidance mechanism. Let me do the same."

"Huh?"

"I need a break from my tragic history. Let's focus on you and your bright future."

I raised an eyebrow at Rufus. "I'm not sure if you can hear as well as you think through all that leather. My plans bottomed out. All I've got is this amateur detective gig going on. No job prospects. No way to leave Hearst and small-town small-mindedness behind."

"You've got friends and family who love you."

I shrug.

"And a dish of a guy chasing after you."

I roll my eyes. "Things with Brad are complicated. Everything about living in Hearst is complicated."

Rufus nods. "Don't I know it. There weren't any options for me here either. None that I could see anyway. But this isn't the same town I grew up in."

"Hate to break it to you, but it is. And I really don't need a lecture on how amazing Hearst is from someone who was smart enough to bail."

Rufus laughs. "Fair. But you and Brad can walk around and live here without concealing everything about who you are. Maybe there's something here for you if you dig into more than this old haunt's history."

I took a deep breath and closed my eyes. I got what Rufus was saying and, sure, I had it better than he ever did. The thing was, it still wasn't ideal and leaving was always about more than getting out of Hearst. It was about proving to people who'd judged me that they were wrong, and that their views were hurtful. They'd finally be forced to see me for who I was in all my magnificent glory. "I thought once I'd gotten out, I'd be on the way to being a huge success. To being someone."

"You already are," Rufus said softly and with such conviction, I could feel his words bore into me and take root. "You don't realize it, but you're paving the way for everyone who comes after you to be themselves and live as they want to because you're not bowing down to convention." Rufus shuddered. "We're trailblazers."

I shivered, then shook my head. "I don't want to be that."

"But you already are."

"I just want to get out of here. I want more than this."

Rufus went quiet for a moment. "I did too." He furrowed his brow and turned almost completely transparent, the basement of Yesterday's Today appearing through him, before returning to his normal opacity. "And we both know how that ended."

I hugged my arms across my body, not convinced Rufus was right. Despite what Rufus had said about making way for future queer generations, that wasn't my responsibility or problem. I didn't owe them my suffering through Uncle Chucks and living rooms full of prom gowns so they could blossom. Didn't I deserve a happier and easier life? The only ticket I had was the Butler and selling it for enough to leave Hearst and its citizens behind forever.

Rufus studied me. "I can see I struck a nerve."

I opened my mouth to argue but he cut me off.

"I want more for you too, Sully. And I want you to know when it's there for you so you recognize when it's in your grasp. Whether you find it in your family or friends or New York City or the arms of a good man, I want you to know it when you find it. I stumbled into impersonation. Literally. Those heels. It was like watching a baby giraffe try to walk. I didn't know it was what I wanted or who I wanted to be. You're young and don't know where you're going to land until you do. All I'm saying is, be open to possibility, even if it seems farfetched."

Rufus moved as if to hug me but stopped short when I took half a step back and pulled my arms tighter around myself, wondering if Rufus was seeing something I couldn't quite. At least not yet. What had Hearst ever offered either of us but the promise of pain?

Rufus let his arms hang at his sides. "Thanks for letting me distract myself from my afterlife by meddling in your life with unsolicited advice."

"Anytime," I mumbled. The reality that Rufus and I were more the same than different was obvious.

I kind of wished Rufus had hugged me—even if I wasn't sure his arms wouldn't slide right through my body—to remind me I had people, living and dead, who wanted the best for me. Instead, we stood in silence, somewhere between his past and my future. The family tree with Rufus's missing name rested not far from us.

At some point I registered the sound of crunching gravel outside.

"Shit, that's Brad," I said, but Rufus had already misted his way back into the Butler, leaving me alone with his tragic family history and more questions than before.

"The pizza man has arrived!" Brad said as he stomped down the stairs, the smell of cheese and dough and the outdoors wafting after him. "Whoa," he said when he saw me, his grin fading. "You found something."

"I found something," I repeated, still in a daze.

Brad set the pizzas down and joined me.

"This is a family tree," I explained after a moment. "It belonged to a man named Rufus. Well, to his family."

He must have noticed me running my finger over where Rufus's name should have been, because after a moment, Brad asked, "Are you going to tell me about this secret mystery that we're investigating now?"

I nodded, but really I was elsewhere, still trying to process everything.

I mean, I'd known queer people must have existed for a long time, but I couldn't help wondering what Rufus's life had been like back then. He didn't have the internet or the language we have. Just a pamphlet for the inevitability of incarceration. How could Rufus have found the courage to be so himself against those odds? He must not have had any role models or guides. How had he navigated all of it?

"Hey, are you okay?" Brad asked, putting his hand on my shoulder.

Instinctually, I turned to face him, pulling Brad's hand to my chest, willing him to feel all the heartbreak and wonder clashing inside me.

Before I could think my way out of it, I kissed him on his smart, handsome mouth. I'd been thinking about his kiss on the cheek, and it felt like permission. Gently, he took my face in his free hand and kissed me back with a firmness that let me know he was quite happy I had made a move. Our first nonparty, nonnight kiss. This could only mean that whatever was happening between us was more than some last-night-in-town fluke. The light was growing dusky in the small basement windows, but something about kissing him again made the possibility of . . . *us* . . . feel more real.

"What was that for?" Brad asked as we pulled apart and I forced my eyes open.

"I don't know. We're so lucky in a way. I was feeling sad and thankful and a little like I might have a crush on you."

Brad shook his head. "I'm trying really hard not to overthink this."

"Oh god, me too." I grinned. "But you're right. I think that's for the best. I mean, I *don't* think."

The moment, whatever it was, had chilled out somewhat, and we both laughed awkwardly.

"So," Brad said, rubbing the back of his neck, "where does this leave us? I mean . . . where does this leave the mystery? What about this Rufus person?"

"Well, there's this," I say, showing him the photograph of Knollwood. "Maybe that's our next stop? It looks nice, I mean, lakes and hills and columns. What I *don't* know is whether this Knollwood Spa place is still open, or if you need an appointment or—"

Brad's eyes dilated to three times their usual size. "You don't know about Knollwood?"

"What? Is it closed? Ugh. I thought this was our big break."

Brad took both of my hands in his and gave me a serious look. "Knollwood wasn't a spa, Sully."

"No?"

"It was a psychiatric hospital."

# 18

The next afternoon, Brad and I agreed to meet up and drive to Knollwood after he'd played a bracing game of pickleball with Ron, who was still apparently hiding from the rest of us over the basement wall incident. I couldn't decide whether I was more excited to spend time with Brad or figure out what the hell really happened to Rufus.

Brad said he would be over at my house around four o'clock, so I spent the day pretending to look for a new job, in case Eleanor asked. In reality, Rufus and I were researching anything I could find about his family's history in Hearst. From the looks of it, the family tree hadn't grown much once Rufus died, so the information online was pretty limited, and we soon exhausted our leads. I even tried free trials of those ancestry sites, but we hit the wall and their paywalls fast and I couldn't justify spending money I didn't have on what was certain to be another dead-end.

A random text came in from Angelika, even though it was, like, midnight her time. Ugh, that queen, always reminding me that she had a life:

Paulo got back to me. Can authenticate but he needs good photos.

I read the text, then read it again. Then I remembered. Her friend Paulo. From Zurich. The one who worked for Sotheby's. With everything that had happened, it almost seemed like this news came from another life.

I hearted Angelika's text and vowed to take great pictures of the Butler, though I worried it might hurt Rufus's feelings. He knew I wanted to sell the bag—we'd both gone into this with eyes wide open—but it suddenly seemed way premature to even think about it. Rufus had just lost his childhood home and his family. This bag was the only home he had left. And solving the mystery was much more important at the moment.

"You and that rectangle again. Everyone in this time is obsessed."

I jolted into the present moment. "Sorry."

"And that thing," Rufus said, looking unimpressed at the sticker-covered laptop Mom had handed down to me. "You said this machine contained all the information in the world conveniently at your fingertips, but . . ."

"I guess it has its limitations, okay? People aren't exactly making TikToks about Hearst's ancestry every day."

"Tick-whats?"

"Oh, hunny."

"I prefer *sis*."

My phone buzzed with another text from Angelika.

Found this, authenticated

Attached was a link to a big-name auction website that featured a Butler that looked very similar to mine. Estimates for this one were upward of $250,000. Literally a quarter of a million dollars. *Whoa.* That was more than enough to get out of here and do New York City in style. With $250,000, I wouldn't need to find a new job. Not right away, anyway. The auction was in five days. If this Butler sold for that much, and I could get my own authenticated, I'd be, like, the non-binary Barbie of historical rare purse finds.

"Who's pinging you?" Rufus asked, seemingly delighted to be using the cool new words I'd taught him. Unsurprisingly, he picked up slang quickly.

Something crunched in my gut. Selling the Butler would be amazing, but it could only happen after Rufus "moved on" or disappeared or . . . we had no idea what would happen. But it was so *nice* having him around. I would miss him. A few days ago, I could never have imagined a talking bag ghost barging into my life. Now, I couldn't imagine him not being here.

BTW you must have seen . . .

This text had a link to Lyndzi's X profile, where I knew she only posted the most basic updates. I figured if she was dead, her assistant might tweet "Am dead. Deets to come." But this was a full-on thread clearly written by the girl herself. Apparently she'd had an allergic reaction to some of the sunscreen she'd done a sponsored post for on the beaches of Tahiti. Oh my god, that was glorious. I scrolled through her increasingly unhinged screed against the manufacturer, the hotel, and Tahiti in general. She'd even posted a pair of selfies, front and side-angled like mug shots, to show her tomato-swollen face.

When I'd finally dried my eyes from laughing, a thought struck me. Lyndzi would need to do damage control. With everything popping off overseas, she'd need someone in the home office to pick up the slack. I scrolled to Gennie of the *We Regret to*

*Inform You* email's profile and opened a DM. What would I write? *Hey I'm available if you need an extra hand!* Visions of a gushing reply full of gratitude and instructions on how to download my e-ticket to NYC danced in my head.

But I hesitated.

"What's up, buttercup?" Rufus asked, balancing his chin on his fists.

A text from Brad interrupted my thoughts:

I'm outside in Olivia Newton-John with an iced matcha for you . . . need to keep our energy up for the drive.

You know what? Gennie and Lyndzi would have to deal with the fallout from SunGlow Co. themselves. I had more important things to do.

"What's up is it's time to get you out of that bag," I said, closing the browser and opening a new message to Brad.

Omg thanks! Be right there, I texted back.

At this point, sliding into the passenger side of Olivia Newton-John had become my new normal . . . and I really liked it. I was well suited for life as a passenger princess. The drive to Knollwood would take an hour, so I did what any young queer Swiftie would do and turned on *Red (Taylor's Version)*. With the drinks between us and Brad already pulling into the street, I wondered if we were at the casual kiss-every-time-we-see-each-other phase yet. I leaned forward, then pretended I was checking my hair in the rearview mirror, then slumped back in the seat. It was okay. We'd figure it out.

"Go ahead, make yourself at home," Brad said, shaking his head but smiling.

Phew. He hadn't noticed my awkward back-and-forth. "We're so modern, we have joint custody. Conscious vehicular uncoupling."

"Oh, yeah?"

"But you pay for gas. Thanks, bestie!"

"Bestie?" Brad shot me an amused look.

"Or something."

We settled into the road trip easily, and for all the negative feelings I had about Hearst, it really was beautiful. The trees were in full flower, everything was green, and I swear I even heard birds singing. It was giving full Disney princess.

It made me think of Eleanor telling me that her favorite memories with Dad were always on road trips, enjoying the "companionable silence." Even though that term was frighteningly boomer, and I'd have to warn her ASAP, I finally knew what she meant—this feeling of extremely cute, easy existence without the pressure to fill every second with chatter. Occasionally, I'd gaze over at Brad's jawline, dappled in stubble . . . oh, my god! I did *not* like what this implied about our relationship. Was that what it was? Was I catching feelings? Had I already caught them? I thought about Guy and Emma, both staying in town. Forever. I still wanted out of Hearst, and I couldn't let these feelings keep me here.

Why couldn't I sit back and enjoy this without overthinking?

I had to end the silence with real urgency, or maybe I'd gotten so used to Rufus's constant soundtrack that I didn't know how to function alone in my own head.

I turned down the music. "Brad?"

"Yes, dear?" he joked.

"Okay, be serious. Why do you love Hearst so much?"

Brad didn't seem totally ready for the question—and to his credit, it *was* a bit of a curveball—so he took his time to respond. "It's not that I'm butt-crazy head-over-heels in love with Hearst, Sully."

"You could've fooled me!"

"It has a lot of problems. There seem to be more bigots per capita here than you'll find in big cities."

"Hard agree."

"And complete ass clowns run the town. Blowhard-regard gets on my last nerve."

"Ooh, good one." I filed that one away—I needed to tell Mom and get the credit.

"But my whole family is here. The friends who've shaped me into who I am. So it's not that I love it. I just don't hate it, and it has a special place in my heart. I take the good with the bad. I'm headed to Penn State this fall, but who knows whether I'll end up back here in the future or not. Either way, I'll always have some love for Hearst."

*Wow.* I hadn't packed a bathing suit for diving into Brad's emotional depths. I guess it was a pretty complicated question, but how was he so thoughtful and emotional and reasonable?

"You know, I'm sorry."

"For what?" Brad looked bemused. Probably since I didn't come to the apology table often.

"I may have made some assumptions."

"Like?" Brad draped his hand over Olivia Newton-John's steering wheel.

"Like thinking you had it completely easy."

"That part still doesn't make sense to me."

I winced. *Was* I making any sense? Wasn't everyone's relationship with themselves complicated? "I guess I assumed that you'd have to like how you turned out in order to seem so happy in the place you came from."

Good golly, the silence that came after that very obvious-seeming comment was decidedly *not* "companionable." I squirmed in my seat.

Brad turned to look me squarely in the eye. "You know, Sully—"

"Eyes on the road, Brad!"

"Don't you want to hear what I have to say?"

*Absolutely not*, I thought. This conversation had gone in some sort of self-aware direction that I was not prepared for. Because, as it turned out, my reasoning might've just exposed me as someone who didn't fully like themselves, and I really wasn't ready to do that kind of heavy lifting today. Or maybe ever. "Of course I do, but—"

"In one hundred feet—" intoned the GPS.

Brad refocused on the road. In all this extremely uncomfortable *sharing*, we'd both almost missed the driveway to Knollwood. Had an hour really passed already?

But then it got even stranger.

Because, apparently, we weren't the only people visiting. In fact, we almost couldn't turn down the winding road to the property because it was clogged with Teslas and SUVs.

"What the hell?" I asked.

"You have arrived," droned the GPS.

Brad and I scanned the scene with the same sense of disbelief. Who were all these people? Some of the drivers were reading their phones; others were puffing on vapes and pacing around their cars;

yet others were clearly taking a snooze. A few girls were fixing their makeup in various dark, tinted windows.

"Is this a funeral?" Brad whispered, even though our windows were closed and nobody else could hear us.

"I don't think so," I said, even if I had no idea what it could've been instead.

We inched our way around the bend, and the main Knollwood structure appeared, perched on a rolling hill, just like it had been in the photograph. It was a beautiful building, but I couldn't even take in the view because it was almost entirely blocked by a very bold, very tacky sign that read Mango-Gasm Reserve Organic Pressed Vodka Juice Presents: An Evening with Mango-Gasm, a Mango-Gasm Event.

Bass pounded from behind the building, so loud that it rattled Olivia Newton-John's windows.

"Oh no," I breathed.

"What?" Brad asked. He might've been confident, but he was still such a summer child.

"It's worse than a funeral, Brad," I said, gritting my teeth. "It's an influencer event."

"Are you kidding?"

This was messed up. Apparently, some idiot publicist had rented out *an old psychiatric hospital* for a massive sponsored party. The horseshoe drive in front of the main building was set up like a red carpet, with influencers posing in front of a flaming orange backdrop. It was a forest of ring lights and selfie sticks. Everyone chatted to their own phones, which were angled at their faces in selfie mode. It felt . . . apocalyptic, and this was coming from someone who understood and appreciated the art of influencing. At least until very recently. *Cough* Lyndzi *cough*. "What in the fresh hell?" Brad asked.

He might've explained the appeal of Hearst to me, but now it was my turn to give him a dose of pop culture. Him and Rufus. Suddenly, I felt *very* trend-forward.

"What do we do?" Brad asked.

"We . . . go. To the party. We have to." I looked him up and down. "We're not exactly dressed for the occasion, but this could work to our advantage."

"Really?"

"Let me think."

We were going to need access to this party, and quick. What would Angelika do? I knew I had to summon the courage of all the Hearst queers who'd come before me. My realization was hastened by the fact that Rufus, who must've heard the brouhaha, started to buck around inside the Butler like a pinball. He clearly wanted out, and I couldn't deny him, because he was the one who'd brought us there. So a figurative *and* literal urging from our queer ancestors, if you would.

"I think I have an idea," I told Brad. "You're going to want to follow the rest of these cars."

"And then what?"

Brad was clearly horrified, whereas I could admit to feeling a teensy bit excited. Finally, something I was equipped for! Besides, I'd always wanted a red-carpet moment, and, hello, I was sort of owed one after what Lyndzi had done. Who could have known there would be one to be had in the greater Hearst area? Sure, renting out a former psychiatric hospital for a party was a perfect example of tone deafness, but I was not going to miss an opportunity to check out Knollwood *and* make an entrance doing it. With Angelika as my witness, and Brad as my muse, I was going to channel some confidence.

"We're not on the list," Brad said, looking worried.

"Leave it to me. I got this."

With some prodding, Brad drove up to the gate, where a security crew was checking phones for credentials. A woman wearing all black and talking rapid-fire into a headset made her way to our driver's-side window.

"Are you sure?" Brad hissed.

"Yes. Roll it down and act like you couldn't care less about being here."

"Do you have your code?" The woman arched an eyebrow, already seeming annoyed that we didn't have our phones out and that our vehicle didn't exactly fit the aesthetic—I'm sorry, Olivia Newton-John! "This is a private event. You two need to get out of here unless you have your invites."

Brad, clearly never having dealt with this type of pressure before, stammered, "Oh, I'm so sorry, ma'am, we—"

"Are on the list, and I can't believe you would assume otherwise." I pretended to check her for a nametag. "*Karen*, is it? My assistant here got lost en route, so you'll have to excuse us, but we're late."

"I still need to scan your confirmation."

"Just a moment," I said, narrowing my eyes. Okay, so being rude and faux confident hadn't worked, and, to be honest, I didn't really have a plan beyond bossing her around a little bit. So much for waltzing in with my head held high. Though I knew there was no email confirmation on my phone, I leaned down to grab the Butler and pretend to rifle through it.

"Oh, shit, is that a real Butler?" Another woman had joined Karen at our window, probably because she smelled a security breach and was preparing to throw us out. I clocked her matching earpiece, but she was clearly a publicist, a few rungs up from event security.

"This old thing? It's just a silly little family heirloom. Honestly, it's exhausting that it gets so much attention everywhere I go. You know how it is."

Rufus glanced up at me through the zipper, his eye makeup flaring somehow while he looked offended, and I tried to communicate with my eyes to *just be cool*.

The earpiece woman nodded at Karen to let us in.

"I'm mortified," the security guard said, scrambling to grab a neon dashboard ticket. "Go right ahead, here's a VIP parking pass. Please enjoy your evening at Mango-Gasm!"

"Thank you." It was so hard to remain cute *and* bored-looking while wiping the sheer smug accomplishment from my face.

Then I noticed we weren't moving.

"What's the holdup?" I asked Brad.

"Your *assistant*?"

"Oh, Brad. Don't take it personally," I responded with a sheepish grin. "It's called thinking on your toes. At least we got in, amirite?"

Brad rolled his eyes. He was so cute when he was fake-mad. We drove right through the gate and toward Knollwood.

# 19

We found our parking spot, thanks to the Butler for having slayed the VIP entry game. With a little assist from me, of course. Angelika would be proud.

I was wearing a wedge that pinched my big toe, which I would have regretted if I hadn't looked so cute, so the short distance to the door was coming in clutch. Brad wasn't as much up for pics, and I hoped I hadn't turned him off with the full supermodel photo shoot I put on. He'd sort of have to get used to it, though, if we were going to keep . . . hanging out.

"Come on, Sull," he said, ducking his head down right as I hit my marks.

I snapped out of it as a gaggle of antsy influencers lined up behind us.

"Let's get a few of us together!" I tried.

Brad's one arched eyebrow spoke volumes.

"Okay, okay, we get it," I sang, and did one last pose with the Butler. "Wow, they must have bused in influencers from Philly and Pittsburgh."

Once the red-carpet photos were taken, we ascended the regal front steps into a massive grand lobby that had been converted for the festivities. More ring lights and content stations lined the room, with influencers aplenty mingling each other to death. I felt very at ease, because this was obviously *my world*, hello, but a peek revealed that Brad was giving tense and out of place.

"My mango has never gasm'd this hard before, *ohhh la la*," I cooed into my phone, raising my voice and pretending to blend in with the content-recording crowd, as if we weren't about to go ransacking this place to discover Rufus's origin story.

It was all so ridiculous, Brad burst out laughing, which made me relax a bit, scattering the tension from our awkward entrance. The more myself I was, the more he seemed to be picking up what I was putting down.

All those losers at Hearst High could eat their hearts out, because we were at the . . . what the fresh hell was this again? An Evening with Mango-Gasm? Anyway, it was a lot better than huffing Coors Light out of funnels off the back of someone's cousin's tailgate.

Out of the corner of my eye, I spotted two very excited influencer girls clearly not from around here, because their fashion was giving extreme luxury, but in a Gwyneth Paltrow culturally appropriative way. Some real subtle old-money wealth. Philly Main Line, maybe?

One of them approached, smelling like a vaginal-steaming soy candle. "Holy fucking oat milk, but is this a real Butler?"

"It looks really, really, really real," her friend said, glomming on to me, too. "I would know. I've been looking for one for years."

For a second, I wondered if they planned to tie me up in a janitor's closet and steal it. Before I could answer either of them, Rufus bellowed, "Hands off the bag, ladies!"

They both jumped back, and it was like a record-scratch moment. It seemed the closer Rufus got to his memories or the more emotional he felt, the more he could interact with the world. There was no other explanation.

"What was *that*?" Faux-Gwyneth asked.

"Oh, um, what?" I attempted to play it off and act natural. "I thought one of you said that."

"We most certainly did not."

"Okay, someone's had too much Mango-Gasm!" I said, too loudly. "Anyway, I just try to keep any unwanted hand oils or lotions off the bag. You know Butlers, so you understand. Okay, excuse me!"

Then I raced off to find Brad, my long-suffering toes be damned. After this whole case was over, I would definitely be getting a pedicure.

When I found him, though, poor thing, he had apparently been similarly sidelined by a very different type of person. A very cute, very much more butch influencer was chatting him up, down, and all around. Totally fine with me, no problem at all, except I looked down to find myself white-knuckling the Butler's handle.

*Is this jealousy?* I wondered, suddenly feeling a tad warm. *Must be heartburn.* I pulled myself aside and took a quick time-out. That's when I noticed Rufus peering over the side, surveying the crowd.

"You know, this is incredible! Look at all these people being completely themselves. They seem so free." A dreamy expression came over his face. "It's just—if everyone now is so open, why do I feel so trapped?"

"You live inside a handbag." It probably wasn't a good look to be having a full-blown conversation with a purse, so I craned my neck to see if Brad was still talking to that . . . other person. He must have seen me looking, because he made a beeline over.

"So what's the plan?" Brad said with that familiar adorable glint in his eye.

Fuck! An adorable glint in his eye? Maybe I needed to try one of these Mango-Gasms. Chill myself out a little.

Shaking off the moment of deep thought and, yes, vulnerability that Rufus had inspired, I said, "Well, if I was a betting person, which I'm not, since Uncle Chuck has a severe gambling problem and my mom forbids us from even playing Pokémon GO, I would guess we're after some records. First priority is anything to confirm or deny that one, Rufus Gratton, was here. And those, if they still even exist at all, would be upstairs in the attic. Sometimes the Allegheny floods, you know, so they obviously wouldn't put that stuff in the basement. As we all know from the great Hearst Records Hall flood of 1968."

"Nice." Brad winked. Now I was speaking his language.

"I know, I surprise myself every day. But what are we waiting for? Let's go!"

"Don't forget anything that sheds light onto Beauregard Hearst or Cygnus Cobpen would be a huge plus if we happened to stumble across it."

"Oh, right! Researching the land claim!"

Brad chuckled. "Okay, Law and Order: Sully Unit, roll out!"

Some *very* bold mango-orange velvet ropes marked off a few areas toward the back of the lobby. The cater-waiters—in neon orange hot pants—seemed to all be coming from that direction, so I knew we needed to make our way over.

"Act natural, and if anyone stops us, say we got lost looking for the bathroom." I couldn't believe I'd doubted myself with that Karen. I was really good at this.

"Sully, I'm seriously impressed. You're such a badass when you're in your element." Brad raised his eyebrows, practically beaming at me. I grinned, awash with the feeling that all was right in the world and so glad we were on the same page.

"Shut up, Brad. We have to go, but thanks. You're gorgeous—I mean great. Okay, let's go."

I could tell that my face was flame red, which *so* clashed with mango orange. *Hello, flummoxed, I'm Sully*, I sang in my head. Brad's cheeks were also full of color.

We successfully slipped past the rope and found ourselves basically alone in the back of the building, in a creepy, echoing corridor with cracked old tiles. Clearly they'd simply cleaned up the "presentable" areas for the party. I bet those mango-drunk idiots out there had no idea what this place was—or worse, that people like Rufus—and me—had been sent here simply for being different and trying to live their lives. I supposed that downplayed the horror of being sent away. And people were still doing it, trying to shove teenagers into conversion therapy, which seemed to be getting more and more legal every day. When would people learn that we couldn't be hidden away or changed to fit society's binary ideal? I shuddered, because for all the progress we'd made, this shit was still happening.

The influencers would've been seriously creeped out and, I hope, sobered up by learning about the real Knollwood. If only Miss

Goop could see what was really going on behind the velvet rope. That only made me sad for, surprisingly, the influencers. They were out there having their curated experience, yet they were missing out on much more real shit.

I realized that this was what I'd have been living by working the Lyndzi job: the influencer lifestyle. For the first time—and I couldn't believe I was saying this—I was glad not to have gotten it. Because it all felt a little . . . empty now.

Our footsteps echoed through the hallways as Brad and I walked more slowly, looking for any kind of staircase that might take us to the top floors of the building. I was just guessing about the attic, but I didn't have any better ideas. It'd been such a high to simply get into the party that I hadn't thought beyond it. There was also the distinct possibility that Knollwood had been cleared out, all its historical documents gone, its previous life scrubbed away.

"Any ideas?" Brad whispered. "Or should I just stick to *assisting*?"

"Okay, okay. Now we're a team. Happy?"

The corner of Brad's mouth quirked up. "Yes."

On either side of us were doors that had fallen off their hinges to reveal dusty, rusty, and, if I'm being honest, *crusty* old beds piled on top of one another against the walls. There were so many of them, the only way they could have fit was to be pressed against one another with almost no floor space in between. Maybe those Mango-Gasm people had gotten a bargain with this venue, because parts looked downright condemned. Or maybe this was a last hurrah before someone like Saul Bunyan came and turned it into an indoor pool or Beauregard Hearst got his hands on it to make condos or sell it for parts.

Brad tried a door on the far wall that wouldn't move, so he, swoon, put his shoulder into it and grunted. It opened to reveal a set of stairs heading down.

Before I could protest, Brad said, "I know you want to see if any important documents are upstairs, but hear me out. There are probably stairs for the staff to move quickly from one floor to another. We may have to go down to get up and it may be hard."

My laughter, fortunately, covered up Rufus's as Brad stared at me with confusion knitting his brows.

"Lead the way," I agreed once our final giggles subsided.

Brad led us down a hallway. I stopped at the entrance of a tiled room. Unforgiving fluorescent lights hung over a metal gurney with straps. A large drain sat in the middle of the floor, the grout leading to it stained a red brown.

I could feel Rufus shaking the Butler.

"Sis?"

"This is where they tried to fix people like me," he whispered so Brad wouldn't hear. "When the fever and electroshock therapies didn't work, they'd bring them down here to chemically castrate or lobotomize them."

I hated having to ask, but I did anyway. "Rufus, were you brought—"

"No," he snapped before I could finish. "I'm sure," he added in a gentler tone a second later.

The Butler continued to shake with agitation. I hurried to catch up with Brad, feeling chills race through my spine.

At one point, we passed a room with papers littering the floor. I reached down and delicately picked up a sheet before it crumbled in my hands—a patient's records from the early 1970s. "Really?" I breathed in surprise.

"What?" Brad popped up over my shoulder.

"There were patients here until, like, not even fifty years ago."

The reality of the history we were traipsing through was starting to wash over me.

Then Brad broke the silence. "It seems wrong to celebrate in a place like this. These were real people with real stories."

Good-looking *and* a little broody? Not to mention great minds thinking alike? I squeezed the Butler to my side with my arm, hoping Rufus was listening and it brought him some comfort.

"It makes that time in history seem so . . . scary," Brad continued, oblivious to the wedding bells ringing in my head.

"Not even *history* history. People who were patients here might still be alive."

We found the staff stairs as Brad had predicted and climbed to the second floor, then the third, then continued up and down corridors, looking for some clue as to where records could be stored. Outside, the sky got darker, and these upper floors weren't well lit. They must've commandeered all the electricity for the dance floor and the twenty frozen daiquiri machines churning behind the bar, full of a mango vodka concoction. I had to admit, I was a little curious. Experience marketing was doing its job!

Down a dingy hallway, we came to a T between two wings of the hospital.

"What do we do?" Brad asked. It was cute that he looked to me for leadership, but I didn't want to break his heart by revealing that I had no idea.

Suddenly, the Butler shook like a 100-pound golden retriever that had just seen a squirrel.

Brad jumped back. "What the—?"

"I just got an idea, follow me!" I yelled, doing my best to act like I was frantically pulling myself this way and that, instead of Rufus and the bag calling the shots.

"I know this is major, but you need to chill," I hissed at Rufus, to no avail. He'd never demonstrated this much strength, especially not in front of someone else. Was my bag going to explode? Had we forgotten all about the resale value?

Come to think of it, when Rufus had pulled me to this room from the bag, that was the first time I'd truly "felt" Rufus. Other than the pamphlet he'd managed to hold, normally when Rufus touched something he couldn't move it, but in here that was no longer the case. He'd been so real and tangible in the moment that he had led me here. A force I couldn't fight. I wished there were clear and defined rules to this whole ghost thing, but I couldn't even imagine what had drawn Rufus to me in the first place. Maybe it was some kind of queer magic between a Mary and their sis.

He dragged me to the end of the hallway, and we arrived at an unmarked door. My feet were killing me. When I got home, I planned on burning these wedges in a ritualistic ceremony so that they could never reincarnate and ruin anyone else's toes again. I would probably throw the espadrilles on the pyre, too. Or hoard them forever in the back of my closet. It usually went either way with me.

"This doesn't look like a records room to me," Brad said. The bag kept jerking around under my arm. Then, more quietly, he asked, "Are you . . . okay?"

"I know, right? That was *so weird*, I just really felt pulled to this room, so let's take a look. I probably *won't do that again*," I intoned, hoping Rufus could hear me.

Maybe we'd unlocked a memory and were getting closer to discovering Rufus's past. I could only hope, because sooner or later, some confused cater-waiter would see or hear us up here. Especially with Rufus throwing a fit.

Brad tried the doorknob and, shockingly, it was unlocked. Dim light from the hallway spilled in to reveal a tiny room, with space enough for only one person. A stained mattress and rusty metal bedframe slumped in one corner. It was giving solitary confinement in a retro sort of way, which was, unfortunately, what we'd come here to find. But I couldn't stand one more minute in that room, let alone imagine living there. I was about ready to nope right out of this place.

"Um, Sully? Is your . . . intuition saying anything?" Brad asked.

I wasn't sure what Rufus had brought us here for, but I was hoping he'd make his intentions known. And soon. Had Rufus been a patient here? Could this have been his room? Or had it belonged to someone important? I was trying to put the pieces together and coming up empty when—

*BAM!* Rufus did a double turn up and out of the bag, bursting into his full glory.

Except, Rufus didn't look so glorious. His normally coiffed hair was stuck to his forehead, sweaty and greasy, and he was dressed in pajamas made of coarse material, a thin slipper too small for him on one of his feet. With his wide, wild eyes, he was more traditionally ghoul-like than I'd ever seen him and clearly panic-stricken, but not nearly as much as Brad. Poor thing, his face was whiter than a Starbucks cup, and he wasn't even the ghost in this equation.

I froze, knowing it was only a matter of time before all my lies came tumbling down, and I'd have to tell Brad the truth.

Because it was safe to say the ghost was out of the bag. Rufus was no longer something I could write off as a fever dream or my imagination. Of course, I'd already believed he was real, but nothing confirmed a ghost's existence faster than sharing him with a friend.

I looked to Brad, whose beautiful mouth was still agape. *Oh, Brad. It was fun while it lasted.*

"Sully, is that a—"

"Um, okay, so, I can explain . . ."

# 20

Rufus went into a tizzy, spinning around the room, looking as though he was cycling through a dozen emotions at once. His normally proper hair and clothes became more disheveled, his mouth stretched out into a wobbly O. If he hadn't already been a ghost, I honestly think the shock of this experience would've killed him. His face was giving excitement at the rush of memories this place had clearly brought back to him, but he was also—understandably—weeping at the sorrow of those memories.

Even though Rufus hadn't said anything, I knew what significance Knollwood held for him. He had been trapped in uncertainty for over half a century, wondering what had happened to him and how he'd lost everything. Now, it was like he was seeing it all at once. I could only imagine the horrible pieces snapping together in his mind.

Brad's mouth dropped open, mimicking Rufus's, and this was definitely *not* a mango-gasm.

"Breathe, honey," I said to both of them at the same time. And then to Brad, "I can explain."

*Shit*. We were in an old psychiatric-hospital-turned-influencer-venue. Maybe I could convince Brad we were both seeing things and that I was as clueless as he was. *Has someone spiked the mango cocktails? Oh no!* But then Rufus dropped down to his ghostly knees and began to sob in earnest, and everything suddenly felt very, very real.

"Um, Sull?" Brad said, slowly. "Are you . . . is this . . . what's going on? Are we seeing the same thing here?"

"That's, that's . . ." I started. Honestly, though, I hadn't planned for this. I'd been spending lots of time with Rufus and Brad, and somehow I'd thought I could keep them separate. But now what? How could I ever explain Rufus to Brad? Even though he must've been wondering what I had been hiding, in his wildest imagination, I'm not sure he would've guessed this.

Before I could fumble my way through an introduction, Rufus clambered up, his movements becoming angry as he whooshed between us. This was some real *Poltergeist* shit, and even though I knew and loved Rufus, I couldn't help backing away, my heart beating quickly.

"Am I seeing a *ghost*?" Brad asked, plastering himself against the wall.

"He's not dangerous; he's just in his feelings. His really big, otherworldly feelings."

Rufus tore through the room with the awareness of someone who had been here before. For the first time, his feet stomped on the ground, making *real* noise. He flew to the bed and ripped the stained mattress off. Broken floorboards became toothpicks in his arms, which were suddenly powerful, weighty. Part of me wanted to reach out and hug him, while the other part wanted to save myself. Plaster fell from the walls, making a mess on the floor.

We had taken great effort to sneak quietly into the off-limits parts of Knollwood, and this ruckus was going to get us caught at any moment. We had to make a quick exit, records or no records. I wasn't mad at Rufus, though. I understood his pain, sort of. I'd never loved and lost so fiercely—or been thrown into an asylum. The wounds we both carried had so much in common, but I couldn't even begin to comfort him now. I worried I didn't know how.

Rufus spun around this small, drab prison like a tornado. "Why didn't someone come back for me? How could they leave me? How could *he* abandon me? And *here*?"

My self-preservation instincts kicked in then, because we did not need another encounter with Security Karen. If I was going to pull this careening train back on track, I was going to need Brad's help. I yelled his name.

He didn't respond. Even though he was standing right next to me, he seemed completely transfixed by Rufus, which was understandable. A person never forgets their first . . . ghost sighting.

"BRAD!" I clapped my hands in front of his face, but in a loving *snap out of it* way, pulling him out of his shock.

"What *the hell* is that?"

"Okay, listen up. That's Rufus. He's my . . . friend. Yes, he's a ghost, but he's a *friendly* ghost even if he might not seem like it right now."

The room we found ourselves in was windowless and incredibly creepy, even for a former asylum. I rushed out to the window on the hallway landing to get a glimpse of the party below.

Behind me, Rufus continued to wail and thrash. The sun was going down, and the courtyard outside had been draped in string lights. They began to flicker with his hopeless yelling, and I worried it wasn't on purpose. The thumping bass coming from the DJ booth cut in and out.

All the lights in the building and outside on the grounds flashed, like a frenetic lightning storm. And Rufus began to change, as if someone was flicking through television channels with a remote. Every outfit I'd seen Rufus in and many I hadn't, big hair, sequined gowns, suits, sweaters, makeup, even facial hair, came and went as Rufus stopped moving in the center of the room and raised his arms. He kept flipping through his appearances and the room glowed green-blue as if we were in a bioluminescent cave. There was the glowing silhouette of the bed with straps hanging from it, bedsheets wrinkled. On a cart was a torturous-looking machine with electrodes dangling while another held an oddly shaped wooden spoon, tubes, needles, and syringes. I turned away as Rufus's memories poured into the space around us and shifted and shimmered with otherworldly light, trying to take shape but not quite there.

There was a sudden creaking, rumbling noise, and then water began to gush from different points as pipes burst. I immediately shielded the Butler from destruction, squeezing it tight under my arm. A few windows shattered, shards glittering like dangerous confetti as an incredible wave of pressure ruptured through the entire property sending electrical sparks from every bulb and outlet. It all happened in a matter of seconds that felt like a stretch of minutes turning into hours.

To my horror, partygoers started screaming and running from the exits, clutching their oversize promotional party yards of orange frosé and mango daiquiris. All the emotion that Rufus had been bottling up for so long was exploding—and if we didn't get out of the way, the whole place might blow apart.

I had to do something. I had to stop this and get us out of here to safety. Hopefully I'd earned Rufus's trust by now, but I didn't know whether it would be enough.

"Rufus!" I shouted. "You don't have to do this!"

"They dumped me here like garbage! Everyone who was supposed to love me!"

What could I possibly say to that? I had Eleanor and Brad and friends whose love I never doubted. That didn't make my life any less hard, but at least there were people in my corner. I couldn't imagine being dumped here and dying all alone. And how gross it was that all these superficial, empty-headed "content creators" were now literally dancing on people's graves?

I turned around, and Rufus stood, raising his arms over his head even higher as if he were conducting an orchestra. His appearance continued to flash rapidly. The lights pulsed in time with his movements. He alone controlled the chaos downstairs, almost as if he had tapped fully into our reality and was able to tune the world to him telepathically.

"Rufus, please, sis. I think I saw cameras. If someone records you, we are so screwed. You're going on YouTube. You'll be on the news—"

"Cameras? I fried them! They don't have anything on us. I'll burn this place to the cursed ground it stands on!"

"Don't do this, Rufus," I tried again. "None of this is worth your energy. Those people aren't worth it. Come on, let's get out of here. If I were you, I wouldn't stay here one more minute. It's time to finally leave this horrific place behind for good."

Rufus's rage seemed to be blowing itself out like a hurricane reaching the eye of the storm. The power flickered, but less forcefully this time, and the water from the burst pipes slowed to trickles. "They left me here, Sully. They *left* me."

"But this time, we're leaving together," I said, more confidently now.

He glanced up at me, his cheeks streaked with luminescent tears.

"That's right. We're leaving, and we're taking you with us. Okay?" I realized I was on the verge of crying myself, but what else did I have to lose? I let it all out. "I've only known you a short while, but I already love you. I don't think anyone who knew you, who knew the *real* you, could abandon you like this."

Rufus's appearance settled, a wild updo and avant-garde asymmetrical eye makeup over a wig. He wore a suit jacket and cravat, stockinged legs ending in a pair of high-shine patent leather pumps. A grizzled beard remained. I reached out a hand to smooth it but I didn't need to touch it before it settled into a groomed state, thick and luxurious.

Rufus touched his facial hair and seemed surprised, his mouth dropping open. "What I must look like," he said. "How people would stare."

"Then let them stare," I said firmly.

We met each other's eyes and nodded in unison.

"Sis," he said.

"Mary," I replied.

Footsteps sounded from the stairs, and there was shouting.

"Sully, I don't want to interrupt a beautiful moment," Brad

said, "but I think people are coming."

"Rufus," I said, "let's go. We can't figure out what happened to you if they catch us. You've come too far to let this place win. And as drop-dead sickening as you look, you're going to have to make yourself scarce."

That did it. Rufus didn't seem happy about it, but he swirled back into the Butler like none of the last few minutes had ever happened. I gave Brad a very serious look. "We'll talk all about it, I promise. But right now let's get the hell out of here, because this girl does *not* look good in prison orange."

*June 20, 1955*
*Rufus, darling,*

———

*I am losing my mind here. Where are you?*

*Here's the truth: I was scared. You knew I was. But not of being with you.*

*I never imagined we could fight like we did that night because until then we'd always fought alongside one another. Against the bullies who teased you as a child. And our parents, who forbade us to be together. But the words we hurled at each other hit their marks and hurt us both.*

*Our love demands a lot of us. And my doubts do weigh on me. The feeling of being watched. Of having to second-guess our every move. But more than anything, I was watching you blossom. And I began to wonder if a boy from Hearst could ever be enough for you when you'd always wanted so much more. I can't deny I envied my cousins or our classmates when they got pinned, engaged, married, celebrated ... while we can't even reside in the same apartment. I want to live freely, easily, normally, as much as I know that confession could lead to other arguments.*

*I hope you understand now why I needed to go home. I simply got the zorros. I know you hate that I still consider Hearst a home but it will always have a piece of me. I needed* to see my family and if there was any chance to repair what was left. But all I did was confirm that where I belong is with the one who holds my heart in his hand as easily as he does the attention in a crowded room.

And now I am scared. When I returned, you had gone. I asked around and heard of recent arrests, but no one has details, and I have no grounds to make demands of any officials.

I'm leaving this letter in case you make it back and I'm not here, so you know I am searching for you, and I won't give up until I hold you again. The world be damned, you are my beautiful swan, the one brave enough to live every day as you are. And I swear, this time I will never let you leave my side.

Yours, if you'll still have me.

# 21

"That was . . . a lot," Brad said once we'd settled into the booth at Denny's and caught our breath. Sure, it was no Balthazar, NYC's favorite brunch hotspot, but we had to make do with Pennsylvania's finest chain option for the moment.

Brad stared blankly across the table, a plate of chocolate chip pancakes steaming between us. I was excited for the sugar to regulate my nervous system and hoped Brad was just tired. But he wouldn't look me in the eye. I guessed I had to start talking. That scene back at Knollwood would be tough to recover from. After our influencer-debut-turned-paranormal-circus, I needed to calm down in a big way, and Brad needed a serious debriefing. I owed him that much.

We'd barely made it halfway down to the driveway when a security guard grabbed us both. In all the commotion, Brad and I were somehow able to divide and conquer. I pirouetted out of the guard's grasp, and Brad beelined for the parking lot so quickly that nobody could catch him. All that lacrosse or soccer or pickleball or whatever had paid off, and he'd looked yummy doing it.

The grand ballroom had disgorged its influencers, who were

running for the hills. The orange carpet was already sticky with spilled mango daiquiri, and a graveyard of broken halo lights only added to the effect. Even the balloon archway had been trampled by TikTokers in their mad dashes to freedom.

Apparently exploding lights, eerie screaming, and decorations flying off the walls was not the kind of "experience" Mango-Gasm had in mind for this party, and a barrage of police cars pulled up to the gate right as Olivia Newton-John, Rufus, Brad, and I made our desperate escape.

I quickly checked to see whether Uncle Chuck was among them and was relieved when I didn't see his squad car. Maybe he was vintage shopping.

Okay, maybe I was still a little salty.

In all the commotion, we were able to edge onto the shoulder and leave Knollwood in our dust. We even went a bit off-road through a field, and our girl did us proud.

Which brought us back to the present moment, and the most awkward, depressing pancakes I'd ever had. And not just because we were at Denny's. Hey-o!

The humming overhead fluorescent lights weren't particularly contributing to the vibes, and the one or two staff working the overnight shift were a far cry from the Mango-Gasm shot girls who'd been making the rounds at the party. There was no sparkler bottle service option, but that was okay. I think Brad and I were both a bit partied out.

My only complaint was the lack of music, or even Muzak, because the silence meant we had to speak more quietly so as not to scare our waitress, Veronica, who lingered annoyingly within earshot. The dining room was a ghost town, pun fully intended, so it wasn't like she had anything better to do, but some privacy would've been helpful.

Under the table, I scrolled through the holy trinity—Instagram, TikTok, and Snapchat—to see if anyone had caught me or Brad—or worse, Rufus—on camera. After not seeing anything under the Mango-Gasm hashtags, I even considered checking YouTube or Reddit, because my post-ghost-in-public doomscroll paranoia was real.

A few minutes passed in silence as Brad let me investigate in peace.

"So, good news. I think we're in the clear," I said, breathing a sigh of relief and bringing myself back to the moment.

Across the table, Brad flinched. I think we'd both forgotten we were sitting at Denny's, or maybe I was just projecting. For me, it had felt good to zone out for a moment.

Reality came crashing back in the form of Veronica, who soon greeted us with our two burgers, fries, and a strawberry shake for moi, of course. She didn't seem to notice that we hadn't even started on our appetizer. Rufus had been whispering in my ear about the milkshakes in his time since we walked in the door, so I figured we all deserved a treat.

Speaking of the man of the hour, inside the Butler, Rufus seemed to be getting agitated again.

Veronica paused to look at my bag for a split second, and I worried that he'd burst out and lay waste to Denny's, too. Her red eyes were fixed permanently at half-mast, so I didn't think we needed to worry.

"Are you okay in there?" I whispered as soon as she faded from earshot.

Rufus huffed from inside the bag.

Veronica appeared again out of nowhere and dropped our bill on the table. "I'm taking my smoke break," she said as she walked off. "I'll be back when I'm done."

"And when might that be?" I asked her.

"When I'm back," she said without missing a beat.

A moment after she disappeared through the kitchen and, presumably, out a back door, I opened the bag and motioned to Rufus. "I think it'd be better if we explained together," I said. Sure, it might've been a bit of a cop-out, but I also didn't want to sit there and tell Rufus's story. He deserved the dignity of sharing his own. "Hold, please."

Looking more solid than I'd ever seen him, Rufus drifted from the bag and sat beside me. It seemed so surreal that the ghost of someone who'd died over seventy years before was sitting with us now, as real as my milkshake-induced brain freeze. Rufus, beard still intact and looking like a big-and-tall thirst trap in his tight jeans and black leather jacket, tried to sip my milkshake but it seemed ingestion wasn't in the ghost realm of power. This was all new to me, too, because I'd just gotten used to him interacting with the physical realm.

"Hello," Rufus said, and Brad flinched again, but kept a tense smile on his face.

"Well, don't be rude, Brad," I said.

"Right. I'm new at this whole talking-to-ghosts thing." He shot me a saucy look, which I chalked up to exhaustion and let slide. "Hi.

Nice to meet you. My name is Brad."

"Oh, I am well aware who you are," Rufus said coyly. "Even more of a flutter bum in the flesh."

"I don't know what he's talking about. He's just transcended space and time and joined the mortal plane, so I think he's confused." I swatted Rufus's shoulder, half-expecting my arm to go clean through him as usual, but it didn't entirely. It seemed he was becoming more solid as his memories came back, which made a weird kind of sense.

"The only thing I'm confused about," Rufus said, gesturing to the menu, "is what Moons Over My Hammy means."

"Don't worry; nobody knows," Brad said, and with that, the awkwardness between them dissipated.

There was no better time to start explaining, and no easier way to say it, so I dove right in. "Okay, well, Rufus is my friend who is a . . . spirit. He's from Hearst; his whole family is—or was—but he, um, *died* sometime in the 1950s. As we just found out, he was likely taken to and institutionalized at Knollwood. In that horrible room."

"So the records hall and the trip to Gratton Farms . . ."

I nodded. "I've been looking for clues to Rufus's history."

Brad chewed on a fistful of fries, nodding to himself. "While I think that's incredible, and I'm not quite sure I believe it yet, I just . . . over the course of the last hour I went from ghosts-are-totally-not-real to everything-I-know-is-a-lie. So bear with me here. But first I have to ask . . . why?"

"That's a very reasonable question," I said. "Well, when Lyndzi pulled my internship, and Eleanor had the whole going-away party when I sold you my car and we made out for the first time—"

"I completely understand the giving in to temptation." Rufus winked and Brad blushed.

"Moving right along. So then I went to Yesterday's Tomorrow and found this fierce bag. The Butler—you've seen it, I'm sure."

"Oh, I know the Butler," Brad said, shooting me the cutest little smile.

"Well, it turns out this bag could be worth . . . a lot of money." I didn't want to tell Brad the exact dollar amount, lest I jinx myself. Speaking of which, I still had to get back to Angelika and Paulo. I had every feeling in the world that the Butler was real—it was too incredible to be some knockoff—but some parts of this story were too personal, too precious, to share, at least at this point. "Of course, Claire didn't know what she had, so I bought it with the money not earmarked to convince you to return Olivia Newton-John to its rightful owner."

"As entertaining as your stories are, Sull," Brad said, "I'm still wondering when we connect the dots to the, you know, *ghost* sitting next to you."

"Stay with me! So when I got home and opened the bag, there was Rufus. I mean, I haven't even been able to investigate inside the bag because I quickly realized . . . that's where he lives."

"Really?" Brad asked. "Like a Keebler elf in a tree."

I nodded solemnly.

"I'm familiar with a cookie company by that name, but don't know how this connects to an elven tree, so let's go with, *sure, yes*," Rufus confirmed.

"Since he revealed himself to me," I continued, "I've been trying to help him piece together his life story, because he has some form of ghost amnesia. I know it's crazy, but *you* see him, right?"

Brad nodded again, his brows knitting together. I was losing him.

"I thought I was going crazy at first, but no, Rufus is as real as this"—I prodded the chocolate chip pancakes—"Um, food?"

"I haven't eaten in over seventy years, and even I have to admit, I'm not enticed," Rufus said, eyeing our meal.

"Anyway. I'm so sorry that I lied, Brad," I said, more seriously this time. "I didn't mean to. Well, yes, I intended to lie, but I thought it was for a good reason. And until tonight, I honestly wasn't sure if Rufus was real in a way that anyone else in the world could see."

"I can't believe you thought I was unreal. You're a real panic and a half, you know?"

"You *are* a ghost though, sis."

Rufus and I smiled at one another, and I took a moment to appreciate our friendship, weird as it was. It was like he'd come along right when I needed him, and, in a way, maybe I had for him, too.

"Okay, okay, that was a lot," Brad said, bringing me back to the moment.

This was all much easier when I had just been feeding him excuses, but now I had to face the verdict of whether he would understand it, accept it, or, least likely of all, want to keep helping.

"I can see how you wouldn't want to share all this with me so fast," he continued hesitantly. "But, Rufus, I have a few questions for you, too."

Rufus sat up straight, seemingly taking pride in being recognized by another breathing human being besides me. "For a looker like you, anything."

Brad shifted in his seat. "How can we, um, help you without getting ourselves into trouble? You know that Sully's mom is a big deal around town, so we don't want to give her a bad reputation—"

"More like a *bag* reputation, amirite?" I said.

Brad side-eyed me, but I could tell from the way his eyes crinkled that he thought I was at least a little bit hilarious. My mind treated me to a quick flash of the future, as Brad and I gossiped about Eleanor the boss lady while making out on my beanbag chair. Okay, maybe it would be a little weird to talk about my mom in the heat of the moment, amazing as she was. I was all about Brad coming to her defense, though.

"You'll have to excuse me, Rufus," Brad said, turning serious. "I thought we were working on something completely different. There's some controversy about who owns the actual land here in Hearst. I thought we were digging around in the records and history books . . ." He trailed off, looking bewildered. "Do you know a Cygnus Cobpen, by chance?"

Rufus made a face. "Gesundheit."

I snuck Rufus a small smile, remembering that this was my exact reaction to Eleanor the first time she said it. Rufus and I were separated by about three-quarters of a century, yet we had a lot in common.

A silence fell over the table, and I worried I was losing Brad. "Well, I think this is even *better* than some dusty old title deed homework assignment!"

Brad nodded, looking down into his lap. Then he glanced up again but didn't look at me. "You probably know more than any of us, Rufus, that Hearst is a small town, after all. Can we trust that if we help out, you can keep yourself from another outburst? People could have really been hurt." He finally turned to me. "Sully included."

Wait, did he just say *we*? Was Brad officially on board the Sull train? And was it me, or was he putting off protective boyfriend vibes? This was giving me all the warm fuzzies.

I turned back to Rufus, waiting for his response, which would be important. I also didn't want to experience the kind of meltdown he'd had at Knollwood again. Not only was it undoubtedly painful for Rufus, but it would easily get us arrested in the middle of Denny's. And if I was being honest, it was scary. I didn't know the full extent of what Rufus could do, and I was sure he didn't either.

Rufus rubbed his hands together thoughtfully. "You have my promise, as much as I can help it. I just . . . I've been confined for so long and so had all the pain and anguish inside me especially at the scene of my . . . incarceration. However, I'm sorry for causing such a big commotion back there." He paused for a moment, and then smirked. "It was fun seeing all those *ridiculous*-looking people running around like wild banshees, though. Wasn't it? Seriously, what were some of them wearing? Those threads can't be normal in the future."

"Oh, they're influencers. Don't pay any attention to them," I said.

Rufus shot me a confused glance. "Influ-what?"

"Don't worry about it."

I was about to refresh my melting pile of whipped cream when Rufus grew quiet. "Now, I'd like to talk about *my* boyfriend."

"Who up until a big argument was his very accepting, very

supportive love," I leaned in to explain. "They started off as childhood best friends, then moved to the bustling metropolis of Pittsburgh together to get away from their families. Discovering who this guy was is one of the mysteries we haven't solved."

"Being back at Knollwood has shaken loose some of my memories. So I may be putting an egg on my shoe and beating it sooner than you think," Rufus said, eyeing the menu and looking melancholy. "It seems that, with my old life flooding back, I am closer to whatever lies ahead."

"Oh, I don't want to be rid of you," I said quickly. I really meant it.

"So what happened to him?" Brad interjected.

"A lot is still hazy. We were happy. But it was always in secret. No one could know we were together. And then we had a big row. His father had never liked me. When we ran off together, he liked me even less. My love decided to go back to Hearst to see his family and, for the first time, I felt as if he was wavering. I remember storming out, feeling betrayed. And then I was there . . . in that horrific place with other men like me. 'Deviants,' they called us. 'Fairies. Perverts.'"

"You mean Knollwood was a place where they would take queer people? Gay men . . . like you?"

Rufus nodded. "And female impersonators. Among others with actual ailments, the elderly who required too much care, and a few women who were too . . . vocal. Hysteria was still a diagnosis. But, yes, there were several of us. I wish I could remember their names and know what happened to them."

With a shudder, I imagined myself being dragged to that

windowless room, shackled to that claustrophobic cot. If I'd been born in a different century, I could very easily have been in Rufus's shoes. I knew history didn't take kindly to people who didn't fit the mold, but throwing them into asylums seemed darker, more organized. And, unlike Rufus, they likely died without a voice. Entire histories that could very well remain untold.

Brad looked at me, and I saw it in his eyes too. Hearst was my own personal hell most days, sure, but it was easy to forget that the only thing separating me and Rufus was the year we were born. "Rufus, we're going to figure out what happened to you and find your boyfriend. You deserve to know."

"What if he left me? Or put me there himself?"

"From what you've told me, I don't think he would do that. He was your best friend, your man. If anything, maybe your father or *his* father had you committed."

"I don't want to think that. I don't want to believe it." A shadow passed over Rufus's face and I could see him working hard to smile again. "That means you'll have to hold on to the Butler for a while longer, until we figure this out. I don't know what might happen if I move too far from it."

"Fuck selling the Butler," I said, only to realize that I meant it. It made me nauseated to think of never seeing that amount of money, or maybe it was the Denny's veggie burger. But Rufus and his history were so much more important. I couldn't begin to think about moving on without getting answers for him—and now for myself, too.

Rufus grinned and looked at my milkshake. "Is that strawberry? I couldn't taste it before."

I nodded my head. "My favorite."

Rufus leaned forward and sniffed it. With a sad sigh that let me know he couldn't smell it either, he said, "It was mine too. It always looked like it tasted like a perfect day with puffy clouds and not too much sun. Kind of like the future."

Kind of, yeah. Still full of challenges, but at least Brad and I could sit here in the open without the same kind of fear that Rufus must've faced. "Super impressive poetic milkshake feelings. Right, Brad?" I angled toward my silent partner, emphasis on the *silent*.

But Brad only sat there, lost in his thoughts, before giving a half-hearted nod.

"Do you three want any coffee? We're closing up soon." Veronica came by with a half-full carafe that'd probably been sitting on the warmer all night.

We all jumped in our seats. Had she said three? So . . . she could see Rufus and hadn't even registered him as a ghost. I guess you would see some weird-ass shit working the graveyard shift at Denny's. Or maybe she'd just smoked the strongest joint in history out there by the dumpster.

"No, we're good," I said. "Thanks."

"Give my compliments to the chef on this milkshake," Rufus added. "It looks a real treat."

# 22

I couldn't believe that Brad and I had been out all night together, even if we had spent part of that time at Denny's with a ghost and a grumpy waitress.

Olivia Newton-John purred as Brad pulled up around the corner from my house and parked in almost the exact same spot where we'd kissed not long ago. I couldn't believe so much had happened since my going-away party even though so little time had passed.

I clutched the Butler between my knees as the air grew thick between us. It felt like Brad was about to say something, but then he nodded at the bag. "Are we . . . alone?"

"Why, Brad? Do you have some ideas?" I flirted, but his face dropped, and I desperately wanted to walk it back. This was why I didn't hit on people. I'd either read the room wrong—devastating in and of itself—or he was still mad about our escape from Knollwood. "Are you okay? I didn't mean to make it weird."

"Is he listening?"

"Not if you don't want him to," I said, but I really didn't know whether that was true. Rufus had changed since we left Knollwood. He was more able to interact with the world, more present. He said that he had boundaries, but I wasn't sure about the logistics. I didn't want to admit that I had no idea about the rules of having a ghostly sidekick. Or wait . . . was I *Rufus's* sidekick? I'd always imagined myself as having main character energy, which Brad had so *helpfully* pointed out on our drive over to the records hall, but if I was going to concede to anyone else, Rufus deserved it.

Brad and I paused for a beat or two, but Rufus didn't materialize or mutter a snarky remark, so either we really were alone, or he'd decided to humor us.

I waited for Brad to speak first, since I'd already messed up my opening, but instead he sighed deeply.

"Come on, you're freaking me out," I said. I wouldn't like where this was going, I could feel it.

He bit down on his thumb cuticle. "I gotta admit, Sully. This is a bit . . . much."

*Whew!* Brad was apprehensive about the whole situation, but not about me. I could work with this, and I'd even let slide the whole "bit much" thing. That wasn't the first time someone had said it about me, though hearing it from Brad pinched a bit. "I know, right? For me, too," I said encouragingly.

"Seriously, Sully. Think about it. Ghosts, deceased drag queens, mysteries, influencers' parties getting broken up by cops . . . I don't know that we should be getting mixed up in all this. If I get a mug shot at eighteen, that's going to hurt me down the line."

"Are you *seriously* thinking about your *political career*, Brad?"

He was right, of course. This was the exact kind of thing some PR firm would one day have to bury. I could see the headlines now: *Mayor's Shady Past Unearthed . . . Footage of Governor Thompson Fleeing from Police . . . Congressional Candidate Babbles about Drag Ghost in Youth.*

He seemed surprised by my surprise. "Well, *yeah*. Obviously. Aren't *you*—"

He stopped and looked sheepish, as my whole stomach dropped down to street level. "What. Brad. Aren't I what?"

"I don't want to say it."

"Nope, no backsies. You were about to say something." I had a feeling I knew what it was, and I wasn't going to let him get away with it. My buzz from the night finally came crashing down, though I tried to keep it light. "I'll summon my ghost on you."

Brad sighed and looked straight ahead. "I'm sorry. I'm tired."

"Say it."

He scrubbed his hand over his face. "Fine. You pull me along on all these 'adventures' and you don't ask me if I want to be involved until it's way too late. Not to mention, maybe you should be thinking more about setting yourself up for some kind of career. A future. Something!"

Tears prickled at the corners of my eyes, and I tried not to cry. Well, I'd asked him to say it—to speak one of my biggest insecurities, because I'd known it was coming—but that didn't make it hurt any less. And here I'd thought he liked me for me, and not for what I "could be" one day. For my*self*, not my job.

Then it hit me. Hadn't I been relying on the Lyndzi job to define me? Wasn't that what I'd been counting on? What a hypocrite I was. In all of this, I'd thought I was being helpful. I liked to think that I'd added a little something to Brad's life. After all, what was the most exciting thing he'd done before our adventures?

Organize his polo shirts? Play in a pickleball tournament?

But that wasn't fair to him. He was his own person. He had his own values. Maybe we weren't as compatible as I wanted to think. Just because he'd kissed me didn't mean he was the Hallmark love of my life.

My cheeks flared with heat, and I sank lower in Olivia Newton-John's familiar bucket seat, feeling like it wasn't my car anymore, and that the boy sitting next to me was not my Brad, for the first time since we'd embarked on this crazy adventure. I shouldn't have been surprised. Brad *was* Bread. His whole family adored him. All of Hearst seemed to approve. He didn't wear his queerness on his sleeve. Like Rufus. Or me.

"Sully?"

"Yeah, um, sorry. Right. It *is* a lot," I admitted, but all I wanted to do was grab the Butler and get out of there. Maybe it wasn't fair to have kept Brad in the dark this whole time, but I'd never exactly navigated a ghost friend and archnemesis-turned-crush-turned-heartbreak relationship threesome before.

For the second time this week, I felt the rug go out from under me. The Lyndzi thing was fine. I was already over it. Okay, sort of. But I *would* be over it. I'd gotten used to those small disappointments, especially in Hearst. Sometimes that meant it was easier to move on, but other times, they still stung.

This, though, felt a million times worse. *This* was me getting my hopes up, and Brad turning out to be exactly what I thought he was. I couldn't change the way he felt, or so the TikTok relationship-advice-slash-makeup-artists kept telling me, but I guess I hoped he would feel differently.

"Yeah, maybe we could take a break from *Scooby-Doo*-ing on Rufus's behalf for a while," I said.

A big, pathetic part of me wished he'd snap out of it and immediately take it all back.

He just nodded.

I looked down into my lap, holding my hands together so they didn't start shaking. "Thanks. For coming with. And I'm sorry I yanked you into all this."

"Sull—"

"No, no, it's okay. Heard it loud and clear." I grasped blindly for the door handle, tears burning at my waterline. God, I just wanted to talk to Emma. "Thanks for the, um, ride—"

He looked up to me, face open and hopeful as he reached for my hand. "I'm not trying to say I don't want to hang out with you. Just that maybe we could take a break from . . ." I pulled away and his words petered off as his brow furrowed.

I nodded curtly. My head spinning, I grabbed the Butler and spilled out onto the sidewalk by my house. The sun was coming up, and Eleanor would be leaving for work soon. I had absolutely no interest in catching her up right now, as I hadn't slept all night. But if she'd noticed, she hadn't called. All I had to do was sneak downstairs and sink into oblivion.

Brad started Olivia Newton-John and pulled away. I watched our—*his*—taillights fade around the corner.

"Okay, I'm sorry, but *what*? Did you hear that?" I asked the Butler. I could use some of that unasked for ghostly perspective I'd had handed to me in Yesterday's Today's basement. "Rufus? Don't leave me hanging."

Unfortunately, it really did seem like Rufus was resting, or just as confused as I was about the last twenty-four hours, and especially the last ten minutes. I looked around my street, wishing I could share this moment with someone, anyone.

I scurried home, completely unable to deal. Down in my room, which felt like I'd last left it three years ago, I tucked the bag into bed with me and passed the hell out, too tired to grapple with *anything* that had happened in the last twenty-four hours.

Before I did, I sent off a text to Emma and Guy for them to read when they woke up in the morning:

Heartbreak 911. I repeat: heartbreak 911.

Too soon, my phone rang, and I bolted awake. It felt like I'd only been asleep a few seconds, but the bright afternoon sun outside my window said otherwise. I wished I could go back to sleep, but the custom ringtone I'd programmed for Guy—"Born in the U.S.A.," of course—told me I should pick up. Even though things between us weren't exactly resolved yet, I was so happy to hear from him. "Hello. Sully's House of Broken Hearts. Sully speaking."

"I need to know everything. And then I need to know who to curse. No one breaks my Sully's heart."

Okay, that was most definitely not Guy. "Emma?"

"No, it's Guy, my voice changed overnight into this husky velvet dream."

I squinted at my screen, with Guy's name on it, trying to figure out what the hell was going on. "Why are you calling?"

"You texted 911!" she said.

"No, I mean why are you calling from Guy's phone?"

"Oh, that," she said. "Well, we never got a chance to have that talk and so, uh . . . Guy and I are doing sleepovers now."

Somewhere on her end I heard a muffled voice. There was a brief struggle on the line and then Guy took the phone.

"Hey, buddy," he said.

"Hey, yourself," I said. "Apparently I'm not the only one in town with romantic drama."

"Yeah." I could hear the grin in his voice. Guy was not exactly complicated, and he didn't mince words. "It's pretty great."

"It's *not* great!" Emma shouted from off-mic. "It's very complicated and fraught and we still haven't talked about it!"

"We've clearly got a lot to catch up on," I said, trying to wrap my head around this new scenario. Guy and Emma doing sleepovers? I was happy for them, I guessed, but that all felt very . . . I don't know, adult. Like Emma had said: What did a high school relationship mean now that high school was over, and the rest of our lives stretched on indefinitely before us? But all this train of thought did was remind me of Brad and his comment about my career, or lack thereof.

"Uh, yeah, definitely," said Guy. "But that's not actually the reason we called you."

"It isn't?" I said. God, was this about to get weirder?

"I wanted to warn you: my dad's heading over to your house."

"Like he does every other day . . . or . . . ?" I didn't know where this was going. Was Chuck coming to formally apologize?

"No, Sully. He's in uniform."

# 23

"Oh." But I didn't have a chance to ask Guy for clarification, as someone was already knocking on our front door so aggressively that I could hear it in the basement. "I guess I gotta go."

This was all so weird. Uncle Chuck never knocked, but I guess he had to when he was on official business. The official business of interrogating me.

"You know who to call if you need a getaway car. I bet Emma's cousin who makes fake IDs could get us some legit-looking passports, too. Mexico, baby!"

"I'm more of a Canada gal—"

More knocking interrupted me, sounding more insistent this time.

"I hope it doesn't come to that," I told him.

"Well, I just want you to know I'm ride or die. Even if it means running from the cops. Especially if it means running from the cops."

"The cops are your dad," I reminded him. But I'd hoped that he was going to reassure me. That he seemed intent on planning our international getaway was *not* helping.

"Yeah, well, I said what I said. Good luck, Sull."

I didn't like the sound of that. Not at all. It implied that I'd need luck to get out of whatever mess I was in. I was about to haul my terrified self up the basement stairs to answer the door when the telltale clicking of business pumps rang out. Eleanor was home? How late had I slept?

The front door opened. Muffled talking. Then more heels, and a knock on the basement door.

"Sull?" she called.

"Coming!" I threw a drapey silk robe on over my rumpled oversize Garfield T-shirt. What could Uncle, I mean, *Officer* Chuck want? Nobody had noticed us at Knollwood. Had they? I'd scoured social media and hadn't seen anything. But what else could it possibly be? Had they reviewed security camera footage from the records hall? That Phyllis was a tough one to read, so maybe her loyalties were—

"Sully!"

That kicked my butt into gear for the last few steps. Eleanor gave me a what-the-eff look as soon as I opened the door. I responded with an expression that I hoped said *I might be in a bit of trouble but I did it for the right reasons which I can't talk about now but I promise that it was worth it and remember you love me very much*. It was a lot to ask of a look, but I'd gone to the Tyra Banks School of Facial Expressions and majored in smizing with a minor in nonverbal facial communication.

Officer Chuck was, indeed, in the house, looking constipated and bulky with his bulletproof vest and chunky utility belt. We settled around the kitchen table awkwardly, with Uncle Chuck shifting uneasily in his tragically brown deputy uniform and looking down at his shiny black shoes.

"Does anyone want to tell me what's going on here?" my mother asked, rolling her eyes. "First, Beauregard is driving me up a wall wanting the council to conclude he's the sole Hearst heir of all time, and now we've got Chuck here in his . . . official capacity."

"Well, I was hoping Sully could clue us in."

"About what?" I asked, all sweetness and light.

Uncle Chuck took a deep breath, an all-business look about him. "First of all, Sully, I apologize for the spectacle at your going-away party."

I found myself having trouble meeting his eyes. Okay, maybe that's all this was. If so, the uniform was certainly a choice. I appreciated that he'd been thinking about it, but it didn't change the fact that he shouldn't have pulled that stunt to begin with. And sometimes I didn't want to give everyone a pass just because they didn't get it. But I had a feeling there was more to this.

Eleanor cleared her throat, looking expectantly at me.

Yes, I was staying in town for the foreseeable future and, yes, I knew he was family, but I didn't automatically want to forgive him yet. And I shouldn't have had to. I knew what was not so subtly expected of me, but instead I decided on, "I appreciate that."

"Okay. But that's not why I'm here."

There it was. The *but*.

Eleanor and I looked at him, and then she looked at me. I definitely had some explaining to do, but I wasn't about to speak first.

"There was, uh, some sort of *influencer* party last night," Chuck began, almost as if he wanted to check whether he'd pronounced the word right. "On the outskirts of town. They all came in from the city for some kind of mango mayhem."

Shit. Had he been one of the responding officers? We'd checked as we were leaving. Had someone snapped a picture of me after all, before the electrical went haywire? Security camera footage? Had Olivia Newton-John been recognized? She *was* a legend around town. . . .

"Oh, yeah?" I played coy, pointedly ignoring Eleanor's loaded glare.

"It was sabotaged. There was a short circuit, people running in all directions. Lots of property damage—"

"I'm surprised it hasn't gone viral yet," I said.

"I recall you wanting to be an influencer," Chuck said.

I gave him a tight smile.

"Were you there, perhaps? You know anything about what might have happened?"

So if I was hearing this correctly, he hadn't seen me, he'd just judged me? Again?

"Okay, that's about enough," Eleanor said.

Here it went. Mom was about to come down on me. I'd have to explain everything. Well, obviously not *everything*. But if I started talking now, I'd have to mention the records hall, Gratton Farms, Knollwood, Yesterday's Today, all of it. Rufus and the Butler, I'd keep to myself, unless absolutely cornered. Brad, too. He didn't need to be dragged into it—he'd made that perfectly clear. If I cost him the internship at Eleanor's office, I might as well jump in the bag with Rufus.

"Sully is not going to answer any questions without our lawyer present," Mom announced.

Record scratch! *Excuse me?*

Even Uncle Chuck looked surprised. "Pardon?"

Eleanor looked at me, serving some serious we'll-talk-about-this-later-and-you're-not-going-to-bullshit-me energy before turning back to her brother. "Sully needs a lawyer present before they talk to anyone, including, and especially, you."

"What's that supposed to mean, Ellie?" he asked. Oh snap, the childhood nickname was coming to the party.

"I hear your department is getting pressure to cut some budget corners and up your quotas. I could certainly put in a good word for the boys in blue. Unless you lean on my kid."

"Ellie, I—"

"If the only thing you 'have' on Sully is that they know what an influencer is, then you have nothing."

For a moment, I forgot that they were quite literally talking about my potential criminal record and future. I was just that dazzled by my badass mom.

"I'm just trying to cover my bases."

"I'd like to believe you, Chuck. I would. But after the stunt you pulled at Sully's party, I don't know what to think of your motives. Was Sully seen there?"

"This isn't some kind of witch hunt," Chuck said, pulling out his phone. "This is a legitimate investigation." He opened an album and scrolled through several images. They weren't social media posts but security-camera footage of the grim upstairs hallways of Knollwood.

I shrank into myself. Oh no. I'd assumed all the power was out up there, but I recognized a blurry but definitely identifiable version of me in at least three pictures. Brad, too.

And honestly, we looked hot together.

*Focus, Sully! Not the time!*

"I see," Eleanor said, her gaze sliding to me. "I was going to give Sully the benefit of the doubt. But apparently I'm the one in the dark."

"Tim"—also known as Chuck's boss, the sheriff—"Wants to bring Sully down to the station. It's over my head. If it gets that far, I agree that Sull should have a lawyer. The reason I'm here"—he leveled a gaze at both of us—"is I'm trying to convince Tim that this isn't necessary *if* I can have a one-on-one talk with you."

"What about Brad?" I blurted. This could be his mug-shot moment, and I felt like I had to redeem myself or he'd never forgive me. "I mean, the other person in the pictures? It's hard to tell who it is. If there even is another person. That hallway was—um, *looked*—pretty dark."

I squirmed in my seat a little.

Chuck's face was unreadable, then he smiled. "What other person?"

*Oh.* We were apparently making a deal. If I talked to him, Brad wouldn't be dragged into this. Between the apology, which had seemed genuine-ish, and Uncle Chuck apparently looking out for me, I knew I had to give him another chance. Those photos did put me at Knollwood, and I owed Mom and my uncle a *version* of events. There was still a way to save this.

"Can we please have the room, Eleanor?" I asked.

Her chest puffed out. "Are you sure that's what you want? You're an adult now, Sully. Don't forget, the legal implications are different."

I nodded, thankful for my mama bear. "Yes, I'm sure."

Uncle Chuck seemed pleased, though he didn't yet know that he was going to get the absolute barest sketch of events.

And asking Mom to leave was to give Uncle Chuck a false sense of confidence, like I was about to spill some deep, dark secrets. That woman would just sit in the living room and eavesdrop anyway.

Chuck leaned forward again, looking painfully earnest. "Thanks, Sully. Again, I'm so sorry about your party. I don't know what I was thinking."

"Thank you."

"Guy was pretty mopey when you were mad at him."

"We're working it out."

"Good. I'm glad to hear that."

We sat in tense silence.

"Right. Unless I'm under arrest, of course. Then we might just have to be pen pals," I said, honestly nervous. Cracking a joke wasn't always a good strategy, but I didn't really have a lot of other coping mechanisms.

Chuck laughed and put up a hand. "No, no, nothing like that. I'm confident I can make this all go away, but I was hoping you'd give me something to take back to Tim and the rest of the team about this party. What the heck happened?"

I wanted to be honest with him—at least partly—but I genuinely couldn't do it. Yes, he was making a real effort, but it was still too raw, too crazy, and part of the story wasn't even mine to share. "Yes, I was there, Uncle Chuck, but it was just me and Brad, cruising around and looking for a party. We got bored, went for a drive, and stumbled upon this event. And even though I've dabbled in influencer culture, it was honestly boring, so we went exploring. While we were inside, things went haywire, maybe an electrical short or something. You know how those historical buildings can be. That's it. Just Hearst kids having fun." Even though I chafed against giving myself that "Hearst kids" label, I needed to make it convincing, so I put on my most earnest expression. "I wanted to see what I was missing out on. You know, with New York and all that."

Chuck nodded, as if he'd suspected as much. "Okay, well, this footage has the two of you coming out of the same part of the house where all the switch boxes were. Not to mention evading a security guard."

"We were making out," I blurted.

Eleanor gasped from the other room, and I couldn't contain my eye roll.

Uncle Chuck bit back a smile.

"And the guard figured out that we weren't actually on the list, so she was probably just mad she got fooled," I finished.

He leaned back in his chair, huffing out a sigh of relief, and then wiped his brow. "Sully, thanks for telling the truth. And you know, Brad is a great kid. I saw a shirt at Target the other day that said 'love is love,' and, uh, yeah. Good stuff. Good message." He coughed into his fist and stood up. "As it stands, I'm going to tell Tim that I don't see how you could be responsible for the chaos, and I'll put that in my report, too."

"I wouldn't even know what an electrical panel looked like," I said with a cute shrug. Too much? It was true, though. Bless Dad's contractor heart, he loved me anyway.

"Yep. Let alone how to short the electrical and burst the pipes.

This ends here, and there's no need to go down to the station. All I have are a few pictures, and all they prove is that you were there. That's no crime, even if you did sneak in."

"No video, then?" I asked, wondering if there was footage somewhere of Rufus's ghost going absolutely ballistic on a crowd of terrified half-drunk Instagram nano-influencers.

"No video. The electrical surge shorted all the CCTV cameras, and they'd already overwritten the footage by the time we got access to the security room."

"Okay, well, thank you for stopping by." I stood up, wanting to put an end to what I hoped would be my first and only police interrogation.

"Thanks again for being honest." He stuck out his beefy, hairy hand, and I had to firmly grip it, which felt more like a test than our entire interview. The mark of a man was a strong handshake, after all. He gripped so hard I swore I heard a knuckle pop. Mine or his, I didn't know, because my entire hand was numb.

"Okay, then," Uncle Chuck said.

"Are you done in there? I was just . . . organizing, so I didn't hear," Eleanor yelled from the living room. Bless her.

Uncle Chuck scurried out the front door, and my mom and I stood there, watching him go.

"I stuck my neck out for you, so you better start talking," Mom said.

"Look, I will absolutely explain, but I need a minute."

"Should I be worried?" She looked at me—*really* looked at me.

"No." But what I meant to say was, *maybe*.

"You know, Sull, it's been amazing having you here. But I have to admit, I'm getting a little concerned, baby."

*Don't say it, don't say it.*

"About the future."

*Ugh. Et tu, Eleanor?*

"You always land on your feet, and though I might not know what direction you're heading, I hope it's a good one."

"I'd like to think so!"

"Do you have any ideas for, you know, what you might—"

"Eleanor, I just graduated high school. Let an enby sweetie get their shit sorted!"

She laughed and gave me a quick hug.

"I want the scoop on Brad, too!" she called as I headed down the stairs.

"That's on a need-to-know basis," I yelled back. "And you definitely do not need to know."

No sooner had Uncle Chuck left than my phone buzzed with a text from Guy:

We goin' to Mexico?

I smirked and wrote back:

Canada. But no. Your dad was actually . . . cool.

Guy texted:

Weird. Emma and I gonna help clean up Claire's basement. You coming?

This reminded me that I'd left Emma and Guy completely hanging, and that Claire probably needed all the help she could get, too. Between Brad and Rufus, I'd really dropped my friends faster than a Hot Pocket. If I was making a life for myself in Hearst, I'd need my friends. Regardless of how permanent or temporary that life might be. But needing was a two-way street, and now it was my turn to be there for them. Even though, yes, I totally wanted to unload all my recent love-life drama.

After I finished getting dressed, Rufus curled out of the Butler, translucent at first, then turning nearly solid. He still had on the jeans and T-shirt, but had ditched the leather jacket. He'd been so quiet since the night before that I'd begun to wonder if he had quit this realm for the afterlife after being hit with so many tough revelations. I wouldn't blame him.

It was good to know he was still here. Like the sweet relief of kicking off my heels after a long day. I'd missed him.

"Going somewhere?" he asked.

"Yes, I need to help my friends."

"You *have* been a big help."

"No, that's not what I mean. I want to help you, of course. And I haven't forgotten about it. But I've been neglecting some of the other people who've been there for me."

"I understand," he said, but Rufus seemed dejected, and I had to wonder if he'd heard my conversation with Brad about needing space. "You don't seem any better off for having found this cursed handbag or me."

"Don't say that."

"All this time you've been trying to help me, but I haven't done anything for you besides the promise of vacating this bag."

I felt instantly bad. Maybe it had started like that, but Rufus and I were the type of friends now that were chosen family. I didn't want him thinking I only cared because of a payout. And while I'd recently been a person of interest in a criminal investigation and that had cost me a romantic relationship, my problems had started before I'd discovered Rufus. "Come with me if you want! I understand if you don't, but I don't think we're getting rid of one another that easily."

Apparently, this was the right thing to say, as Rufus's face lit up. "Lead the way!"

# 24

The next thing I knew, I was walking up to Yesterday's Today with the Butler under my arm as if the last few days hadn't even happened. It almost felt like the basement party had been eight years ago.

Though I was feeling a bit more charitable about helping, I was still sorting through my feelings about Hearst. But community was community, especially the store. It'd be nice to feel a part of things again.

My replacement cashier wasn't around to give a perfunctory smile, so I patted Clementine— who had shed even more glitter from when I last saw her—and let myself downstairs. Claire wouldn't mind, especially since I was there to help. In fact, the ruckus coming from the basement was so loud that someone could come up here and rob the place and nobody would notice. Apparently, It was all hands on deck down there.

I might not have been able to solve Rufus's mystery or fix my own life—*yet*—but this clean-up was something I could do.

Emma and Guy had beaten me to it and were already taking a water break. Claire was crushing a soda can, as per ushe. Then I caught sight of Brad and immediately froze, gripping the banister like Kate on that broken *Titanic* door. Brad, who'd made me feel like I had gotten *everything* wrong. Brad, who'd driven off in Olivia Newton-John earlier this morning, claiming he needed space. Well, what if *I* needed space, Brad? What if I had been busy keeping his name out of the tabloids all afternoon and defending him to the police?

Okay, that might've been a little dramatic, but I was honestly shook to see him. I hadn't dressed to impress, either, with Garfield peeking out from under my caftan.

"Make him yours or make him sorry he's not," I heard Rufus hiss from the handbag.

I plastered a smile on my face as Brad marched up to me as though nothing had turned awkward.

"Am I stalking you, or are you stalking me?" I asked, laughing, but really, his answer to this question could determine the entire course of our future relationship, if there was one, so no pressure or anything.

"I'm here to help Claire."

"Great. So am I," I said a little defiantly.

He shrugged. "Great."

I fought the urge to seal our mutual, helpful presence in this basement with a businesslike handshake. A girl could work alongside her crush. Not a problem. Totally not weird.

"I can't believe you're here, Brad," Emma said, coming up to both of us.

Where was she going with this? I'd just made it unawkward-ish, and I hoped she wasn't about to set us all back.

"What do you mean?" I asked, low-key scouting for information.

That's when I noticed Brad blushing, which was beyond cute. The Butler puffed up, like my own moral support purse.

"Brad?" I asked. "So you *are* stalking me?"

"Brad has become a little local historian," Claire said, giving him a weird look. "He showed up, asking questions about the building and former tenants. Oh, and something about a signet ink pen that I didn't follow at all."

Say *what*? Had Brad gotten on board with our mission after all? Or was he just preparing for his Eleanor internship?

"Well, well, well, looks like you've been doing some *Scooby-Doo*-ing of your own," I pried once Emma and Claire had buzzed away to yell instructions at a few volunteers. "I thought you were done with that."

Okay, maybe I'd been a little harsh, because Brad winced.

"I panicked last night," he said. "Or this morning, I mean. But when I got home, I couldn't stop my brain from spinning. About Rufus. But about us, too."

I could tell he was being honest. Though he'd hurt me, at least he recognized it.

"I don't want a break. I just didn't know how to deal with everything feeling so intense."

He glanced over his shoulder. Guy was tearing down drywall, wearing a completely ridiculous American flag shirt with the sleeves ripped off, and cutoff jorts.

"You go, babe!" Emma yelled.

*Babe?* We definitely had to talk.

Brad's expression became sheepishly adorable as he turned back to me. "I couldn't sleep, thinking about everything."

*Everything* could be referring to *anything*. Did he mean the kiss? Rufus's mystery? All of the above? Could he possibly itemize and prioritize that list? I waited to see if he'd elaborate.

"Are you here to chat or to work?" Emma said, coming up behind me and scattering the tension immediately. "Because we need to take this wall down. Masks?" She thrust respirators in both our hands, giving me a serious look that shamed me into participating. The wonderful news, of course, was that Brad was back on Team Haunted Handbag, as far as I could tell. He was into this. Together, we'd unravel the mystery of Rufus, and then get to work on nailing down whatever it was we had going on.

*He was into me. He'd been thinking about us. That's what he had to mean, right?*

I hid my blossoming grin behind a mask.

In a beat, Brad had figured out his mask and was making for the wall. Emma hung back to help me adjust mine, because of course I needed help.

But for the first time in, like, our entire lives, there was an awkward pause between Emma and me.

"I think I owe you an apology," I said. "Actually, I know I do."

"Oh?" She kept her eyes on the tangle she was working to unknot. She definitely wasn't going to do *this* part for me.

"I don't want you to think that just because I've wanted to bail on Hearst, I want to bail on you. Or us."

"And yet . . ." My best friend of all time handed me back my respirator and gave me the same knowing look she'd given me the day we'd met in first grade and I'd tried to smuggle a handful of malt balls into Mrs. Fischer's class in my mouth.

"And yet I've totally been off in my own world when you needed me. You're full-time now, you and Guy are official, and these are the big life things I want to be there for. I don't want to miss out on being your friend, no matter where I am. And I'm sorry."

Emma looked like I'd just grown a second head. She blinked, then looked up at the ceiling and blinked a few dozen more times.

"Are those tears?" I asked.

"Damn it, Sully."

"Does that mean I'm forgiven?"

"Damn it, Sullivan!" she shouted and hammered my chest with her fists. In the next second we were laughing and she was scooping me into one of her legendary hugs.

"I'm going to try to be less self-involved from now on," I said.

"And not blame haunted handbags when you can't talk about your feelings?"

"What? Oh!" How had I forgotten I'd tried to tell Emma about Rufus? "Oh, right. Ha! Well at least my excuses are entertaining."

"Are they, though?"

"Shut up."

Guy came up to us, looking expectant, and Emma slipped her arm around his waist as if they'd been doing it for years.

"So this is new. Or old?" I asked. "I'm guessing this isn't like the other thousand times you guys have casually hooked up."

Emma beamed up at Guy like she hadn't just been freaking out about him two seconds ago. "No, it's different this time."

"We're making it official," said Guy. "Like an actual post–high school, uh, relationship."

Emma let out a long breath as if this last word were the most terrifying thing either of them had ever said, but her eyes were all smize. Then it hit me, why this was a big deal, and not just in the oh-my-hook-up-drama! kind of way, why she'd been freaked when we talked the other night. We were making life choices now, choices that mattered and set you on a course. Like saying *I love you* or *Will you move in with me?* or *How many cats can we fit in this studio apartment?*

Whether I left Hearst or not, things were changing.

I pulled them in for a hug, and it felt so good to know that, no matter what, I had them both in my corner.

"Now," I said, "my only question is, obviously, why Guy is dressed like someone who lost their way at a Trump rally."

He grunted. "Hey! These are my work clothes!"

"And you are *working* them." I smiled, and I could tell from the crinkles around his eyes that Guy was smiling back at me under his mask.

"Okay, kids, let's stand back a bit. The rest of that wall is coming down!" Claire shouted.

But I noticed a look of concern on Claire's face and sidled over to her.

"You okay?" I asked. "It's only a wall, and bringing it down will give you more space down here."

"It's not about the wall. Beauregard Hearst has some new documentation and filed paperwork that would force me to find a new home for Yesterday's Today."

"He can't do that!" I exclaimed. "Can he?"

"I'm talking to Saul later and Eleanor will call a community meeting, of course."

"Saul?" I asked. "As in Bunyan?"

But before I could press Claire for more salacious details, Guy trotted into position, and, at his urging, together, we all counted down from three.

Muscles straining, Guy, Ron, and Brad all pulled, and the wall disintegrated with a crash, sending up a plume of drywall dust and regular old building dust. *Oh, no! The Butler!* Getting dirty was *not* good for her resale value, which I was conflicted about but couldn't abandon completely, so I lunged for a nearby plastic bag and threw it over the goods. Priorities, obviously, especially since it was still Rufus's home. Besides, it was cute. Like a little purse poncho. All this smashing was getting me excited to bring Rufus out and talk about everything . . . after this crowd left, of course. My eyes burned, and I was glad Emma had insisted on the masks, but soon the cloud settled.

"Woo! Guy!" Emma hooted, clapping.

"It's not celebration time yet, kids," Claire said, handing Brad the largest sledgehammer I had ever seen, and I'd been in Dad's workshop. "Let's start clearing this junk out, and then we can party."

"Mr. Speaker disagrees!" said Guy, pulling his ancient Bluetooth speaker out of his backpack. I hadn't seen Mr. Speaker since . . . well, high school. Which didn't sound all that impressive since high school had only ended a few weeks ago.

There was immediate chaos as everyone scrambled to pair their phone first. Being the only one not wearing work gloves gave me an edge, though.

"Sorry, babies, I win!" I said and started blasting my most

energizing morning shower playlist. First up, "I Wanna Dance with Somebody," obviously.

As soon as the song started, Rufus seemed to shimmy in the Butler. So he was a Whitney fan. I'd have to remember that.

"Okay, I can break rocks to this," Guy said, hefting his own sledgehammer.

I had never thought clearing out a thoroughly wrecked basement could be fun, but before I knew it, we were all letting our rage and energy out. The boys smashed what was left of Claire's wall, with Guy trying to look sexy and Brad . . . not even needing to try.

Brad went to take another swing, but he caught me staring. *Damn.*

"You want to try?" He offered me the handle of the sledgehammer.

"You're kidding."

"Come on, I'll show you."

Next thing I knew, I was standing with Brad six inches behind me, demonstrating how to hold a sledgehammer and positioning my hands. This was not how I'd expected today to go.

"Please don't hurt yourselves," said Emma nervously.

"Shut up." I grinned, amazed by how heavy the hammer was.

"Okay," said Brad, hands on my hips. "Now just make sure you swing from here."

"Stop distracting me!"

Silence fell over the room. I got the feeling everyone was watching me as I tried to stop blushing, charm Brad, balance the Butler, and look effortless, all at the same time. Brad's hot-cold-hot affection was giving me some whiplash, but I could work with it.

"The wall's right there," said Brad, pointing.

"I can see the wall!" I nearly fell over laughing, but I refused to let him sidetrack me. I raised the big stupid hammer over my head and swung, missing the chunk of drywall by about a foot and burying the sledge in the neighboring wall.

The one that wasn't supposed to come down. The good wall.

"Oh shit," I said, letting go of the murder weapon. The entire head of the sledge disappeared, and it clattered with a dull metal thud somewhere on the other side. "Oh shit, oh shit."

"That's the wrong wall!" Claire shouted, rushing over to the scene of the crime. "Damn it, we're not trying to do *new* damage, Sully."

Brad and I slunk backward to give her some room.

But her tirade, which I totally deserved, dried up the moment she examined the damage.

"What's with this hole?" she asked.

"'Cause Sully—" Guy started, but Emma shushed him.

"No, I saw what happened"—and here Claire shot me a look—"but why did it go *through*? There's not supposed to be anything behind this wall but dirt and bedrock." Claire looked at Brad, then at me. "Guys, I think there's another room back here."

"Hold up," I said. "So I'm *not* in trouble?"

*August 5, 1955*

*My swan, Rufus,*

*After I convinced a court teller who's light in the loafers like us to help me, I discovered you'd been taken in for "disorderly conduct" and "open lewdness." But you weren't booked, which hit us as odd.*

*I know you won't be pleased, but without knowing what else to do, I went back to Hearst. We have sympathizers there, more than we ever knew. They told me to speak to your father. You can imagine how that went. After he strongly suggested I hit the asphalt, your mother caught me before I left to fill me in about the deal he struck—or, rather, paid for—to keep you out of legal trouble and instead have you committed at Knollwood. Strangely, he seems to believe not having you convicted was the compassionate option.*

*The staff at the hospital have turned me away numerous times. They won't even confirm if you are being "treated" there. I have no legal recourse. I am pressing your mother and working in the shadows with people in Hearst to have you released.*

*I can't imagine how alone you must feel. How scared. I regret our fight so much and would do anything to undo it all.*

# 25

Not only did we take down both already damaged walls, but before you could say HGTV, the four of us had smashed a hole into a third wall at Yesterday's Today. It was giving design makeover on a budget and, yes, I made sure to stay away from any and all sledgehammers.

"It's dark in here," Guy said, sticking his head into the hole once some of the dust had cleared.

I quickly swallowed any jokes about big holes, because this was very serious.

Claire went upstairs to find flashlights, and by the time she returned, we'd opened a crack large enough for a person to slip through. I once again held my jokes.

Since I began investigating across the decades, everything was starting to feel a little surreal, but I wanted to know what was back there.

"Let me see," I said, taking one of the flashlights from Claire.

"Wait, you're just going in?" said Brad. He peered into the dark as though it contained an entire ancient army of spiders, which it probably did.

But after Knollwood, I liked to think that my ick tolerance had risen a few notches.

"Be careful," Claire hissed, and gave me a pointed look.

"Don't you want to see what's back there?" I asked. "It could be anything!"

"Probably asbestos," said Emma.

"Whatever it is," I said, "it's our history. Right?"

Brad smiled. "Yeah. Right."

"Then step aside!" I said, sweeping the Butler in a wide arc, its poncho crinkling. "I'm going in."

It took me about five hot seconds to regret that decision. As it turned out, mysterious hidden rooms in thrift-store basements were dark, dank, and extremely dusty. My eyes almost sealed shut with all the drywall flurries flying around.

The flashlight's beam only lit up a few inches ahead and caught the swirling motes in bright flashes, keeping my eyes from adjusting. My imagination filled with images of sewer alligators and mole people and . . . *get a grip, Sully.*

I squeezed the Butler to my ribs and pressed forward. Rufus was oddly quiet. For a second, I thought about ducking into a corner and coaching him to stay calm so as not to risk a repeat of the Knollwood Freakout.

Obviously, I couldn't see much, but as the edges of the room failed to materialize in the gloom, I could tell the space was surprisingly big. The crunch of glass under my feet echoed in the stillness. It almost felt like everyone behind me—Emma, Gus, Claire, Brad—was holding their collective breath. I swept the light but could only see indistinct shapes and the occasional gleam of something metallic. I tried shining the beam down and it finally caught something useful.

"Hey, there's tile back here! Like on the floor!" I called. I wasn't sure what that meant, but it helped to notice something I recognized, or this whole place would be too otherworldly.

A moment later, another flashlight beam joined mine, and I heard Brad cough, muffled by his mask. "I really hope Emma was joking about the asbestos. Wow, is it me, or is this place huge?"

"It's at least twice the size of the basement. Like, it shouldn't be this big," I said. The main sales floor was about the same size as the part of the basement we could see, so that meant we had to be either in the next building's basement or this had been dug under the street somewhere.

"Are we under the parking lot?" Brad asked, looking at the ceiling as if it would tell him the answer.

That's when I looked up and noticed hammered tin, with ornate flower patterns stamped into it, glinting in the dim light.

"You guys looking around, or are you just making out?" Emma called from the other side of the wall, her voice echoing too loudly in the cavernous space.

"We can multitask!" I called back.

"Hold on," Claire grumbled, sounding distant. "I'm getting more flashlights."

Soon, the space started filling up with people, echoes, and light, the thick layer of dust on the ground getting churned up from all the footprints. We were leaving tracks on the tiles, which spread all the way to the walls. The mysterious dark lumps in the darkness turned out to be the backs of booths, decorated with glass gas lamps that looked like they must be a hundred years old.

Maybe because they were. I looked closer and while the fixtures seemed to be authentic in the beam of my phone's light, they had been retrofitted with modern electric bulbs.

"Was this a *restaurant*?" asked Guy.

A restaurant? No. Not underground. But a gathering space tucked away in secret? That sounded historically accurate. Then it hit me, with shocking clarity. "It was a speakeasy!" I shouted, my voice slapping off the walls. "Oh my god, how dare Hearst have the nerve to be this hip?"

It almost felt like the place *wanted* noise. Wanted music.

"A speakeasy?" Emma asked breathlessly.

"Don't you think? A secret spot underground with booths and—where's the bar?"

"I think I found it!" Brad called. He'd wandered over to the far wall, where a dark, curved shape shored up the space like a hug.

We followed his flashlight beam, taking in the full measure of this strange, subterranean enclave. Our lights picked up something big and gleaming, a long brass rail running the length of the basement, and beyond it . . .

Faces?

*More ghosts?* I didn't know if I could handle that.

I was about to scream when I recognized my own fierce self, staring back, distorted by dust and cobwebs. A mirror, maybe thirty feet across, loomed behind the entire bar, reflecting us back to ourselves. Behind us was a raised platform a lot like a stage.

"Holy shit!"

Hanging overhead was, of all things, a disco ball on a rotating mechanism. I wondered how to get it spinning.

"This is incredible," Emma whispered.

I could almost hear the wheels spinning in her head. By the end of the day, guaranteed, she was going to be scheming with Claire about reopening this place. After all, the pinnacle of Hearst nightlife was Denny's. So she'd have a point.

Eleanor and I could probably help with permits, but I was getting ahead of myself. It almost seemed like this place didn't want to be forced back into the spotlight. Not yet, at least. Not until we'd coaxed out its secrets.

I felt hairs standing on the back of my neck. It wasn't just the surprise of finding this place. It was something more. I liked the way it felt here. I liked the way *I* felt here. The booths were covered in burgundy leather, and the brass accents on a beautiful, curving mahogany bar, the old mirror that had stayed down here, unbroken, for who knows how many decades. Based on the mishmash of items, I'd guessed the place had seen a fair few decades itself. I'd probably spent years cluelessly walking around on top of this exact spot, trying on this or that from different eras, daydreaming of New York while ringing up purchases. And the entire time, *this* had been hiding down here.

No, not hiding. Waiting.

The Butler seemed to give a jolt. For a second, I felt a deep flash of fear. I knew now that Rufus could appear to people. We'd found that out in no uncertain terms at Knollwood. Would he blast out of the bag here, in front of everyone? Spooking random influencers was one thing, but showing Rufus to everyone I knew? On the one hand, I almost wished it'd happen, because I was tired of carrying around all these secrets. On the other, letting Brad into the whole improbable mess had been hard, and I'd almost lost him. Still, I didn't know how much longer I could stay strong and keep all this to myself before something had to give. Maybe Rufus was about to make the choice for me.

"Holy hell, look at these!" Claire squealed, beaming her light over the walls, which, as it turned out, were hung with photographs in frames ranging from the gilded kind like the remnants we'd pulled out of Gratton Farms to more contemporary, thin, plastic ones.

There was so much to explore, I couldn't handle it.

This wouldn't be my first time looking at old documents and ephemera, so I traipsed over to check it out.

Aiming my own flashlight at the walls, I found in black-and-white photographs that looked like they were from the 1920s and '30s, maybe even a little earlier, taken right here in this space. First, I checked out everyone's amazing flapper costumes—well, I guess they weren't costumes, if these were really from the early twentieth century. The clothing styles jumped dramatically forward. I guessed that the speakeasy had closed during wartimes. When it resumed, the people within in the photographs were as varied as the frames, coming from different backgrounds. The '50s styles morphed and gave way to the '60s before there were no more photos. This bar was a time capsule perfectly preserved.

I looked to Brad. "But how?"

He shook his head and shrugged. "We're not the first queer people from around here," he stated simply. "Some historians have said Pennsylvania has always had liberal leanings and credited the

Quakers for their live-and-let-live belief system."

"The oatmeal people?" Guy asked. "We have more to thank them for than awesome cookies?"

Emma patted his arm. "We'll talk more about this later."

Brad stood so close to me we were almost touching as we both studied the photographs again. Then I noticed something that seemed to completely contradict everything I knew about Hearst.

The women were leaning into other women. Men were holding hands, looking flushed and happy and . . . free. There were performers in drag, people sitting on one another's laps, dancing together, mugging for the camera. Two women kissed in a booth, limbs carelessly entwined, as if nobody was watching.

As if nobody cared.

It dawned on me slowly, but as surely as I knew anything, as surely as I knew that Rufus was real . . .

This was a *queer* speakeasy.

Right in the heart of Hearst.

I'd developed a connection to Rufus, I'd promised to help him uncover the mystery of his life and death, and now that thread of intuition seemed to have led us to this. A living, breathing haven right under our feet.

# 26

Before I had a chance to completely study these new-to-me-but-nonetheless-iconic hometown legends, Brad called out from the far wall, under the mirror.

"Guys!"

Guy spun around. "Yes?"

"No, I mean everyone," Brad said, laughing. "You too, Guy."

We all crowded into the narrow space behind the bar, but it was incredibly hard to focus because everything in view was so ornate and beautiful. From the crystal glasses wreathed in dust to the old-timey cash register to the tincture bottles and old-fashioned liquor bottles that were likely filled with colored water and kept for the aesthetic. Although I expected to find more modern glassware and alcohol bottles under the counter when I peeked, there was not a single bottle of Mango-Gasm or can of White Claw on display here, folx.

But that's not what Brad wanted us to see. Or wanted *me* to see.

Brad shone his flashlight on a photograph mounted on the wall, next to the mirror.

With a jolt, I realized the building looked familiar. Sort of like Yesterday's Today but maybe with a different facade? I squinted in the low light. The numbers 728 were painted on the transom window above the door. So this *was* the same building.

Then I noticed something else. Or, well, someone. A man with kind eyes and an infectious smile peered coyly out of the shadows of the doorway from under a fedora.

"That's this building!" I said, glancing at Brad.

"Right. But that's not all," he said, his green eyes bright with excitement.

He angled his flashlight beam above the mirror, and inlaid with gold leaf in the frame, aged but undeniable, was one word: *Robby's*. Two gold leaf swans, their necks curved to create a heart, followed the singular word.

"Robby's," I whispered, and it almost felt like the Butler warmed a bit beneath my arm, humming with its own heartbeat. I had the fleeting urge to keep the bag in its poncho but—resale values be damned—including Rufus in this moment was just too important. It really felt like we were about to learn what happened in the Rufus saga.

"I think we found him," Brad breathed. The Butler shifted and Brad patted it to settle Rufus.

"Him?" I asked, the Butler radiating such a warmth I am sure Brad must have felt it.

The Butler almost pushed off my side to jump into Brad's arms as if to urge him on.

"Rufus's . . . *you know*," Brad whispered, widening his eyes."

"What are you two whispering about?" Emma asked.

I quickly changed the subject. "Robby's . . . speakeasy. Holy shit."

"What's this?" Guy asked, pulling a metal box out from beneath the cash register. It looked like the kind of steel cash box they had at school bake sales. "And there's a safe down here too but I couldn't find a key."

I took the box. "Let me at it, by the power vested in me by Eleanor," I said. Part of me knew we'd have to share this place soon. But not with a wide-eyed crowd of Hearst citizens coming in for craft cocktails. First, we'd have to throw on the lights and let the city inspect it. And there would be some in the city who wouldn't be thrilled with what we'd found. Who wouldn't appreciate seeing all those adorable queer couples making out in the pictures. Who wouldn't know about Robby or Rufus and wouldn't like them very much once they heard their story.

I'd just discovered this place, and already I felt protective of it. Like I didn't want anyone else in here, poking around. Like it should stay the haven that it was obviously meant to be. I shuddered at the thought of Beauregard and his cronies running their greasy hands over the photographs and tainting everything Robby had built.

The box lid opened with the creak of rusty metal. I was hoping for some ancient money, I'm not going to lie. But inside was something much more valuable. Something that could potentially help us protect this place and keep it in the rightful hands of the owner.

First, a business certificate made out in the name of Robert Feldman.

My entire body thrummed. This was perfect. Exactly what we needed. Guy had no idea what he'd just helped us find. Was this about to be *too* easy? After Knollwood, I was grateful that this particular adventure wasn't going to end with cop cars and running through a field in platform wedges. Fingers crossed, at least.

Brad lifted out a stack of pamphlets. I recognized them as being identical to the one I'd found hidden with Rufus's family tree and the photograph of Knollwood, *If you are arrested* . . .

Despite the somberness of the pamphlets, the piece of paper beneath them sent my hopes soaring to the point that I lost my breath. It looked like the deed to the building. The address was correct. The letterhead belonged to the city of Hearst.

"Wait," I said, to myself, but also to the room. I almost didn't care who saw this stuff anymore or who wondered what I was doing. I needed as much help as I could get to figure this out. I pinched my flashlight between my cheek and shoulder, just so I could have my hands free to handle the thin, flaking pieces of paper and read what they said. Phyllis from the records hall would be so proud of my respectful handling of these old documents. Brad and Emma gathered around.

But then my hopes came crashing down. "What the hell?"

The name on the deed was . . . Cygnus Cobpen?

*What?*

Details of my dinner with Eleanor came flooding back. Cygnus Cobpen was somehow connected to the missing landowner of Hearst.

"Look at this, Brad," I said, angling the paper toward him. "Cygnus Cobpen!"

"Actually, I think you said Walrus Trash Can."

"You need to get your ears checked, Brad!" I playfully swatted his shoulder. Then the ramifications of our discovery hit me right in the solar plexus. "Holy shit, did Hearst's long-lost heir own a *gay bar*?"

"What in the hell are you two talking about?" Claire demanded. "Can someone explain?"

Here Brad and I were, murmuring like conspiracy theorists, and I realized that everyone else was about ten steps behind. "Did anyone see the recent story in the *Bugle* on who actually owns the land in Hearst?"

Everyone shrugged, even Claire. Unfortunately, Jack Spangle might've been right about our generation and the newspaper, but I certainly wasn't going to tell him. Brad took over and explained—thankfully leaving out the whole Rufus thing—while I dug back into the lockbox to see if there was anything else to find.

"I'll be right back," Brad murmured, almost to himself.

"We're sort of in the middle of a once-in-a-lifetime—"

But he had already disappeared in the gloom.

I couldn't believe what we'd uncovered, yet everything about this also somehow felt meant to be, as if we had just uncovered an amazing piece of Hearst's queer history, a badass queer-owned business, and the missing piece to Rufus's story. And here, staring me in the face, was a document proving that Cygnus Cobpen had, in fact, existed and owned this very building.

The only thing I couldn't piece together was how Robby fit into things. His name was on the business license, but not on the deed. Was Cygnus Cobpen an ally, or another fascist like Beauregard who sat on his butt and collected hard-earned rent payments?

I did know one person who could help, and who'd be all over this new historical record, but when I called Eleanor's cell phone, she didn't pick up.

Damn it, Councilwoman! It was usually so inspiring to know

that my mom was changing the world one city code at a time, but very inconvenient when I needed her. I delicately placed the piece of paper into the Butler, then pushed past Guy, Emma, and Claire and hauled myself up the basement stairs, feeling woozy.

"What were you doing down there?" Claire called after me.

But I didn't care. I looked for Brad among the few people gathering at the thrift store but came up empty. Where had he gone?

Next, I tried calling Mom's office, and Aaron, her secretary, picked up.

"Is my mother there?" I asked.

"Sully?"

As I threaded my way through the racks of Yesterday's Today, I couldn't help thinking of what lurked beneath my feet. It made me wonder what else I didn't know or see every day but took for granted.

"I really need to talk to her," I said, my lungs burning for some fresh air. Emma was probably right about the asbestos dust, and mesothelioma was *not* a good look.

"I'm afraid she's in the chamber."

"Can you have her call me? Maybe sneak her in a message," I said, bursting out into the dazzling early summer sunshine and heaving a grateful breath. "It's about the heir to the Hearst throne."

Aaron suddenly turned serious. "Are you joking?"

"Do I sound like I'm joking?"

I imagined Aaron marching down the hallway to the council chambers in his sensible loafers, grim with determination, waving my phone message around.

But then there was a disturbance on the other end of the line. I overheard some garbled speech and Aaron *rudely* hung up.

Ugh. My tax dollars at work, amirite? In the golden light of a balmy June afternoon, I dug the piece of paper out of the Butler and smoothed it out so I could read it more closely.

It was a deed all right, and though I was familiar with the hall of records and had seen my fair share of historical and legal municipal documents, I didn't really know what else I could glean from it.

Claire tapped me on the shoulder and I jumped. Go figure being around a ghost for a few weeks hadn't made me more shockproof. "What's that?"

I handed it over and she scanned it. "A deed?"

"*In*deed," I joked, but Claire just waved me off. Rude.

I really wanted to sneak Rufus out of the bag in the bathroom and give him all these new details. As I stepped back toward the building, Olivia Newton-John squealed into the parking lot of Yesterday's Today, spitting gravel.

*Brad?*

He emerged from the driver's seat, triumphantly hoisting his city hall badge. "Government privileges!"

"What?"

Then I saw a certain councilwoman in the passenger seat. "Eleanor?"

"Sully! Brad fetched me!" She left the door open in her excitement and came running out, looking flustered, her sensible pantsuit all off-kilter.

"Aww, Brad!" I said, cartoon stars and hearts practically beaming from my eyes. He'd interrupted a meeting to fetch us Eleanor. Aaron didn't even have the courage to do that. It'd be a frosty summer in Mom's office if Brad kept kicking ass and taking names like this.

"Sully . . ." Brad intoned.

"What?"

"Show her!"

"Oh!" I gingerly plucked the deed from Claire and presented it to Mom. "It's the deed to the Yesterday's Today building."

"Cygnus Cobpen," Eleanor read, finally stopping to catch her breath. "The missing heir." She shook her head frantically. "Sully, where did you get this?"

"Are you ready?" I asked.

"For what?"

I gripped her shoulders, preparing to drop this colossal bomb. "To know that Hearst had its very own secret queer speakeasy behind a false wall in the basement of this building?"

Eleanor looked at me as if I'd been getting into that ancient gin. "Come again?"

"I'm serious. Run by a guy named Robert Feldman. Cygnus Cobpen might've owned this building, but a queer man was running a full-on gay bar in the basement, and I think the long-lost heir must have known about it. There's a business license downstairs and—"

"Wait, wait, wait, how old is the space?"

"There are photographs easily from the 1920s in there, but it could be older." I squeezed the Butler to my body.

"Now, *this* I have to see."

October 3, 1955

*I am broken beyond repair. I was turned away from Knollwood a final time. They told me that you died from a TB outbreak. That it swept through that awful place. Yes, we were together for most of our lives, but I wanted an entire lifetime.*

*I asked to bury you. Your parents said they'd handle matters privately, it was a family affair, and informed me they are selling Gratton Farms to the Hearsts and leaving the state.*

*I will never forgive myself. I swear, I will find a way to keep you with me, to honor you, to make sure you are never forgotten.*

*My swan, my beautiful Rufus.*

# 27

Later that night, at home and alone in my room for what felt like the first time in weeks, I finally let my hair down, and the ghost out of the bag. I was buzzing. So much had happened today. After a tour of the surprise secret basement of Yesterday's Today, Eleanor had been buzzing too. "People need to know about this," she'd said, a wild look in her eye. Brad followed on her heels, documenting every pamphlet, photograph, nook, and cranny with his phone as they went. By the time we'd come back upstairs, she'd decided to call a press conference. Knocked out on my bed, I could hear her pacing above me, swapping calls with the local press and Hearst's comms director.

I'd never been prouder of my mom. We were standing up for people who had quite literally been driven underground, simply because of who they were and who they loved. They were vilified as though they were infiltrating society with their sick behavior. It's not so different from how people nowadays spout bullshit lies about how perverse trans people are, like we're some sort of invasive species. And they were supposed to respond how, by being thankful that they didn't get worse treatment, like legally sanctioned persecution, losing their jobs, being publicly outed, or condemned to prisons or psychiatric wards?

They'd never had a chance to be fully and truly themselves, but I did. With Eleanor's support, I could stand up for every other kid like me, growing up in places like Hearst and not feeling seen. My sinuses prickled, and I thought about Rufus—what it would've meant for him and Robby to be able to live openly. I didn't know if this life would ever be easy for me, but I certainly felt less alone now knowing about those who had come before me and found joy in unexpected places like Robby's. Or like Yesterday's Today.

Now, we just had to figure out how Robby and Cygnus Cobpen were connected. Worst-case scenario, Cygnus really was related to Beauregard, but I didn't trust this "new documentation" he had.

At least we knew for sure now that Robby had settled back in Hearst. That Hearst could, in her heyday, apparently throw one *hell* of a queer party. The pieces were falling into place.

"Can you believe it?" Rufus laughed. "You found him. My Robby."

"No. Yes. Oh my god. I'm sort of freaking out," I said. "There are still some missing pieces, but Rufus, we have answers. Real answers!"

A few weeks ago, I couldn't wait to get out of here and jet-set with Lyndzi. If I'd left, though, none of this would've happened. I never would've met Rufus, or come to new and better terms with Guy, or, *ahem*, connected with Brad.

And now the very place I'd been trying to flee had a secret gay history.

We both sat there in silence for a moment, processing. I suddenly felt a real weight against my shoulder. Rufus had slumped toward me dressed in a pair of slacks and baggy sweater, silent tears running down his face. I wrapped my arm around him, pulling him in for a hug. Our first one.

Then Rufus quietly added, "I can't tell you how good it felt to *see* him again."

"Robby?"

"Of course, Rob. It's always been my Robby. But there are still so many gaps in the story. It's almost worse to know some of it, but not everything, because the questions become even more glaring."

I lay down in my beanbag chair and fiddled with all the pieces coming together in my mind. "Well, he clearly came back here from Pittsburgh."

"Oh, yes. He always retained the good memories from Hearst. How we met here. How we used to play together. The birth of Tallulah. The birth of our feelings for one another... There *was* still good here."

My throat went dry. I wished I could give Rufus a second chance at life. Bring him back to our modern time. Offer a do-over. "So as far as Robby knew, you were with him one day, you had a fight, and the next day—*poof*."

"Gone." Rufus nodded solemnly. "It must have been so confusing for him. He must have thought I'd hit the road. But I would never."

"I know," I said with a smirk. "I can't seem to get rid of you, no matter what I do!"

For a second, Rufus looked wounded, but then he cracked a grin. Did I sense a little bit of comedic timing there? "You are haunted, sis."

"Mary, I wouldn't have it any other way."

The smile dropped from Rufus's face and he shook his head. "I haven't been able to stop thinking about it, though. Rob looking for me, not being able to find me. Thinking I'd abandoned the life we'd built together, even if we had to keep it hidden."

"I don't think he would, though," I said, and meant it. "He must have known you weren't capable of that."

He shook his head, brow furrowed. "Our last fight, though, it was bad."

"Still."

"He told me that he wasn't sure he could live with . . . me. I was the impersonator, not him, and being together meant too much acting in public. He wanted to come home, here, to Hearst. And as much as he supported my dreams, he had his own to enter the political sphere and worried what being with me would mean to that. He was simply scared; I know that now. But at the time it felt like the most bitter rejection."

My heart sank. The simple thing would be to judge Robby for chickening out on Rufus the same way I had judged Brad for nearly the same concerns, but I couldn't even fathom what their lives had been like together back then. There was a *real* danger—especially for Rufus/Tallulah, but also Robby. "It was a different time," was all I could think of to say.

"You're telling me!" Rufus laughed. Then he turned serious. "I still don't remember how I ended up at Knollwood, though. Did Rob send me away? Maybe I *needed* to go away. Maybe I lost my humanity in that fight, and he couldn't handle me anymore. What did I do?"

"You know," I said, "when I first started seeing you, I thought *I* was going insane."

Rufus smirked, placing one hand behind his head and the other on his hip. "Because you'd never glimpsed such a beautiful specimen in your life?"

"Something like that." Now it was my turn to be serious. "But I don't think Robby sent you away. From what little I know about him, he wouldn't have done that."

Rufus nodded slowly, his eyes shining. "I believe you're right. He'd never abandon me. I was wrong to think he'd dumped me at that hellhole."

"Right. He couldn't have been *that* hurt, because he must have come looking for you. Why else would he have ended up in Hearst running a hidden gay bar?"

"Maybe he tried, but he didn't find me in time." Rufus shook his head. "All I can hope is that he figured it out at some point even if it hurt him that I was being kept here, so close and not beside him."

"He had to have known what was in your heart. Anyone who knows you can see how fabulous you are. And look at everything he built here!" Tears pricked at the corners of my eyes. "He came looking for you. He must have never given up. Robby invested in this place, he made it his legacy, your legacy, so that nobody would go through the same pain you two went through."

Rufus's eyes turned glassy again, as if he was holding back tears. "I don't think that's the point, though."

"What?"

"That nobody ever felt pain again. Pain is an inescapable part of being human."

"So says a *ghost*."

"I'm serious! We can't prevent pain from happening. But I do think we can use it. We can fuel ourselves with it. We can hold others up, no matter how much we hurt. That's what Robby did. He made a place where we could support one another and lift each other up." He paused to wipe his eyes. "At least we had our love."

"You're right. Yours ended tragically, but you got to experience it."

Rufus nodded. "He was always so proud of me, but now I'm so proud of him. Look at what he did, despite such adversity. He came back, and he stood up for people like us. He faced this town head-on when I wouldn't come back . . . couldn't come back. I can't help feeling like he did it, in part, for . . . me."

"I'm sure he did." I smiled. "Did you see the place? It screamed Tallulah."

How lucky Rufus was to have had Robby. And how lucky *I* was to have a friend like Rufus, and to be able to help him with his pain.

But Rufus had helped me, too. He had appeared—literally—in my life at a time when I'd felt purposeless and lost. Those worries still hadn't gone away, but now they came in and out like a tide. For so long I thought I could escape it all by leaving Hearst, but that theory didn't seem so certain anymore. And now, knowing that I wasn't alone—that other badass queers had come before me—had me thinking that maybe being here in Hearst for a while longer might not be so bad. Maybe I could bloom where I was planted. At least for a little while.

"But what about Cygnus Cobpen?" I wondered out loud. "Who was he?"

Rufus shook his head, drifting around the room. "That's the only part that doesn't make any sense. If he's indeed connected to that square, Beauregard, that would be the pits."

We were both silent for a moment before I said, "Okay, before we watch *Grease* and you meet my car's namesake in the role of Sandy, Robby and your couple name would be . . . Robus? Rufy?"

Rufus wrinkled his nose.

"Ruby!"

"Tallulah Ruby Bouvier Beale," he said slowly, tasting each syllable. "It's a touch long, but I can pull it off. Now what about you and Brad? Breadly is all I can come up with."

"Good thing we're not a couple because that is terrible."

"You're not yet. Come on, let me help you. Until the bag sells, we can't figure out what the rest of your life looks like, but surely we can figure out you two crazy kids. What's holding you back from really going for it?"

I wasn't sure how to answer. Maybe Brad and I were meant to never really get started. He was Hearst and I was New York. Or, I had been New York. Now I didn't know what I was.

A small sound shook me out of my thoughts, and Rufus froze, ready to vaporize again at a moment's notice. I looked around, only to see another rock hit the basement window with a *tap*.

"Hello?" I called, raising an eyebrow at Rufus.

Two boat shoes came into view, and Brad bent down to wave. A jolt of guilt flashed through me. Here we were, talking about Rufus's lost love, who he would never see again, and there was Brad in the flesh.

"Speak of the devil!" Rufus nearly cheered, whizzing around my head.

"Do you... mind?" I asked Rufus, swatting at him as I headed for the stairs.

"No, go enjoy yourself. You two have earned some alone time without your resident ghost *haunting* around." He winked. "Seriously, go. I could use a moment. I'm still catching my breath. Metaphorically. I'll just be down here, alone, puzzling over it all."

I didn't trust Rufus completely after that wink, but I wasn't about to keep Brad waiting longer than needed. I swept up the stairs, trying to play it cool, even as Eleanor shouted so loud that Phyllis could hear her all the way down at the records hall, "Oh, Sulllllly, your *friend* is here!"

"Okay, Eleanor, yep, got it, thanks a lot," I gritted out and practically leaped for the door, stopping Brad in his tracks.

"Hey, Sull—"

I shooed him in the other direction. "Let's take this party outside, shall we?"

"Well, hello to you, too!" Brad said, laughing as the door shut behind us.

"It's just very crowded in there, with parents and ghosts and stuff. I thought we could go somewhere a little more—"

"Private?" Brad gestured to good old Olivia Newton-John, a grin playing on his lips.

"Yeah, something like that." But I suddenly felt shy. Would Brad and I still have the same chemistry without our shared mission of solving the mystery of Rufus? What if he got to know me and found out that I was secretly an old lady who liked to spend their nights testing out face masks and watching best-of *Golden Girls* compilations on YouTube?

"So, pretty wild stuff, huh?" I hedged.

Brad raked his hand through his hair and glanced at me out of the corner of his eye. "Which part?"

"Well, I was thinking the handbag ghost and then the secret gay nightlife of Hearst. You?"

Brad opened the passenger door for me, and we got in the car, even though we had no destination planned. For the first time in a while, that felt nice. Like I wasn't running anywhere. Like I was happy right where I was, Great-Grandma Josephine–style, which I never thought I'd say about Hearst.

"Did you, um, want to talk about anything?" I was maybe still trying to fill the silence, though.

"I have a question for you."

"Oh . . . kay?" I squirmed in the passenger bucket seat. Was Brad about to ask me out, officially? Was I nervous? I didn't know why, but I felt oddly at peace, like I expected it, and like I knew exactly what my answer would be. "Any minute now, Brad. I'm at the edge of my seat. Your seat. Maybe even *our* seat, if we were to revisit our shared custody arrangement?"

He smiled and shook his head. "You're impossible."

"I know. That's why you like me," I said boldly.

"I do. That's why I have a question."

"Brad! Out with it!"

"Okay, okay. I . . . I like you, Sully. A lot."

It was actually happening. My chest heaved with anticipation. Stop the presses. I swallowed a shriek of delight.

"But . . ."

Say *what*? I gaped at him. "I'm sorry, but . . . *what*?"

"But I want to know if you're . . . staying."

"Oh."

"At least for the rest of the summer. *Because* I like you." Brad fidgeted with his keys, looking down in his lap. "You seemed so set on leaving that, well, if you're still on your way out, I want to know."

"Aren't you leaving?"

"We'd still have the summer," he said, then shyly added, "and Penn State isn't a long haul. Especially since I have a car now."

The hugeness of his question pinned me to the seat. The last time we'd sat here like this, I had been on my way out. My suitcase was packed, and I was set on moving to NYC and working for Lyndzi. That's when I thought that there was nothing for me in Hearst. Kissing Brad was just one final *fuck you* to my hometown. Now, though, not only was there some*one* for me in Hearst, there was also a whole community to explore, one I'd never dreamed of.

For the first time since I'd realized that other people weren't going to let me be myself that easily in Hearst, Pennsylvania, I could see staying here and fighting for it. Fighting for myself and my friends, but also for Hearst's queer past . . . and its future.

I'd seen, firsthand, how Rufus and Robby had suffered when they didn't get to live the way they were meant to. If I ran away now, I'd be giving up on something potentially special. With someone who saw me and *really* liked that person. It didn't have to happen somewhere else. If Robby and his joyful group of misfits could thrive in Hearst . . . maybe I could, too. My whole take on Hearst, and on what places—and people—could be, had changed. For the better.

"I am . . . staying. For now." I took a deep breath. "Claire told me she's thinking of hiring me back as she was locking up earlier. Maybe letting me do some vintage buying for her, and I get a parking space, even though I don't have a *car* anymore . . ."

"Darn," Brad said, and my heart stuttered in my chest.

"*What?*"

But he was grinning. "That means we're going to have to share custody of Olivia Newton-John after all."

"*Bread*, you flirt!"

"I was thinking Monday, Thursday, Friday . . . maybe every other week—"

I shut his dumb mouth up with a kiss, practically leaping across the console. Brad laughed into my mouth. He could be so damn cute. And I could be . . . happy.

Here.

"Or maybe we can just use the car together," I offered. "That back-seat bingo Rufus mentioned sounded kind of interesting."

After some very hot gymnastics moves to get into Brad's lap and maybe accidentally honking the horn with my butt once, I stared down at him, into his eyes. His smile made me feel dreamy as his breath warmed my neck.

"I like the sound of that. And . . . I'm glad you're staying," he admitted, his voice thick.

"Yeah. Me too." I leaned in for another kiss and—

"I Wanna Dance with Somebody" started blasting from the speakers and shaking the whole car, as if sent as a seal of approval by a poltergeist who'd discovered his electricity-manipulating powers along with the once-in-a-generation powerhouse vocal talent that is Whitney.

I buried my face in my hands. "Oh no!"

"What's going on?" Brad asked, jolting up and almost knocking me in the chin.

"I think Rufus approves."

Brad laughed, his forehead pressed to mine.

"Knock it off with the cheesy stuff!" I yelled. "If this is you trying to help, quit it!" I had no idea if Rufus could hear me though he apparently had a great sense of when Brad and I were getting hot and heavy. (AH! Hot and heavy! I had someone to get hot and heavy with!)

Brad reached to claw at the radio button—even though the car wasn't even on—when the song suddenly cut out.

"*Thank* you! That's better!" I called before turning my attention back to Brad. "Now, where were we?"

Olivia Newton-John jolted on again, this time blasting '70s funk that could have been straight out of a porn, the bass vibrating the seats.

"Rufus!" I shrieked. There was no winning with him.

Brad burst out laughing, and the moment was broken. He swatted at the volume dial, but the music only got louder, until the entire frame rattled.

"Turn it off!" I yelled, but the volume only cranked up.

Brad and I tumbled out of the car, but nothing we did turned the radio off. It was so loud that Eleanor came out of the front door, her hands over her ears. Neighbors peeked from their windows. It was a handlebar-mustache porn party on Allegheny Lane. Brad's face flamed red, but I didn't care. They could stare.

Rufus could have his fun. We'd all earned it.

"Turn that shit off!" Eleanor screamed, right as the song cut out. The echo of her swear word rang up and down the block.

"That's your councilwoman, ladies and gentlemen, looking out for you! Your next campaign platform should be noise violations!" I yelled, and sagged into Brad's arms, the two of us laughing our heads off.

# 28

When Councilwoman Eleanor Hartlow said she was holding a press conference, she wasn't kidding. If my mom knew how to do one thing well, it was make a statement. I like to think she got it from me. Brad, Emma, Claire, Guy, and I—wearing the Butler, of course, and a very profesh pantsuit, if I do say so myself—all gathered to be part of the historic announcement at Yesterday's Today, which she'd whipped together in less than twenty-four hours. We'd all pitched in, setting up the basement as our staging area. Claire had arranged three rows of folding chairs, just outside the massive hole in the wall that led through into Robby's. The press, as they started to arrive, could almost but not quite see past the makeshift stage to the hidden room beyond. Soon the little basement was cramped and noisy, the assembled reporters scraping chairs and sipping their coffees.

"Love that pantsuit," Eleanor mouthed when I joined her at the front.

"I love *your* pantsuit," I said, as if we hadn't just been touching up our makeup together in the break room upstairs.

Dad had told me the same thing when I left him in the audience. She gave me a smile. "I am so proud of you, Sully."

"Why? I'm not the one calling a press conference like a boss bitch."

"This press conference wouldn't even be happening if not for you, kiddo. You've given me a focus bigger than myself, and I can't wait to see what we can do together."

"Mooooom," I hissed, feeling a blush rise on my cheeks. "Are we having a moment?"

A camera shutter clicked and I smiled, proud to be standing beside her. Proud to be a part of this very important day. The press had shown up in droves, our local TV news affiliate and Karl from the *Hearst Bugle*, plus reporters from just about every city in the state. This was probably the biggest thing to happen to this town since we got a Krispy Kreme at the Speedway truck stop.

"How we doing?" I whispered into the Butler, working to look natural. There were cameras all over, but I hoped the earbud in my right ear might make people think I was taking a call instead of just plain old delusional.

"Ready for your mama to tell the world about Robby's," Rufus whispered. Rufus was dolled up in a sultry, red bodycon dress and looked amazeballs even if no one could see him. "And look good doing it."

A late arrival came stomping down the basement stairs. Despite my good mood, I'd been flinching every time someone new arrived. I was worried Beauregard Hearst was going to crash the party and hit us with some kind of gag order to keep Mom from telling the story of counterculture in Hearst.

Instead, Uncle Chuck appeared on the landing in full uniform. *Shit.* Whose side was he on in all this? He'd seemed to come down on the side of Team Sully during our last conversation, but with politics and city budgets involved, he probably had a tough choice in front of him.

"Don't worry," Guy said, leaning in to whisper in my ear. "Dad's here for extra security, just in case."

*Whew.* I grinned at Uncle Chuck, and he smiled back. Free speech, baby. And this was going to be one for the ages.

"Welcome, welcome, to this very special announcement on the hidden history of Hearst," Eleanor began.

I went to take my seat in the front row of folding chairs, but Eleanor motioned for me to stay. To stand beside her.

"In the 1920s during prohibition, this basement was a thriving speakeasy." Eleanor gestured broadly behind her. "That's right, we are learning that Hearst's history was far richer and more complex than we realized. And this incredible discovery is just the beginning. In a moment, we'll go inside and you can all see the space for yourself. But first, there's something else you should know," Mom said, like she knew she had everyone in her thrall. Of course they were! She was captivating to watch. "Robby's, as this speakeasy was called, was owned, along with the rest of the building, by none other than Cygnus Cobpen. Those of you who have been following Karl's coverage"—she nodded to the *Bugle* reporter in the front row—"Will recognize this name as the presumptive missing Hearst landowner, whose existence was hinted at in documents unearthed this month during the demolition of the Old Hearst Schoolhouse. Now, I'm excited to announce we have confirmed documentation that proves Cygnus Cobpen was indeed a previously unknown landowner in Hearst."

This was followed by several impressed gasps from the crowd, though at that moment my attention was on the growing commotion upstairs. As Mom had been talking, the sound of the front door opening with its familiar double-chime sent alarm bells echoing in my head. Footsteps thundered on the floorboards above us, and I got the feeling this wasn't a reporter running late.

Sure enough, Beauregard came clomping down the basement steps. His suit was rumpled like he'd slept in it, and his rat's-nest toupee was askew. He was holding several loose sheets of paper in one hand. He had the look of a guy about to object to a wedding—or have a massive coronary event.

I froze, gripping the Butler tightly. I really did not want Rufus bursting out, because a press conference could only take so many disturbances.

"Stop the presses!" Beauregard yelled, almost tipping over a metal folding chair and waving his clutch of paperwork around.

Mom started, "Beauregard, I'm sure you think you have a good reason for interrupting this press conference—"

"New evidence has come to light!"

"It sure has," Eleanor said, keeping command of the crowd, but I could tell she was nervous.

"That's not what I mean!" Beauregard marched up to the makeshift stage and physically hip-checked my mother to the side.

"Sir, I'm not sure that this interruption is appreciated," Uncle Chuck said, putting his hands on his hips, conspicuously close to his service weapon.

"I beg your pardon, Chu—Officer," Beauregard said, smoothing down his hairpiece. "Thank you to Eleanor, uh, the councilwoman, for her part in this discovery. When I heard we'd found property owned by Mr. Cobpen—"

"Who's *we*?" I put in. "And *when* did you learn that? We only found this place yesterday."

I figured Phyllis, Beauregard's administrative gal pal, had probably called him last night when Mom put in the comms request. Though why he was so excited I still couldn't guess.

"That's not important right now." He waved me off like a fly. "What *is* important is the probate records for 1985 to 1995"—he waved the papers in his fist—"Which clearly show that Mr. Cobpen is definitely, well *almost* certainly, *my* direct ancestor."

My stomach dropped down to my sensible flats. Was that true? Were the Hearsts and this Cygnus Cobpen hanging on the same family tree?

The assembled press seemed as confused as I was, but considerably more excited. Red recording lights on phones and cameras reminded me that this was all being logged for posterity.

"Well, Mr. Hearst," Eleanor said, trying to maintain some kind of professionalism, "your family's genealogy has been a favorite topic of yours for years now, and there's never been any mention of Cygnus Cobpen having ties to your family."

"Well, you may not understand this quite yet, as a *junior* councilwoman," Beauregard said, a smug smile stretched across his fleshy face, "but new findings come to light all the time. And this is a prime example." He gestured to the building around us. "Our history is still very much alive."

"Unlike that dead stuffed chipmunk on his head," Rufus whispered just loud enough for me to hear—and I burst out laughing.

"What's so funny, mister?" Beauregard snapped.

"Actually, Beauregard, I use 'they/them' pro—"

"This has nothing to do with you," he shot back. "Or any of *that*."

Eleanor's eyes narrowed, and I saw her cheeks go tomato red. This wasn't good. The last thing any of us needed was my normally even-keeled mother going ape on Beauregard with the cameras rolling—although I knew she'd hand him his ass in the most educated and articulate way possible, I couldn't let Beauregard steer today away from what was important.

"That's where you're wrong. It has *everything* to do with *that*," I said, squeezing the Butler to my side. Mom gave me a look like *Sully, what are you doing?* I winked back. "So if we have this *straight*," I said to Beauregard. "You are claiming that Cygnus Cobpen is your ancestor. Correct?"

At this, Beauregard drew himself up taller, puffing his barrel chest out. He grinned at the reporters like he was posing for his front-page photo. "That's right."

"And he owned this building, and was associated with any businesses in it."

"Correct again."

"Well, what are we waiting for?" I said. "Let's see the place!"

With that I turned on my heel and shoved aside the tarp we'd hung as a makeshift curtain.

The room behind me filled with gasps as the crowd got their first look at Robby's. Soon chairs were pushed back as everyone clamored to squeeze through the small opening into the speakeasy on the other side.

"This is . . . *extraordinary*," Beauregard said, with the same fake reverent hush he used on the campaign trail. "What an important historical moment for Hearst."

"It sure is!" I piped in.

"Robby's?" he read from the mirror above the bar. "My word. You know, I had an Uncle Robert. He married my father's sister, Maude. They left Hearst in the early '70s to pursue political careers at the state level. I wonder if he was involved with this *wonderful* discovery for my family? And the town, of course. This is exactly the sort of thing I campaigned for, Hearst traditional family values. Uncle Robert and Auntie Maude would be so proud."

"So proud," Eleanor sweetly echoed, a smile of understanding starting to spread across her lips.

A photographer began snapping shots of the frames above the bar. I pointed to where he'd directed his lens. "Well, then I think you'll *love* these framed family photos."

Beauregard practically floated over to the far wall. I followed him. I really wanted to be front and center for this moment. To show him those gorgeous pictures, and to see his dumb face, which he was now sticking in front of each photograph.

A beat, then two, and then he reared back, like he'd been slapped.

"What . . . what *is* this?"

"What's the matter?" I asked. "This is Uncle Robby's! Right? Isn't that what you were just saying? Don't you recognize it?" Then I pointed to the two men dancing in one of the older photographs. "Maybe this was your great-great-cousin? And his *husband*? I mean, I guess technically it was probably just his boyfriend, given the time period. What do you think?"

Beauregard backed away, shaking his head furiously. "This must be some elaborate prank."

Guy was grinning, and Brad looked at me with—if I was going to put words to it—absolute wonder. Even the Butler seemed to relax on my shoulder. I had the trust of everyone in that room, past and present. The crowd that had shown up to Yesterday's Today gathered in around us, pulling together. There had been a podium set up for the official press conference, but it seemed we were starting off the cuff.

"It's not a prank, Beauregard," Eleanor said, marching up to him, holding the deed. "You say you're related to Cygnus Cobpen?"

"Yes?" But all of Beauregard's machismo from earlier was gone.

"Well, that name is inexorably connected to Robby's, the queer speakeasy you are standing inside at this very moment." Eleanor took an embossed and antique-looking deed of sale from her sleek black folder and thrust it in his face (but I noticed she was very careful not to let him grab it).

"The . . . the *what* speakeasy?" he said, scanning the deed.

"If you want to claim Robby's . . . if you want to claim Cygnus Cobpen, Beauregard"—I liked calling him by his first name, like we were golf buddies, and more importantly, equals—"Then you have to claim *this*, too. All of it."

He shook his head at the deed, the pictures, everything.

"You know," I said, "Hearst's *traditional* family values you always went on about are pretty much in line with progress. And you're all about progress. It looks like your family has been progressive for a long, long time."

"This has to be a forgery. I refuse to believe it," Beauregard said, looking around like he was Scrooge, rejecting what the Ghost of Christmas Future was showing him. And in a sense, that's what we were: the future. But we were the past, too, and we now had the undeniable evidence to prove it and link the two together.

"If you'd let me finish my speech," Mom was saying, "I was about to share how it looks like Robby's was a hub of a queer community in the 1950s and 1960s. That's right," she said into Karl's waiting microphone. "Hearst had a lively underground scene where people of all gender and sexual identities and expression could come together and escape the social strictures of the day. More than a hub, a haven, really. With the proper documentation, the name *Hearst* will be synonymous with queer rights and activism."

A few people gasped, and I thought I even caught someone literally clutching their pearls. But I had to look past that, to all the people who seemed excited and genuinely happy about the news—and not just my friends, either, but the majority of faces in the audience that nodded along to the announcement.

"This is a sick joke," Beauregard muttered, backing out of the room. "It has to be."

"You'll have to ask your family, I guess," I said, shrugging innocently.

Beauregard went apoplectic, spluttering and turning red in the face. The vibes of the entire place seemed to change, from a beautiful, supportive refuge to something hostile. It was as if the entire basement wanted him *out*. And I couldn't have agreed more.

Instead of providing an answer, Beauregard, that drama queen, straightened and tried to retain what was left of his dignity. "This is clearly an ongoing development, therefore and hitherto—"

I caught Mom rolling her eyes in my peripheral vision.

"We should all vacate this property before anyone gets the unsubstantiated idea that any *relative of mine* was a part of this . . . *lifestyle*." Beauregard gestured with disgust at Robby's, which glowed in the shadows. "The good Hearst name does not deserve this sullying—"

"Excuse me!" I said, mock-offended, but also maybe truly offended. "'Sullying' is a compliment, thank you."

The joke got a solid laugh, and once that was done, I could worry again. After everything, we were somehow further than ever from figuring out who Robby's belonged to, who the mysterious founder was, just what the hell happened back then. Despite how far we'd come, we still might never know how Rufus was truly connected to everything.

Beauregard waved me off. "This deed is clearly a hoax and this councilwoman is attempting to defame the character of our good town of Hearst, not to mention my family's name and reputation! I will take you to task for defamation. Besides, Uncle Robert was a *Feldman*. Who even knows who this Cygnus Cobpen is?"

"Didn't you just say that new evidence had come to light and Cygnus Cobpen is a relative of yours?" Brad shouted.

"The only *Hearst* relation beyond a doubt is Maude and I can guarantee that my aunt, who ran every church bake sale and attended every Founders' Day parade my entire childhood, certainly had no idea about the sort of debauchery that was going on down here."

Eleanor's face fell, though it was too subtle for anyone but me to notice. For the first time since I'd found the Butler, I worried that all this had been for nothing, and this wasn't actually Hearst's big gay glow-up, after all. Every single sign pointed to our version of history, with Robby at the center, but all we had was some dusty paperwork to back up our case and the original records were probably lost. If Robby's was meaningless and Yesterday's Today wasn't about to be saved from Beau and flooded with tourists, did I not have my job back anymore? And what about Brad?

Seriously, what about Brad? He whipped his phone out, tapping and scrolling wildly. He moved his thumb and pointer finger apart on the screen, the signature motion to enlarge whatever was on it.

Brad stood and approached Beauregard, his phone held out. "Is this your auntie Maude?" he asked, nearly shoving the device in Beau's face. "At the Founders' Day parade in the '50s?"

Beauregard adjusted his glasses and stared. "Yes. See. A good woman with good *family* values."

"And might I be so bold as to suggest that the child on her knee is you?"

Beau squinted. "Yes. She always took me to the parade."

Brad swiped and did the thumb and pointer finger thing again. "And this is your aunt again?"

Beauregard adjusted his glasses and nodded. "I'd know her anywhere."

"Then she must have known all about Robby's," Brad said, pinching his screen.

"I can't see how."

"That image was zoomed in but the original is on the wall behind us. It shows the woman you confirmed as your auntie Maude sitting on the lap of another woman in the exact speakeasy behind us."

"That can't be!"

"It can, especially when queer people who were forced only to exist as they were in private spaces like Robby's got married to people of the opposite sex for public appearance. Ever hear about the cufflink crowd? Marrying a gay man would have worked for Auntie Maude to hide the fact that she was taking a deep weekend dive into—"

"Brad!" Eleanor and I exclaimed together, her from shock and me from delight.

Brad went red.

A speakeasy. A sham marriage. A potential lesbian aunt. This was getting into juicy daytime soap opera territory.

"It doesn't matter," Beauregard said smugly. "Cygnus Cobpen can't be my relative if no one can prove evidence of his existence. That makes me the sole heir and sole claim holder on this property. That also means that I, and I alone, can make unilateral decisions on the future of my land. You may be able to issue an injunction to stop me from bulldozing this place, but you can't force me to let it become some kind of . . . of . . . of whatever. Once I get possession, I can kick that thrifting weirdo and her lot out, lock the doors, and throw away the key. No one will ever see this place again. I can pave it over even if I can't destroy it."

"You can't do that!" Claire said from the audience, Saul Bunyan at her side shooting daggers at Beau.

"You can't go paving queer paradise and putting up a parking lot," I added.

"Ooh, bop-bop-bop-bop," Brad added, and if this wasn't a serious moment, I'd have been all over him.

"Can't I? I know the laws and bylaws inside and out."

From the small street-level windows in the basement, we watched as another car screeched into the parking lot at a sharp angle, and I was about to ask for a Victorian fainting couch because it was all getting to be too much.

"Oh, for fuck's sake, we're trying to have a press conference here!" Claire yelled over the crowd. We were maybe one more revelation away from a riot.

"What's happening now?" Rufus whispered.

"I have *no* idea."

"Beau, that is *enough!*" hollered . . . Phyllis from the records hall?

Beauregard slumped, looking like he'd been dragged to the principal's office. And maybe he had.

"Phyllis," Eleanor said, nodding her head in deference. "To what do we owe the pleasure?"

"I'll tell you exactly to what," Phyllis said, marching up to the podium and clutching her own manila folder, "but I'm not sure it's going to be a pleasure. Especially for Beauregard Hearst, here."

"What is *happening*?" Emma mouthed to me.

I shook my head. "I have no idea."

"Beau, I will have you know that I am, first and foremost, a civil servant," Phyllis began.

"Woo!" Mom chimed in.

"Phyllis, I'm sure we can discuss this somewhere a bit more pri—"

"No. I am done listening to you."

I leaned forward. Why did it feel like we were witnessing some kind of lovers' spat?

Phyllis stood up straight, shoulders back, cardigan flapping as she shuffled down the stairs in sensible shoes. "When you asked me to keep this to myself, I really thought about it. I did."

"Oh shit!" Claire breathed. "Are they . . . ?"

"Wait, let her talk," Brad said.

Beauregard looked thoroughly chastised. He refused to raise his eyes to the crowd. You better believe that the camera was rolling, and Karl tapped so furiously into his Notes app I worried his phone would overheat.

"But I cannot stay silent!" Phyllis raised her voice. "Not for your promises, and not for the chance to be first lady in the governor's mansion one day."

Her meaning dawned on me. Oh *no*. Beauregard had apparently been writing checks that he couldn't cash, and promising Phyllis the sun, moon, stars, and that unfortunate peen. I wondered whether Beauregard's wife was watching the press conference. I sure hoped so! These were some *real* traditional family values, amirite?

I wondered who was going to run and make popcorn. There were always microwavable bags in the grimy thrift-store break room.

"I can best serve Hearst in my position as its primary historian. Which means revealing what I've discovered."

This had the ring of something monumental, and I knew Rufus had to hear it. For the first time in weeks, I let go of the Butler and put it behind the riser platform. Emma gave me a weird glance, but I knew I had to take the risk. That way, Rufus could see this for himself.

"You're right, Beauregard," Phyllis continued, "that Cygnus Cobpen wasn't your relation, because he wasn't a person at all."

A confused murmur went up through the crowd. Even I was stumped.

"Cygnus Cobpen was the name of an incorporated entity, and its principals were Robert Feldman and his wife, Maude Feldman, née Hearst, and a third individual, the widow of Mr. Thomas Gratton, a Ms. Evangeline Gratton."

I gasped. So Cygnus Cobpen wasn't a person, but that only inspired more questions. What did he represent? There were people behind every company; I knew that much. This was more drama than a Netflix binge. Phyllis kept talking and I raced to put the facts together. Over seventy years after Rufus's death, and these names that were so precious to him—that were wrapped up in so much loss and pain—were being spoken into a microphone in modern-day Hearst. Tears prickled at my eyes. Phyllis's every word was proof.

Robby *had* existed, and he had come to Hearst, looking for Rufus. Then he'd stayed to honor Rufus's memory. Along the way, Robby had apparently found and joined forces with another queer person who couldn't live freely and they'd found a way to at least have one space where they could be who they were. And somehow they kept finding people like them or allied with them right here in Hearst and made sure they had a place where they could bloom.

"Be that as it may," Beauregard huffed, "I am the only living descendant in the Hearst bloodline, and, as such—"

"That's true," Phyllis interrupted. "But only because Evangeline Gratton died within the last few years at over a hundred and ten years old, bless her soul. And I have a copy of her final will and testament that clearly states that all properties once belonging to the corporation functioning as Cygnus Cobpen are donated back into controlling possession to the city of Hearst in honor of her son who prematurely predeceased her, one Rufus Gratton, who performed under the stage name Tallulah Bouvier Beale."

I should have known that a drag queen always stans a good reveal to stop the show. Forget daytime soaps and Netflix, this was some telenovela-level scandalosity and I was here for it.

As this statement reverberated over the crowd, Rufus clung to the edge of the Butler, looking like he was about to burst.

"These three individuals formed a shell company, and I have the incorporation papers right here. Including an agreement that, upon the death of one of the principals, all holdings would belong solely to the remaining survivor. In this case, Evangeline Gratton, whose will is clear and ironclad."

"Why the name?" Guy asked.

"Good question," Brad said.

"Okay, king, go off!" I laughed, anticipating being impressed by whatever Brad was about to disclose.

He quickly winked at me. Winked! "Cygnus is the scientific genus for *swans*, like the two on the mirror in the *Robby's* logo." Everyone in the room gave him an equally blank look. "Swans are known for forming same-sex pairs in the wild. Am I the only one who knows this?" He shrugged. "I follow *National Geographic* on TikTok."

"Oh my god!" Emma said, making half the room jump. "Male swans are *cobs*. Females are called *pens*. It was a covert message for other queer people."

And swans mate for life. Even though Robby and Evangeline had lost Rufus, they had never stopped thinking of him. They never forgot him, or who he was. I hoped he knew that. I wanted him to see it. They loved him so much that it showed in everything they did. Everything around us.

Karl raised his pen in the air and Phyllis called on him. "But how did these three know each other?"

Brad glanced my way, because what could he say? That Gratton's son and Robby's lover were the same man, whose ghost just happened to be in the handbag at my side? I knew exactly why they'd bonded. It was their love of Rufus. I turned and found his eyes peeking from the bag. And I knew what I had to do.

"Robby's swan," I said out loud, "was Rufus Gratton. They were each other's life mates even though Rufus died right here in Knollwood asylum, where he was unfairly incarcerated for being openly queer. The discovery is a testament to the forgotten and erased *queer figures* of Hearst, may they long be remembered now!"

The Scooby Squad went nuts, whooping and dancing, so much that I worried someone would get tangled up in the reveal curtain and send the whole thing crashing down. Karl and the assembled crowd looked at us like we'd lost it, but whatever. I was used to getting sideways glances. What a victory!

Brad smiled at me, and my eyes stung. This time, though, they were happy tears.

He knew, too. He felt their love across the decades. Even when all had seemed lost, love is love, and love won. It just took a little time.

# 29

As soon as the basement emptied of everyone but Claire and Karl, Beauregard seemed to snap out of his revisionist-history gay-erasure panic.

"You," he breathed, narrowing his eyes, "you and *what*ever you are."

"I'm Sully. Nice to meet you," I said, matching his low, menacing tone of voice and not taking the bait, thank you.

Beau kept advancing, forcing me back into the speakeasy behind the curtain where we were out of view of the onlookers and their cameras.

"You and your mother think you're very clever. But I am not going to forget this. How dare you embarrass me and drag my family name and history through the mud. I will dedicate my remaining years to making sure both of your lives are a living hell." His voice was low but he spoke in a speedy whisper, like he knew this situation had quickly become much bigger than anything he could possibly keep quiet with his usual threats and schemes.

Not long ago, I'd have been trembling in my flats to know I'd made enemies with a powerful man who could make so many things difficult for me here in Hearst. But now, this living, breathing hemorrhoid-cream ad of a human being couldn't touch me.

Down here, robbed of his podium and his microphone and cronies, Beauregard looked exactly like someone who had missed the boat, who was becoming irrelevant more quickly than the latest Hallmark Channel Christmas movie every December 26, and who was firmly going to be remembered as standing on the wrong side of history.

He didn't get to decide who had power anymore. The Butler shook on my shoulder. It was time to really send Beauregard for a loop.

"And why are you always wearing that damn *purse*?" he sneered.

"It's an authentic Butler, you uncultured asshat. And it's also where my dear friend Rufus lives." Before Beauregard could walk away thinking he had the upper hand, I opened the bag. Mary Poppins had nothing on me. Either I was going to look just as senseless as Beauregard already believed me to be or—

"What?" Beauregard said, without even a hint of interest.

Rufus took his cue, whooshing out of the bag in full ghostly regalia, looking every inch a terrifying phantom. The lights began to flicker as Rufus cycled through his drag as he had in Knollwood, except this time I knew Rufus was in full control. The bioluminescent light lifted on a breeze like a mist from the tiled floor, this time purple and pink, and music crackled like a radio trying to tune itself with snippets of songs sounding through the static. Rufus stood tall, proud, and strong, and I stood by his side.

Then he began to grow and morph. His face elongated into a snout and sharp teeth sprouted, his fingers contorted into glittery talons, and he grew a tail from under his gown, but the hair and makeup remained over the scaly skin. I clutched my pearls. Literally. Both hands grabbed at my necklace before they slid over my open mouth. Rufus was fierce, honey!

Beauregard shrieked, looking like he was about to lose the contents of his bowels. "What *is* that?"

"This is Rufus, and he's more man than you'll ever be," I said. "You're acting like you haven't seen a spectral She-Rex before.

"You might claim an illustrious lineage through some genetic accident that saw you born a rich white man and not a dung beetle, but blood isn't the only thing that makes a family. Or a legacy. We were here, we are here, and we're not going anywhere no matter what you try to pull," I continued, as Rufus and I advanced on Beau.

In his Mae West voice, Rufus added, "If you come for us again, bring protection because I'm afraid my bite is worse than my bark." He snapped his jaws.

Beauregard tripped all over himself to get away from us and reach the stairs. With shaking hands, he grabbed the banister and launched himself up, step by step.

"I'll see you in your dreams, Beauregard!" Rufus sang after him.

I raced to the bottom of the staircase to see Clementine, midair, floating after Beauregard. He raced upstairs, and we listened to his heavy footfalls pounding all the way to the exit.

Rufus whirled back into his human-ghost form with all the haunting theatrics gone again, and he hugged me. He was as solid as I'd ever seen him, and now he could share in this moment with all of us, standing out in the open. Brad gave me a big raised eyebrow, but I just shrugged. Rufus deserved this.

Now the whole town would know his story.

"We did it," I whispered as I hugged him back.

"*You* did it, Sully. None of this would've been possible without you."

When we released each other, I said, "I didn't know you could do that."

"Me either," Rufus admitted. "But now that I can, I'm sure I can scare off that sales clerk who took your job and get it back for you."

"Rufus!"

Upstairs I heard someone popping champagne and my mother laughing.

"Shall we join them?" Rufus asked.

"Let's wait until things clear out a bit more. Back in the bag for now?"

"Oh, all right. Once more, for old times' sake. Play it again, Sull."

I stopped in my tracks, wondering if he was right. Since we'd technically done what we'd set out to do, did that mean Rufus would be leaving now? Where would he go? Was this the end? I'd known we would part ways one of these days, but I hadn't expected it would happen so soon. I would miss him so much.

"Of course, there are more details we still don't know," I muttered. "How did Robby find out about Maude? What did he know about you at Knollwood? How did your mother feel about you being incarcerated? What did you even die of? We never even got to watch *Grease* together. I know you'd go wild for Rizzo. It can't be over now. We have more answers to find."

"I don't think we will ever definitively discover everything. It was a different time." Rufus looked at me sadly. "There's more to history than any of us will ever know, but I have the most important answers now. It might be time for me to look to the future. And for you, too."

Brad gave me a sudden and surprisingly sweet kiss on the cheek, but even that couldn't restore my smile. "Sull, what's wrong?"

"I'm going to miss him," I said honestly, my chest beginning to tighten.

For his part, Rufus dematerialized and slid back into the Butler while nobody was looking.

"Oh." Brad's brow furrowed in concern. "I was trying not to think about that. How does all this work?"

"I don't know. There's no rulebook for owning a haunted handbag."

A little while later, I picked up the Butler and drifted back down the stairs to the basement. Claire was just wrapping up giving a few quotes to Karl, who'd burned a hole in his camera taking pictures, and soon, I was alone down there.

Someone had put up a few work lamps, and the speakeasy was better lit this time around. I could imagine how warm and inviting this place had been, especially to the people who needed it, despite being underground.

I set the bag on the bar, in front of the big mirror with the row of photographs looking on, including the one of Robby in his fedora.

Slowly, Rufus drifted back out in his gray suit, his beard intact again but looking like he'd been pulling at it. There was a heaviness in the air, as if we both dreaded what was coming.

"So," I said.

"So . . ."

"Are you happy?" I asked. "To know that they cared for you? That they didn't abandon you?"

Rufus nodded, his eyes gleaming in the low light. "Of course."

"What's the matter?"

"Oh, Sully. You know what."

I nodded. I'd never thought I'd get to keep Rufus in my life forever, but I also hadn't really thought about what saying goodbye would be like. How empty I'd feel without him. "So you're going? You're moving on?"

At that, Rufus laughed. I was about to swat at him, because we were supposed to be having a moment, until he said, "Heavens and hells, no. I'm not moving on. I'm moving *in*!"

"What?"

"To Robby's, if you, Claire, and Emma will have me." Rufus did a graceful swirl around the place, whooshing up some dust, the gown with the silk flowers blooming over him along with his wig and full drag. "The speakeasy is a little roomier than that bag, no offense," he said, though I wasn't sure if he was talking to the bag, me, or both. "But this place Robby and my mother created and left for me—*this* feels like home."

I tried to smile but it fell flat.

"Cheer up, buttercup. This means I'm going to stay around, *and* you can sell the bag. I see it as a win-win, as people in your era say."

"Yeah, but I'll miss having you around all the time."

"You know I'll be watching."

I grinned. "Okay, creep."

"It's *sis*. Remember?"

"I remember, *Mary*."

He was right, of course. It *was* time to move on. For him, so he could be the friendly ghost at Yesterday's Today while we figured out what to do with Robby's. Which I totally didn't mind, by the way. I'd always thought the shop could use a ghost and, frankly, was surprised that one didn't already live there.

And for me, so I could figure out what my calling was, especially now that I knew I'd be staying in town for a bit. Going back to the thrift store was going to be a great start, especially if Claire let me turn it into the vintage resale palace of my dreams. Brad was also going to be . . . great, I hoped. But other than that, I needed to figure out my next steps, too.

"Okay," I said.

"Good. It wasn't up to you, of course, but I'm glad you agree."

"So what do we have to do? Is it like giving a genie his freedom so he can leave the lamp?"

"I don't know, to be honest. Why don't you try it?"

I picked up the Butler, feeling unsure. We'd taken so many risks—hello, breaking and entering at an influencer party, and Rufus making his modern-day debut at Denny's, of all places—but this felt like the biggest gamble of all. I took a deep breath. "Okay, um, Rufus. I . . . release thee."

"*Thee?*" Rufus laughed. "I'm not *that* old!"

"Come on, just leave or something. Agitate that gravel. Pedal to the metal. Did it work?"

Rufus swept out of the Butler one last time, with full smoky ghost effect.

"Wow! So I really did say the magic words!"

"No, I can do that whenever I want to. I guess we'll just have to see if it sticks."

I laughed, but it came out a bit strangled, because I was trying not to cry. "I'm going to miss you."

"You can see me whenever you want. Come on, now. I have some thinking to do, and I want to see what happens with this place. Oh, I know! That's a promise you can make me."

"What's that?" I asked, looking down at the Butler. It seemed different now, a bit slouchy and faded. It was still in perfect condition, don't get me wrong, but it was as if some of the life had gone out of it. Which, I guess, it had.

"Whatever happens with this spot, you must promise me that it'll live up to Robby's vision for it. That it serves the same purpose for this town and the people who need it most."

"Don't worry about that, boo. I already have some ideas."

Rufus looked down at the bag, too, as it rested on the dusty tile floor between us. "Are you going to sell it? The bag?"

"Obviously. I gotta get *my* bag, amirite?"

"I don't even know what that is. You're still such a curious mystery."

"I'm funny, Rufus. I'm sorry if you can't appreciate—"

"You know, if you have to tell someone that you're funny, it means you're not actually that funny."

"Oh, hush." And just like that, we were laughing again, but only for a moment. I picked up the Butler and felt its weight in my hand. Maybe it was my imagination, but it felt lighter. "But why the Butler?" I asked. "Do you think it was the bag you brought with you to Knollwood?"

Rufus's brow furrowed. "I can't say, but I suppose that's possible. No, wait. I carried my clothes in it. Whether I was Tallulah or Rufus. It housed my costumes or male threads in case I needed to make a quick change. I remember now. It was always by my side."

If I sold it though, it wouldn't always be by mine. But I hoped Rufus would.

I walked behind the bar and held the corner of the photograph of Robby. "We really need to get a better frame for this," I said, but my voice trailed off as I leaned in closer to look at it, shining my flashlight. Tucked under Robby's arm was . . . "Rufus, the Butler. It's right there in the picture."

Rufus zoomed through me, hello, I guess not having physical substance was a choice he could make now, to inspect the photo too.

"It looks like there's proof he kept you beside him wherever he went."

Rufus looked around at Robby's. "I suppose the least I can do is stay here by his side now as long as he'll have me."

I held out the bag for Rufus. "I can't. It belongs to you."

Rufus shook his head. "We made a deal. I belong here." He pushed the bag back to me. "Get to know your new accessory, already."

I turned on my phone flashlight and peered inside the Butler. I hadn't really dug around much, as I'd always seen it as Rufus's space. Apart from putting a few documents in there, I hadn't even checked the pockets or looked for any marks to signal it was authentic.

The lining was silky, no stains, and I was remembering for the third time that I still owed Angelika's friend Paulo some pictures . . . when my fingers slid over something hard underneath the lining.

"Hold on," I said, carrying the Butler to one of the work lights. My heart thundered in my chest. Of course, I had gotten so much more than money from having this bag, and nothing could ever replace my friendship with Rufus, but I *had* been hoping to sell it eventually. Was there some kind of label or identifier hidden in the bag? If there was a rip here, or something someone had stitched up . . .

"What is *this*?" I squinted inside the bag, then felt inside the pocket. The lining was split there. Ugh, this was bad news. And there was . . . something behind it. Something hard, almost like a small piece of metal. "Rufus?"

"Yes?" He drifted over from where he'd been further examining Robby's photograph above the bar.

"Do you know what's in here?"

"What?"

"Inside the lining. How did you not notice? You were in this thing for more than sixty years!"

"Do you ever think to look inside the walls of your house?"

"No, and yet"—I gestured around us—"That clearly doesn't mean nothing's in there!"

"Touché," Rufus said, then gestured to the bag. "So what do you want to do?"

"Claire always has a seam ripper or tiny sewing scissors somewhere. Hold on." I took off for the stairs, hoping I could carefully cut the seam open and retrieve whatever it was, all while keeping the Butler in the best condition possible. Maybe, given its history, we could overlook the whole torn-lining thing. Especially since I had a feeling that whatever we were about to find was much more valuable than even the most priceless haunted handbag.

I opened enough stitches to work two fingers inside and sandwiched the hard, metal item between them. As carefully as I could, I pulled the item out. It was a key.

"What does that open?" Rufus asked.

I shook my head then remembered what Guy had found behind the bar. I hurried to the locked fire safe, and slid the key in. It went in but didn't turn. Dangit. I took a deep breath, and tried again. The door swung open with a creak.

Inside the safe were a stack of papers, letters, and a photo of a beautiful, curvy person posing in a dress that looked like it was blooming with flowers.

November 6, 1956

My beautiful Rufus,

I can practically hear you laughing at me for still writing you letters. But old habits die hard and, besides, it lets me feel close to you.

I'm writing with a lot of news.

First, I got married. To a woman, no less. It's nothing at all like what you'd think. My parents were elated, as you can imagine. Maude Hearst was in a bad way. She's one of us, you see. Once I knew about her and her beloved, it was a protection I could give to them that I wish someone had given us. We both said our vows to other people although we faced each other.

The second piece: your father passed away. Your mother phoned to tell me. She'd never forgiven him or herself. That makes the two of us quite a pair. He believed he did what was best for you, but that isn't any consolation. She and I have been speaking regularly and she has come to understand more of the man you were because of my love for you.

And third, we three are an industrious trio, your mother, Maude, and me. We've been buzzing about land. It's where we've set our sights. And a tribute. To you. To all of us. A place where we can gather those who've been told they are ugly ducklings and let them be the swans they always were. It turns out Hearst was more than we thought once we looked below the surface. Do you remember the rumors of the old prohibition speakeasy? As it turns out, they're true.

You would have loved it. You would have shone. But even though you're not here to see it, I know you're with me in spirit.

Maybe because we do it in your name, and in your memory.

Robby's officially welcomed its first customers, and more come down the stairs and through our magical doors each day. Your mother has helped me secure the title to the building; Evangeline Gratton is a wealthy woman now, able to make decisions for herself, and she suits the role. We three have created an alternate identity, Cygnus Cobpen, named after you, my swan, to let the others know there are more of us working among them. You would be so proud. I am tempted to add, "Wherever you are," but I know where you are. You are with me, you are in my heart forevermore, you are with all of us at Robby's, the most dazzling bird in the bevy. I don't need to pray that I will see you again—I see you in every detail, in every patron, in every happy heart. You are always by my side and I, by yours.

Yours, eternally,
Robby

# Epilogue

## Two Months Later

For the first time in my life, I was excited to celebrate the Founders' Day Festival and to celebrate *all* of Hearst's history. After watching it pass by me and rolling my eyes for years, I was now in it, bitches!

The parade had just gone down Main Street, right past Yesterday's Today and the all-are-welcome Robby's Speakeasy that would be opening in the basement in a few weeks' time. My dad was donating his time in between jobs to restore the space to its former grandeur. And even Uncle Chuck and his crew pitched in, cordoning off the street and opening it to pedestrians to dance, drink, and eat from local food trucks. (Apparently, Hearst had food trucks!)

While it was great to see the whole town getting into it, I only really cared about what was going on at Robby's, which wasn't technically open to the public yet . . . unless you knew someone. And I did, in fact, know someone. Me! Claire had entrusted me with the keys, of course. She was also hosting a private afterparty, so once the parade ended and Mom and I had finished our waving-from-the-back-of-a-dealership-sponsored-convertible duties, I met up with Brad to head over.

Of course, we rolled in a tad late because I loved to make an entrance and, okay, maybe I got distracted by his lips. The beautiful sequined gown that I'd worn to the parade had come in from an estate sale, and Claire pulled it aside for me because, as buyer (hello, promotion!), I got first dibs. (I let it air out for a few days to confirm that it wasn't haunted.) I was even learning how to authenticate stuff, with constant FaceTime freak-outs to Angelika, of course. There were hidden treasures everywhere, as it turned out, and Claire thought we could really turn the store into something special. We even had plans to start selling curated pieces online.

With the full support of Claire, Eleanor, Guy, Emma, and Brad, I was really feeling myself, and showing that self to everyone in town too. I knew I couldn't keep every juicy thing that came into the store, but this gown . . . oh, baby. I wasn't ready to let go of her just yet.

"You look great," Brad said, squeezing my hand as we rounded the corner.

"Really?"

"Of course, and you know it."

I didn't want to admit that I was nervous, but then I reminded myself that it was okay to have a vulnerable moment. I squeezed his hand back.

Soon, we were downstairs in the basement of Yesterday's Today again, but everything felt different. The last of the false wall had come down, and my friends were milling around, looking at the art on the walls, inspecting the antique bar, and drinking classic mocktails (and cocktails for those over twenty-one)—Manhattans, Gin Rickeys, and French 75s alongside three bespoke bevvies, the Rufus, the Tallulah, and the Swans.

Okay, so Claire had been a bit preoccupied with Saul Bunyan lately and didn't technically have a liquor license yet, but if anyone snitched, I was confident we'd sort it out. Because in addition to *being* somebody, I also knew somebody on the city council. *And* in the records hall. Beauregard probably wouldn't be coming around this building anytime soon. If his wife had even let him out of the doghouse yet. Or he'd gotten over his fear of dragalicious dinos.

"Boo!" someone said in my ear.

"Rufus! You need some new material, sis. A ghost who says boo? How cliché."

"I know, but you should've seen your face."

Rufus smiled, looking handsome with his beard and full makeup in a vintage Chanel-style tweed jacket and skirt I swore I'd brought in just last week. He was looking very Jackie O. with an extra touch of Jack.

I smacked him with my clutch. What? Rufus had evacuated the Butler, I had dibs, and it was currently off in Chicago getting authenticated by a leather goods historian Paulo had recommended. I didn't know what I'd do with the bag, or how the valuation would shake out, so I let that be Future Sully's problem too.

"Are you letting people see you now?" I asked while Brad bustled off to get us some drinks.

"Every once in a while. And only the allies."

"Nice lingo!"

"Oh, Sully, I've got to tell you, I'm having the time of my afterlife!" Rufus grabbed my chin and tutted. "Sis, no offense but we've got to do something about your paint . . . or lack thereof."

Before I could protest, Rufus had levitated a tube of lipstick and applied it to my lips, then pressed the tube firmly into my hand. Ruby Woo. I grinned at him with my freshly applied color.

Rufus surveyed his handiwork. "It's perfection. Same as you. Don't you even dream of wiping it off."

"Mary, I wouldn't dare."

Since getting in touch with his past, Rufus had gained more and more control over what form he took. He could materialize, but mostly he just humored everyone as Robby's resident ghost, getting up to minor mischief (like stealing Clementine from front cash and posing her in the speakeasy downstairs) and making a few misty appearances or casting unusual shadows. I even thought I'd once seen him frolicking inside the pictures with the old crowd.

Claire and Emma were very into it and quickly decided that Robby's was officially the most haunted place in Hearst. It was a real selling point, honestly. Emma even had plans to cordon off her own corner and do tarot readings on the weekends. Claire was happy for any little boost to the business, and Saul thought we could draw in the paranormal-hunting crowd who, he swore, loved pickleball. A haunted basement speakeasy? That was better marketing than a Mango-Gasm influencer party. (Which isn't saying a lot.)

Brad had also discovered through good old Google that Robby and Maude had taken creating safe space seriously and really were a political power couple, advocating for equal queer and other human rights legislation in Pennsylvania throughout their terms in the 1960s and 1970s. It was clear, honoring Rufus's memory couldn't be confined to one small drag bar in Hearst.

"Hey, now that I think about it, have you ever seen Robby down here?" I asked, but Rufus had disappeared. I guess he was off to haunt someone else, or to stir up trouble.

Sensible heels clacked down the basement stairs and—

"Sully, baby!" Eleanor yelled over the noise and pounding music.

"Mommy dearest!" I called back. "How'd the rest of the festival go?"

"Good," she said, coming over. "Someone from a political action committee out of Philly was there."

"The big city?" I asked, and we both laughed. "You're not running off on us, are you?"

"I don't know, Sull. He thinks I could have a shot at a state representative seat." She broke into a dazzling smile. "Especially with how I got this place declared a historical landmark due to its importance to the queer community in an unprecedented power move."

"Shut the front door! Are you going to do it?"

She shrugged but couldn't hide the smile curving along her lips. "If I'm being honest, you inspired me to get this far. Who knows how much further I can go? I never planned to leave Hearst, you know, but splitting my time between here and Harrisburg could be a new experience."

"Mom!" I said, a sudden lump in my throat. "You're going to make me cry!"

"Well, you better save it, hon."

"Huh?"

"Because I'm gonna need a speech . . . speech . . . *speech*!" She grabbed a French 75 and started banging a knife against it. The ringing eclipsed the music, and soon, Emma—that traitor—turned down the volume.

I shot Mom a glare, but who was I kidding? I wasn't about to miss my moment to shine and take a second stab at my big speech.

Claire swiveled a work light at the bar, and it took both Brad and Guy to help me climb on top of it in my heels. The makeshift spotlight caught on my sequins, making it look like the bar was alive with flickering candlelight.

Watching everyone gather to listen to me and knowing that I stood in such an important place, framed by the heavy wooden mirror with *Robby's* on it, I couldn't help but feel that I was not only taking my place in history but putting in a vote for a better future.

Two months ago, all I'd wanted to show the people of Hearst was a middle finger and my backside as I left and never thought about this place again. But now, I needed them to know about the hidden history of Hearst, and that everyone who'd lived there—out in the sun or hidden in the shadows through no fault of their own—mattered. Still, to this day.

I hadn't prepared a speech for my going-away party, and I didn't have one for what I was now thinking of as my sticking-around-for-now party. But as Brad and Eleanor gazed up at me, with Emma and Guy flanking them on each side, I realized I didn't need anything fancy—for once. I could just tell Rufus's story.

So I did. I talked about two boys, childhood friends, who grew up in Hearst, feeling alone and lost but for each other. I talked about how they had decided to leave for the city, only to find more bigotry and hatred there that forced them to lead two lives, private and public. How Rufus and Robby had struggled with knowing who to trust, and whether they had the courage to continue their relationship. How we guessed Rufus had been picked up by the Pittsburgh police, who were not very understanding to discover a man dancing around in women's clothing despite the obvious star potential.

I didn't know the whole story, of course. Nobody ever would, because the trauma of being thrown into jail and then being shunted off to Knollwood to die in a tuberculosis outbreak had had such an effect on Rufus that his memory of the end of his life was still gone. But we did have Robby's and Rufus's letters from over the years, even those Robby wrote to him long after Rufus was dead and Robby was established in Hearst. There's a lot about the letters we'll never fully know, like how Rufus got the letters to begin with. But I guess some mysteries will always belong to the past.

"Just like there was a secret speakeasy perfectly preserved behind a false wall in this building the whole time we've lived in Hearst, there are hidden stories everywhere," I said. "And this is the story of Rufus Gratton. He might've had a very different existence had he been born in our time. Unfortunately, he was denied the kind of life that queer folx can claim now. That's not to say that it's always easy."

"Woo!" Guy said, then shrank back when everyone looked at him. "I mean, not 'woo' about it not being easy but 'woo' that you're you!"

Emma made a big show of doing an exaggerated face-palm as he kissed her on the cheek. And I had to laugh.

"Robby loved Rufus, even though society and the law told him that he shouldn't, and that people like Rufus shouldn't even exist. When Robby learned that Rufus had been arrested by the police in Pittsburgh and outed as a female impersonator, which I can only imagine was a horrific process, completely without dignity, Robby chased him to Knollwood, where Rufus had been thrown into an asylum. That's right. Let that sink in. Thrown into a psychiatric hospital simply for having the courage to be himself in a society determined to make him and people like him deny their truths and conform . . . or perish for resisting, and some considered it better that they be dead rather than exist at all."

Eleanor and my dad found my eyes from the audience and both nodded. Everyone around the bar was completely silent. I could practically hear the ice cubes sweating.

"For Rufus, it was too late. But Robby would remember their relationship for the rest of his life, and he would use this tragedy to turn their love into a triumph. Rufus may not have gotten a chance to live the life of dignity and love that every human being should be free to experience, but he will always be a hero. And thanks to Robby, he has the opportunity, now, to inspire a whole new generation right here in Hearst."

I held up my virgin mojito and turned to face the bar, where a photo of a man in a fedora hung beside one of a man in a gown blooming with flowers. "To Rufus. You may have been lost, but you are not forgotten. Tonight, we remember you."

At this, the lights in Robby's flickered and I swear I heard the opening notes of some classic Whitney. Just a tiny bit—I would've missed it if I'd blinked or sneezed. I was sure that most people did, because the crowd broke into raucous applause. But I knew exactly what it was, and I held it close to my heart as I took a bow.

It was Rufus, and maybe even Robby, wherever he was, saying *thank you.*

# Authors' Note

Dear Reader,

Grow where you're planted. That has been the mantra of *Let Them Stare* from day one. We're so excited to finally share this story of finding the extraordinary in perfectly ordinary places and learning how to take up space, even in places where you're certain you don't belong.

But let's rewind for a sec. We should probably start with our meet-cute.

It was May of 2019 at BookExpo in New York City. Jonathan was wearing a boot, and not the fabulous kind of boot that you'd normally find in their closet. More like an orthopedic boot. Julie was signing copies of *Dear Sweet Pea*, and Jonathan was there for *Over the Top*. Julie rushed to meet Jonathan backstage after the signing. Jonathan touched her hair and said it had "great movement." Julie rode that compliment all the way home to Texas.

Fast-forward to the summer of 2022, when Jonathan had an idea for a book. A book about a haunted handbag. (Yeah, baby, you read that right. A haunted handbag.) Jonathan began mulling over an idea for a story that linked our present queer community to the community that came before us.

Jonathan knew they wanted a writing partner to be there every step of the way. So Julie was asked if she'd like to chat with Jonathan about coauthoring a project. Julie immediately said yes. (She was still dreaming about her hair having "great movement"—and so was Jessica, her hairstylist, to be honest.)

The call went like this: our agents pointed us at each other like Furbies, and we haven't stopped talking since. We clicked immediately, and both believed deeply in this project from square one. But our friendship has turned into so much more than a plan to write a book together. We've bonded over ice-skating, gymnastics, animal rescue, surprise mutual friends, Texas, *Harriet the Spy*, and our problematic fave, *Grand Theft Auto*.

And, somehow, despite us both having a serious case of ADHD, we found Sully's story. A little bit of each of us lives in Sully and their world. Between being genderqueer and being a bi fat lady, we've both known what it means to be gawked at. Like Sully discovers, we've decided that sometimes the best solution when people don't know what to make of you is to just Let Them Stare. Because queer people have existed everywhere since the beginning of ever, honey.

With that, we will wish you happy reading! And don't forget to check your handbags for loose change—and potential ghosts.

xo,

Julie & Jonathan

# Acknowledgments

We owe our deepest thanks to our agents, John Cusick, Gwen Beal, and Albert Lee. To Alessandra Balzer and Kristin Rens, thank you for shepherding this project and seeing its potential so early on. Thank you to everyone at HarperCollins who touched this project in any way, especially Jenna Stempel-Lobell as well as Alison Donalty for bringing their vision for this cover to life. Thank you as well to each artist they worked with to make Clementine happen. Also, to Paul Coccia and Chad Hall, for your invaluable help. Last, and perhaps, most important, to Mary Kole for getting down in the trenches with us every step of the way. The story of Sully and Rufus doesn't exist without you.

—JVN & JM

Thank you to my family, my friends, my entire team, everyone at Bittersweet, the queer historians who have educated me over the years on my podcast, especially Bob Skiba, and to the people who have helped shape me into the person I am.

—JVN

Huge and immeasurable thanks to my family and friends. Especially John and Mary. Jessica Weckherlin, for your electric enthusiasm. Jonathan, thank you for bringing me along for the ride of a lifetime!

—JM